Praise for *New York Times*

"A gu███████████████████████████hor
███████████████████████████am

"Joan████████████████████████
Weste████████████

—*Publishers Weekly*

"Johnston warms your heart and tickles your fancy."

—*New York Daily News*

"Joan Johnston continually gives us everything we want…fabulous details and atmosphere, memorable characters, a story that you wish would never end, and lots of tension and sensuality."

—*RT Book Reviews*

"Absolutely captivating…a delightful storyteller…Joan Johnston [creates] unforgettable subplots and characters who make every fine thread weave into a touching tapestry."

—*Affaire de Coeur*

New York Times bestselling author **Joan Johnston** started reading romances to escape the stress of being an attorney with a major national law firm. She soon discovered that writing romances was a lot more fun than writing legal bond indentures. Since then she has published a number of historical and contemporary category romances. In addition to being an author, Joan is the mother of two children. In her spare time, she enjoys sailing, horseback riding and camping.

New York Times Bestselling Author

Joan Johnston

Hawk's Way: Carter & Falcon

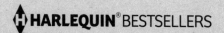

HARLEQUIN® BESTSELLERS

ISBN-13: 978-0-373-40104-8

Hawk's Way: Carter & Falcon

Copyright © 2009 by Harlequin Books S.A.

The publisher acknowledges the copyright holder of the individual works as follows:

The Cowboy Takes a Wife
Copyright © 1994 by Joan Mertens Johnston

The Unforgiving Bride
Copyright © 1994 by Joan Mertens Johnston

Recycling programs for this product may not exist in your area.

This edition published by arrangement with Harlequin Books S.A.

For questions and comments about the quality of this book, please contact us at CustomerService@Harlequin.com.

® and TM are trademarks of the publisher. Trademarks indicated with ® are registered in the United States Patent and Trademark Office, the Canadian Intellectual Property Office and in other countries.

Printed in U.S.A.

CONTENTS

THE COWBOY
TAKES A WIFE

CHAPTER ONE

DESIREE PARRISH HAD BEEN secretly observing Carter Prescott throughout the Christmas pageant. So she saw the moment when his jaw tightened, when he closed his eyes and clenched his fists as though he were in pain. A bright sheen of tears glistened along his dark lashes. Moments later he rose from the back pew in which he sat and quietly, almost surreptitiously, left the church.

For a moment Desiree wasn't sure what to do. She didn't want to leave because her daughter, Nicole, hadn't yet performed her part as an angel in the pageant. Nicole *was* an angel, Desiree thought with a swell of maternal pride. But it was because of her five-year-old daughter that she needed Carter Prescott's help. Desiree had to speak privately with the cowboy, and she wasn't sure if she would get another opportunity like this one.

According to his grandmother, Madelyn Prescott, Carter had come to Wyoming from Texas looking for someplace to settle down. What if Carter moved on before she got a chance to make her offer to him? What if he decided to leave town tonight? Without giving herself more chance for thought, Desiree rose and headed for the nearest exit. She made a detour to grab her coat and wrap a scarf around her face to protect her from the frigid Wyoming weather.

Desiree was alarmed when she stepped outside to

discover her quarry had disappeared into the night, hidden by the steady, gentle snowfall. She frantically searched the church parking lot, running through the fluffy snow in the direction his footprints led, afraid he would get away before she could make her proposition known to him.

She cried out in alarm when a tall, intimidating figure suddenly stepped from behind a pickup. She automatically put up a hand as though to ward off a blow. There was a moment of awful tension while she waited for the first lash of pain. In another instant she realized how foolish she had been.

She had found Carter Prescott. Or rather, he had found her.

"Are you all right?"

She heard the concern in his voice, yet when he reached out to touch her she took a reflexive step backward. It took all her courage to stand her ground. She had to get hold of herself. Her safety, and Nicole's, depended on what she did now.

Disconcerted by the growing scowl on Carter's face, she lowered her arm and threaded her fingers tightly together. "I'm fine," she murmured.

"Why did you follow me?" he demanded in a brusque voice.

"I..." Desiree couldn't get anything more past the sudden tightness in her throat. The cowboy looked sinister wrapped in a shearling coat with his Stetson pulled down low to keep out the bitter cold. He towered over her, and she had second thoughts about speaking her mind.

But she had no choice. It was two weeks until Christmas. She had to have a husband by the new year, and this cowboy from Texas was the most likely candidate she had found. She examined Carter closely in the stream of light glowing from the church steeple.

From the looks of his scuffed boots and ragged jeans, life hadn't been kind to him. His face was as weathered as the rest of him. He had wide-set, distrustful blue eyes and a hawkish nose. His jaw was shadowed with at least a day's growth of dark beard. His chin jutted—with arrogance or stubbornness, she wasn't sure which. From having seen it in church, she knew his hair was a rich, wavy chestnut brown. He had full lips, but right now they were flattened in irritation. Nonetheless, he was a handsome man. More good-looking than she deserved, everything considered.

"Look, lady, if you've got something to say, spit it out."

Desiree responded to the harsh voice with a shiver that she chose to blame on the cold. Plainly the cowboy wasn't going to stand there much longer. It was now or never.

Desiree spoke quickly, her breath creating a cloud of white around her. "My name is Desiree Parrish. I know from having spoken to your grandmother before the pageant this evening that you're looking for a place to set down some roots."

His scowl became a frown, but she hurried on without stopping. "I have a proposition to make to you."

She opened her mouth and then couldn't speak. What was she doing? Maybe this was only going to make things worse, not better. After all, what did she really know about Carter Prescott? The grown man standing before her was a stranger. She wondered whether he remembered the one time they had met. His eyes hadn't revealed whether he recognized her name when she had spoken it. But, maybe he had never known her name. After all, they had only spent fifteen minutes together twenty-three years ago, when she was a child of five and he was a lanky boy of ten.

It was spring, and Carter Prescott had come from King's Castle with his father to visit the Rimrock Ranch, since the two properties bordered each other. She would never even have met him if her kitten hadn't gotten stuck in a tree.

She had been trying to coax Boots down by talking to her, but the kitten had been afraid to move. The ten-year-old boy had heard Desiree's pleading cries and come to investigate. She thought now of all the reactions Carter could have had to the situation. He might have ignored her. Or come to see the problem but left her to solve it herself. He might have made fun of her or taunted her about the kitten's plight. After all, she was just a kid, and a girl at that.

Carter Prescott had done none of those things. He had patted her awkwardly on the shoulder and promised to get Boots down from the tree. He had climbed up into the willow and reached for the kitten. But Boots evaded his reach. He had finally lurched for the kitten and caught her, but cat and boy had come tumbling down in a heap on the ground.

Desiree had screamed in fright and hurried over to make sure Boots was all right. She found her kitten carefully cushioned in the boy's arms.

He had handed Boots to her with a grim smile. "Here's your cat."

She was too busy fussing over Boots to notice Carter's attempts to rise. It was his gasp of pain that caused her to look at him again. That was when she saw the bloody bone sticking out through his jeans above the knee.

Her second panicked scream brought their fathers on the run. Her father picked her up and hugged her tight, grateful she was all right. She babbled the problem out to him, her voice too hysterical at first for him to realize what had happened.

Carter's father bent down on one knee to his son. His lips had tightened ominously before he said, "Your mother will give me hell for this."

Carter hadn't made a sound when his father picked him up and carried him toward their pickup. His face had been white, his teeth clamped on his lips to stop any sound from escaping. Desiree had tried to follow him but her father had held her back.

"Let the boy be, Desiree," he'd said. "He won't want to cry in front of you."

"But, Daddy, I have to see how he is," she protested. "He saved Boots."

Her father relented, and she ran after Carter and his father.

"I'm sorry," Desiree called up to Carter, her tiny legs rushing to keep pace.

"You ought to be," Carter's father said.

Stunned at the meanness in his voice, Desiree stopped in her tracks. But Carter turned to face her over his father's shoulder. He nodded and tried to smile, and she knew he had forgiven her.

But she and Carter had never crossed paths again. When she asked about him several days later, her father had told her that Carter had been visiting Wyoming for only a few days. His parents were divorced and Carter lived in Texas with his mother. He wouldn't be coming back.

Desiree had never seen Carter again, until he showed up at the Christmas pageant in Casper tonight. Was she willing to gamble her future on a man she had known for barely fifteen minutes twenty-three years ago? It seemed idiotic in the extreme.

Desiree wasn't an idiot. But she was in urgent need of a husband. Carter might not be the same person now as he had been then. But she remembered vividly how he had cradled the kitten to keep it from harm at the expense of his own welfare. Surely he could not have grown up a cruel man. She was staking her life on it.

Carter was already turning to walk away, when she laid a slender hand on his arm. She tensed when she felt the steely muscle tighten even through the sheepskin coat.

"I need a husband," she said in a breathless voice.

Carter's head snapped back around. His icy blue eyes focused intently on her face.

"I'm willing to sign over half the Rimrock Ranch to you if you'll agree to marry me. Of course," she added hastily, "it would be a marriage in name only."

His eyes narrowed, and she found herself racing to get everything out before she lost her nerve. "The Rimrock is the second largest outfit in the area, nearly as big as King's Castle, your father's place. It's got good water and lots of grass. The house was built by my great-great-grandfather. You'd be getting a good bargain. What do you say?"

Desiree gripped his arm tighter, as though she could hold him there until he responded in the way she wished him to answer. She chanced a look into his eyes and was surprised by the humor she saw there. His lips twisted in a mocking smile.

"Surely you could get a husband in a little more conventional way, Miss Parrish," he replied.

This wasn't a laughing matter. The sooner Carter Prescott realized that, the better. Desiree reached up and pulled aside the heavy wool scarf that was wrapped around her face.

"You're mistaken, Mr. Prescott." She angled her face so he could see the vivid scar that slanted across her right cheek from chin to temple. "No man would willingly choose me for a bride."

She raised wary brown eyes to the man before her and shuddered at the cold, hard look on his face. Her shoulders slumped. She should have known better. She should have known even the promise of the Rimrock wasn't enough to entice a man to face her over the breakfast table for the rest of his life.

Desiree hurriedly wrapped the scarf back around her face to hide the scar. "This was a stupid idea," she muttered. "Forget I mentioned it."

Desiree quickly stumbled away, embarrassed by the stinging tears that had sprung to her eyes. It would have been humiliating enough to have him refuse her offer. She didn't want him to see how devastated she was by his reaction to the scar on her face. It had been so long since she had exposed herself to someone for the first time that she had forgotten the inevitable horror it caused.

She would have to find another way to save herself. But merciful Lord in heaven, what was she going to do?

Meanwhile, Carter had been so stunned by the entire incident that Desiree had nearly reached the door of the church before he recovered himself enough to speak. By then he was glad she was gone, because he wouldn't have known what to say. He stared after her, remembering the look of vulnerability in her deep brown eyes when she had exposed her face.

He was amazed even now at the strength of his reaction to the awful sight he had seen. He had felt fury at the destruction of something that had obviously once been quite beautiful. And pity for what it must be like to live with such a scar. And disgust that she had been reduced to begging for a spouse.

If he was honest, he also had to admit that his curiosity was piqued. How had she been wounded so horribly? Why was she so anxious to find a husband? And why had she singled him out?

Carter wondered if she remembered the one time they had met. It was a day he had never forgotten. He unconsciously rubbed his thigh. His thigh bone—the one he had broken saving her blasted cat—still ached when the weather was wet or cold. If he got tired enough, he sometimes limped. He never had liked cats much since.

For other reasons that day was etched in his memory like brutally carved glass. The scene between his mother and father when his mom had arrived at the emergency room of the hospital had been loud and vicious. It was easy to see why his parents hadn't stayed married. They had been in the process of a divorce when he was conceived, and he had been born before the divorce was final. His mother just hadn't seen fit to inform his father of that fact. She had only brought him to Wyoming to meet his father because Wayne

Prescott had accidentally found out about his son and demanded visitation rights.

The incident at the Rimrock Ranch had convinced his mother that his father was not a fit custodian. That day had been the first and last he had seen of Wayne Prescott. So Carter remembered well his first meeting with Desiree Parrish. It had been a dark day in his life.

Desiree was correct in her assumption that he wanted roots, but his wants and needs had culminated in a specific objective. He wanted the land that would have been his inheritance if his mother and father hadn't divorced. He wanted King's Castle.

Unfortunately, on his father's death the land had gone in equal shares to his father's very young widow, Belinda Prescott, and his father's bastard son, Faron Whitelaw. Carter had already made a generous offer to them for the land. They had promised him an answer tonight.

He felt queasy at the thought that they might refuse him. Where would he go if he couldn't stay at King's Castle? Where would he find the solace he so desperately needed from the memories that relentlessly trailed him wherever he went? He had been running for so long—six years—that he had begun to wonder if there would ever be an end to it.

As he stepped into the cab of his pickup and headed back to King's Castle, he couldn't help thinking about the offer Desiree Parrish had made to him. He remembered well the lush, grassy valleys to be found on the Rimrock. A river carved its way over the prairie, right through the ranch. The ranch house was a two-story, wooden-planked structure, simple but enduring. He had never seen the inside.

To tell the truth, before he had discovered King's Castle was on the market, he had inquired about purchasing the Rimrock. His agent had been told, in no uncertain terms, that the ranch was not for sale. So why had Desiree Parrish offered him half the place for his name on a marriage certificate? And how could she have believed that someone rich enough to buy the Rimrock, lock, stock and barrel, would bargain away his freedom for it?

Unless she doesn't know you're rich.

Carter found himself chuckling as he realized the image he must have presented to the young woman, unshaven, with his jeans frayed and his boots worn to a nub. Apparently his grandmother hadn't told Desiree his true circumstances. He sobered abruptly. He had learned, to his sorrow, that wealth couldn't buy happiness. In fact, it had been the source of great tragedy in his life.

Carter felt the tension pounding behind his eyes. He never should have given in to his grandmother's pleas for him to attend the Christmas pageant. Tonight the memories had come back to haunt him. Listening to those childish voices, seeing those angelic faces, had brought all the pain of betrayal and loss back into sharp focus. He wanted to forget the past, but he wasn't sure it was possible. Guilt rode heavy on his shoulders. And regret. And anger.

Carter stopped his truck in front of the ranch house at King's Castle, a three-story stone structure with turrets and crenels, which his father had called The Castle. It didn't fit this land anywhere near as well as the simple house on the Rimrock. He headed around back to the kitchen door, which he knew would be open. He found his way through the darkened house to the elegant parlor, where a fire still glowed in the grate. He stirred the ashes and added a log from the pile nearby. Finally, he poured himself a whiskey and settled into the chair near the fireplace, where he could empty his mind of the painful past and concentrate on the future.

It was Desiree Parrish who filled his thoughts. He remembered how tiny, almost delicate, she had seemed next to his great size, how the snowflakes had gathered on her dark hair and eyelashes. Those memories were overshadowed by the look of fear in her huge brown eyes when she had revealed her scar to him. And by the way she had braced herself for his revulsion.

It was true the scar was ugly, but Carter had shifted his gaze to her eyes, which had called out to him. He had seen a wounded spirit that was the equal of his own. It had taken a great deal of effort to resist reaching out to fold her protectively in his arms. Fortunately, she had run before he could do something so foolishly impulsive.

Carter didn't know how long he had been sitting there, when he heard Madelyn and Belinda Prescott and Faron Whitelaw returning. He felt his gut tighten, reminding him how much their answer mattered to him. He wanted this place; he *needed* this place, if he was ever to forget the past and go on with his life.

Madelyn entered the room scolding. "What happened to you, young man? There were several more people I wanted you to meet, although I suppose we can have a party here and—"

He had risen the instant she came into the room and was already there to help her out of her coat. "I'm not much interested in parties, Maddy."

"You should be," she countered. "Why, a handsome young man like you ought to be settled down now, with babies and—"

"I just want an answer from Belinda and Faron, one way or the other," he said sharply, cutting her off again. He laid her coat across the sofa, which gave him a chance to focus his attention anywhere except on Belinda and Faron. He was afraid he might see their answer to his offer on their faces. He was afraid that answer would be no.

At last, he forced himself to look at them. They were staring at each other, and he could feel the tension between them. His heart began to pound, sending blood rushing to his head, making him feel dizzy. He reached for his whiskey and swallowed a restoring gulp. He met his half brother's eyes and said, "Well, what have you decided?"

"Give us another few minutes," Faron said. "Belinda and I have some things we need to discuss before we can give you an answer." Faron quickly ushered Belinda out of the room and into the ranch office across the hall.

Carter crossed to the bar so he would have his back to his grandmother. He didn't want her to see the frustration—and fear—he felt. He poured a glass of port and turned to hand it to Madelyn. His casual calm was hard-won. The hell of it was, he didn't think he was fooling Madelyn for a minute.

His grandmother settled herself on the sofa. Instead of launching into a thousand questions, she sipped her port and stared into the fire.

He was too nervous to sit and too proud to let Madelyn see him pacing anxiously. He hooked an arm over the mantel and focused on the map of King's Castle that hung above it. The boundaries had changed over the hundred-odd years the land had been owned by Prescotts, but even now it was an impressive spread. He froze when he heard the office door open.

"Maddy, can you come in here for a minute?" Faron called.

"Excuse me, Carter," the old woman said. "I hate to leave you alone. I'm sure I won't be gone long."

He didn't look at her, afraid that his feelings were naked on his face. "Don't worry, Maddy. I'm used to being alone."

He could have bitten his tongue after he'd said the words, knowing how much he had revealed in that simple sentence. He felt more than saw, her hesitation. But he heard her set her glass down on the end table and leave the room.

He shook his head in disgust. How had he let possessing The Castle matter so much to him? He was only setting himself up for disappointment. He should have come sooner, when Wayne Prescott was still alive, and demanded his heritage. But he hadn't needed Wayne's land then. He hadn't yet experienced the tragedy that had left him rootless and alone.

"Carter?"

He forced all emotion from his face as he turned to face Faron, who was flanked by the two women. He knew the answer before Faron spoke.

"We've decided not to sell."

CHAPTER TWO

DESIREE CONCENTRATED ON the road, which was slick with a layer of ice and difficult to see through the blowing snow. She had been among the last to leave the church, since she had helped with the cleanup. The storm had worsened in the past hour, and Desiree wished she had asked someone to follow her, at least until she got to the turnoff for the ranch. She didn't want to end up stuck on the road somewhere overnight, although if she ended up frozen to death that would solve the worry of finding a husband.

Beside her, Nicole chattered on happily about the Christmas pageant. Desiree responded to her daughter, but her thoughts were elsewhere. She was mentally kicking herself for being so foolish as to confront a perfect stranger with a proposal of marriage.

"Did you see me, Mommy? Was I a good angel?"

"You were wonderful, sweetheart. A perfect angel."

Desiree worried her lower lip with her teeth. Why hadn't she stood firm until she had an answer from Carter Prescott? Because she was afraid, that's why! But although the ragtag cowboy's eyes had been cold, they hadn't been unkind. And while he had towered over her, she hadn't felt threatened. It had been the fear of rejection, not the fear of physical harm, that had sent her fleeing into the night.

"Did you see me fly, Mommy?"

Desiree smiled at the image of her daughter flapping her angel's wings. "I certainly did." She had watched the finish of the Christmas pageant from the shadows along the side aisle of the church, her chest aching with love—and fear. She *must* find a husband before the new year. Her safety, and Nicole's, depended on having a man's presence in the house. If only she had been less fainthearted about confronting Carter Prescott!

"Look at me, Mommy. Look! I can fly even without my wings!"

"Nicole! Sit down, and put your seat belt back on this instant!"

Nicole quickly dropped down on the seat and began hunting for the end of the seat belt in the darkened cab.

Desiree had taken her eyes off the road only for a second, but that was enough. She caught a patch of ice and felt the pickup begin to slide. She turned the wheel into the skid and resisted the urge to brake, knowing that would only make things worse. But she could already see the truck wasn't going to recover in time to stay on the road.

Nicole gave a cry of alarm as the pickup began to tilt. "Mommy! We're falling!"

"It's all right, Nicole. Sit still. Everything will be fine." Desiree's heart pounded as the pickup slid sideways off the road into a shallow gully.

The truck thumped to a stop at a sharp angle with the right wheels lodged in snow two feet deeper than the left ones. It took a second for Desiree to realize they really were all right. Nicole whimpered in fright.

Desiree reached over and grabbed Nicole and pulled

her daughter into her lap, hugging her tight. "It's all right, sweetheart. We're fine. Everything's fine."

"We're going to fall, Mommy."

"No, we're not. The truck is stopped now. It's wedged in the snow. It won't tip any more." But she wasn't going to be able to drive out of this gulley. Which meant that unless she wanted to spend the night in the truck, she was going to have to walk back the two miles or so to the church and call for help.

"You'll have to wait here for me, Nicole, while I—"

"No, Mommy! Don't leave me! I'm scared!"

Despite her daughter's cries, Desiree shifted her onto the seat. "I won't be gone long."

"Don't leave! Please, Mommy." Nicole clambered back into Desiree's lap and twined her arms around her mother's neck.

Desiree hugged her daughter, fighting the tears that stung her nose and welled in her eyes.

She had been on her own for six years. She had gone through her pregnancy alone and had raised Nicole without help from anyone. Forced to cope with whatever life had thrown at her, somehow she had survived. She and Nicole were a family. Sliding off the road wasn't nearly the disaster that loomed on the horizon. Soon their very lives would be in danger.

So what if she was stuck miles from home in the middle of a snowstorm with her daughter clinging to her neck like a limpet? They, and the truck, had endured without a scratch. There was no reason to cry. But her throat had swollen so thick it hurt to swallow, and she could feel the heat of a tear on her cold cheek.

It wasn't the accident that was causing her distress,

she conceded; it was the knowledge that she had so little control over her life.

Desiree took a deep breath and let it out. She had managed so far to keep things together. She just had to take one step at a time. She retrieved the blanket she kept in the well behind the seat and wrapped Nicole snugly in it.

"Mommy has to call a tow truck to haul us out of here," she explained to Nicole. "The closest phone is at the church. You need to wait right here for me until I get back. Don't leave the truck. If you wander off, you could get lost in all this snow. Okay, sweetheart?"

It was a sign of how much more quickly the child of a single parent had to grow up that Nicole sniffed back her tears and nodded reluctant agreement to her mother's order. There was a risk leaving Nicole alone, but there was even greater risk in taking her out walking in the bitter cold.

"I won't be gone long," Desiree promised as she closed the truck door behind her. Desiree wished she had a warmer coat to keep out the bitter wind, but at least she had warm boots. She would be cold when she arrived at the church, but anyone who lived in Wyoming was inured to the harsh weather.

To Desiree's amazement, she had been walking no more than two minutes, when she saw headlights through the snow. She was afraid she would be lost in the dark at the side of the road, so she stepped out onto the pavement and waved her arms. She knew the moment when the driver spotted her, because the pickup did a little slide to the side as it slowed.

As soon as the truck stopped, she raced to the driver's window. The door had already opened, and a tall man was stepping out.

"I need help! I—"

"What the hell are you doing out here walking on a night like this? Where's your car?"

Desiree felt her heart thump when she realized she was staring into the furious eyes of Carter Prescott. "My truck slid into a ditch. I was going back to the church to call for a tow. Can you give me a ride?"

"Get in," he said curtly.

Desiree raced around to the other side of the pickup before Carter could reach out to touch her.

As he pulled his door closed he said, "It's doubtful you'll get a tow truck to come out in this storm. I'll give you a ride home."

Desiree debated the wisdom of arguing with him. But she would rather have Nicole safe and warm at home than have to wait with her daughter in the cold until a tow truck arrived. "All right. But I left something in my truck that I need to pick up. It's only a little way ahead."

When Carter pulled up behind her truck he said, "Do you need any help?"

"I can handle it." Desiree was struggling with the door on Nicole's side of the truck, when it was pulled open from behind her. She whirled in fright—to find Carter standing right behind her.

"I figured you could use some help, after all."

Desiree took a deep breath. This man wasn't going to harm her. She had to stop acting so jumpy around him. "Thank you," she said.

The instant the truck door opened, Nicole came flying out. Desiree barely managed to catch her before she fell. In fact, she would have fallen if Carter hadn't put his arms around Desiree and supported both her and the child.

"This is the something you needed to pick up?" he asked.

Desiree heard the displeasure underlying his amazement and responded defensively, "This is my daughter, Nicole."

"You didn't say anything about a kid earlier this evening."

"It wasn't necessary that you know about her until we had reached some agreement."

"I don't think—"

Desiree cut him off. "I would rather not discuss this further until we're alone." Which was tantamount to a suggestion that they ought to have further discussion on the matter in private, Desiree realized too late.

"All right," he said.

"You can let go now. I've got her."

He was slow to remove his support, and Desiree was aware suddenly of how secure she had felt with his arms around her. And of being very much alone without them.

She carried Nicole the short distance to his truck. He held the passenger door open, but she found it awkward to step up into the truck with Nicole in her arms.

"Give her to me." Carter's tone of voice made it plain he would rather not have handled the child. Before either Desiree or Nicole could protest, he had the girl in his arms.

Desiree had barely settled herself in the truck when Carter dropped Nicole on her lap, shoved her thin wool coat inside and slammed the truck door closed.

"The turnoff for the Rimrock is about five miles ahead on the right," Desiree instructed.

"I know."

"How—"

"I drove by there on the way to my grandmother's. I haven't forgotten visiting your place when I was ten."

She watched him rub his thigh and wondered about the bone he had broken so many years ago. "Does it still bother you?"

"Sometimes."

"I'm sorry."

"No need to be. It was my own fault."

He looked sinister in the green light reflected off the dash, not at all like the savior she had sought out in the parking lot of the church.

"What's your name?" Nicole asked. "Do you know my mommy? I was an angel tonight. Do you want to see me fly?"

Carter's lips flattened in annoyance.

In the uncomfortable silence that followed her daughter's questions, a frown grew in the space between Desiree's brows. Carter's refusal to answer Nicole was rude—or at least, inconsiderate. Did Carter simply not like children? Or was it just Nicole's behavior he didn't approve of?

Carter's lack of response did nothing to curb Nicole's curiosity.

"Are you coming to our house?"

"Yes," Carter replied sharply.

Desiree realized he had probably been curt in hopes of shutting her daughter up. But Nicole wasn't deterred by Carter's antagonism. The little girl had learned through dealing with a mother who was putty in her hands that persistence often won her what she wanted.

"Do you want to see my room?"

Carter sighed.

Desiree could see that he wanted to say no. He sought out her eyes, his lips pursed in displeasure. She decided to rescue him from her daughter's clutches.

"It's nearly bedtime, sweetheart. You'll have to wait to show Mr. Prescott your room until some other time." It was all she could do to keep her own displeasure at the cowboy's surliness out of her voice.

"Are you going to be my daddy?"

"Nicole!"

Desiree was mortified at the question because she had, in fact, proposed to the man sitting across from her, and because she hadn't realized Nicole was even aware that she was seeking a husband. The little girl's next words made it clear that she had thought of the idea all on her own.

"My friend Shirley has a daddy, but I don't. I asked Santa Claus for a daddy, but so far I haven't got one. Are you the daddy I asked for?"

"No," he said in a strangled voice.

"Oh. Well, it's not Christmas yet," Nicole said cheerfully. "Maybe Santa Claus will bring me a daddy."

Desiree was chagrined at her daughter's outspokenness. However, if she had anything to say about it, Nicole would get her wish, although Carter's attitude toward Nicole was a matter that needed further exploration before their discussion of marriage continued.

Carter was pleased when they reached the Rimrock ranch house to discover it was just as he remembered it. The two-story frame structure had been built to last by people who cared. Someone had planted pines and spruce around the house, and with the drifting snow it was a scene worthy of a picture postcard.

"Follow the road around to the back," Desiree said.

Carter didn't volunteer to carry Nicole from the truck, and Desiree didn't ask. But halfway to the door, and though it made his stomach clench, he took the little girl in his arms to relieve Desiree of a burden that was obviously too heavy for her.

To his surprise, when he reached for the doorknob, he discovered that Desiree had locked the back door. Most ranches, even in this day and age, were left open, a vestige of range hospitality from a time when homesteads had been few and far between.

"Afraid of the bogeyman?" he asked with a wry grin.

Desiree didn't smile back. "I have to think of Nicole's safety." She stepped inside, turned on the light and held the door for him.

Carter immediately set the little girl down. His heart thudded painfully as he watched her race gleefully across the room, headed for the hall. She turned on the light and kept going. Carter could hear her running up the stairs.

"Make yourself comfortable while I put her to bed," Desiree said, following Nicole down the hallway that led to the rest of the house. "We'll talk as soon as I get her down. There's coffee on the stove or brandy in the living room. Help yourself." Then she was gone.

Carter hadn't been in the house before, but he knew the moment he crossed the threshold that this was a home. A band tightened around his chest, making it hard to breathe. This was what he had been seeking.

There was warmth and comfort here, not only for the body, but also for the soul.

The kitchen was cluttered, but clean. There were crayon drawings taped to the refrigerator, and a crock full of wooden spoons and a stack of cookbooks sat on an oak chest in the corner. The red-and-white linoleum floor was worn down to black in front of the sink, and the wooden round-leg table and ladderback chairs were scarred antiques. An old-fashioned tin coffeepot sat on the stove. Carter decided he would rather have the brandy.

He followed where Desiree had gone, down a hallway, past a formal dining room, to a combination office and parlor, where a stone fireplace took up one wall and a large rolltop desk took up most of another. A picture window took up the third wall. The fire had burned down to glowing embers, and Carter took the poker and stirred the ashes before adding another log.

A spruce Christmas tree stood in the corner, decorated with handmade ornaments. Above the fireplace, a set of longhorn steer horns a good six feet from tip to tip had been mounted.

Carter looked longingly at an old sofa and chairs that invited him to sit down. He heard a *whoosh* from the vents as the furnace engaged. As he surveyed the room, he realized that the aged quality he had admired so much in the furniture was as much the result of poverty as posterity. Certainly there were heirlooms here. But there was a shabbiness to the furnishings that could only be the result of limited funds.

Carter felt sick to his stomach. Maybe Desiree Parrish knew more about him than he had thought. Maybe she had come after him because she knew he had the money to restore this ranch to its former glory. He had been married once for his money. It wasn't an experience he intended to repeat.

He spied the wet bar where he found the brandy and glasses. "Would you like me to pour one for you?" he called up the stairs.

"Please. I'll join you in a moment," Desiree called down to him.

Desiree took a deep breath and let it out. She had another chance to persuade Carter Prescott that he should marry her. She had to do everything in her power to convince him that she—and the Rimrock—were a bargain he couldn't refuse.

She leaned over and kissed Nicole good-night. "Sleep tight, sweetheart." She left a small night-light burning. Not for Nicole. It was Desiree who feared the dark. She had made it a habit to leave a light so she could check on her daughter without the rush of terror that always caught her unaware when she entered a dark room.

Desiree closed her daughter's bedroom door behind her and hurried across the hall to her own room. She slipped out of her coat, which she hadn't even realized she was still wearing. But she had turned the heat down before she'd left for church to conserve energy, and it took time for the furnace to take the frost out of the air.

She crossed to the old oak dresser with the gold-framed mirror above it and checked her appearance. This was a heaven-sent second opportunity, and she wanted to look her best. It had become a habit to sit at an angle before the dresser, so only the good side of her face was reflected back to her. She forced herself to face forward, to see what Carter Prescott would see.

There was no way to disguise the scar. It was a white

slash that ran from chin to temple on her right side. Plastic surgery would have corrected it, but she didn't have the money for what would be purely cosmetic work. She put another layer of mascara on her lashes and freshened her lipstick. And she let her hair down. It was the one vanity she had left. It spread like rich brown silk across her shoulders and down to her waist.

She smoothed her black knit dress across a body that was curved in all the right places, but which she knew had brought her husband no pleasure. Desiree forced her thoughts away from the sadness that threatened to overwhelm her whenever she looked at herself in a mirror. She had to focus on the future, not the past. This was her last chance to make a good impression on Carter Prescott. She couldn't afford to waste it.

But it took all her courage to open the bedroom door and walk down the stairs.

Carter controlled the impulse to gasp as Desiree entered the parlor. It was the first time he had seen her when she wasn't shrouded in that moth-eaten coat. She moved with grace, her body slim and supple. Her dress hugged her body, revealing curves that most women would have died for. His groin tightened with desire.

He thought maybe his hands could almost span her waist. There wasn't much bosom, but more than a handful was a waste. His blood quickened at the thought that if she were his wife, he would have the right to hold her, to touch her, to seek out the secrets of her body and make them his.

He wasn't aware he was avoiding her face until he finally looked at it. His eyes dropped immediately to the brandy in his hands. He forced himself to look again, but focused on her eyes. They were a rich, warm brown, with long lashes and finely arched brows. It was clear she had once been a very beautiful woman. Once, but no more. The scar ran through her mouth on one side, twisting it down slightly.

"Did you pour a brandy for me?" she asked.

Carter realized he was staring and flushed. He welcomed the excuse to turn away, and shook his head slightly, aware he ought to do a better job of hiding his feelings. She had to look at that scar every day. The least he could do was face her without showing the pity he felt. He turned back to her with the drink in his hand and realized she had turned herself in profile, so he only saw the good side of her face. Desire stabbed him again.

He wondered if she had done it on purpose or whether it was an unconscious device she used to protect herself when she was with other people. At any rate, he was grateful for the respite that allowed him to speak to her without having to guard his expression.

Desiree took the drink from him. "Why don't you sit down and make yourself comfortable?" She gestured to a chair near the fire and sat down across from him on the sofa so he saw only her good side. "I never gave you a chance earlier this evening to respond to my proposal."

"I was glad for the time to think about what you had to say." Carter took a sip of his brandy.

"And?" Desiree held her breath, determined to wait for his answer. Her nerves got the better of her. She couldn't help making one last pitch. "You can see the house is comfortable." She forced a smile. "And I'm a good cook."

"Tell me again why you want to get married," he said in a quiet voice.

Desiree debated the wisdom of telling Carter the real reason she needed a husband. She had always believed honesty was the best policy. When she opened her mouth to speak, what came out was, "I've been on my own for six years. Nicole needs a father. I…the winters are long when you're alone. And I could use a partner to help me do the heavy work on the ranch.

"As you've seen for yourself, my face makes it impossible for me to attract a husband in the conventional way. I decided to take matters into my own hands."

"Why me?"

"Your grandmother speaks highly of you." She smiled. "And I haven't forgotten how you saved Boots."

"Boots?"

"My cat."

He rubbed his thigh and grimaced. "Right."

So maybe she didn't know about his money, Carter thought. She wanted company. And a father for her child. And someone to do the heavy work on the ranch. That made sense. And he could understand why she didn't trust a man to see beyond the scar on her face. He was having trouble doing that himself, although his body had responded—was responding even now—to the thought of joining hers in bed. She had beautiful eyes. In profile, the scar didn't show at all. And in the dark…

He would be giving her something in return for something he wanted very badly. Carter knew he could put down roots here. This place felt like a real home. He wanted to make it his. Though Desiree apparently didn't know it, he had the money to restore the Rimrock to what it had once been, to make it even better.

He wanted to ask her when and where she had gotten

the scar on her face, but he figured that could wait until they got to know each other better. Assuming they did.

"I have two problems with your proposal," he said.

Desiree had been certain he was going to say a flat no, so she welcomed the opportunity to overcome his objections. "What problems?"

Carter's lips thinned. "I hadn't counted on the girl. I'd want her kept out of my way."

Desiree bristled. "This is Nicole's home. I wouldn't think of confining her to any part of it to keep your paths from crossing. If you can't handle the fact that I have a daughter, this isn't going to work."

Carter was amazed at how Desiree's eyes flashed like fire when she was angry. In that moment, her scar made her look like a fierce warrior. He nodded abruptly. "All right." He supposed it wasn't necessary for her to keep the child out of his way; he would do whatever was necessary to keep his distance from the little girl.

"And the second problem?" Desiree asked.

"I can't agree to a marriage in name only."

Desiree paled. Her heart pounded, and her stomach rolled over so she felt like throwing up. She couldn't couple with any man, ever again. "Why not?" She forced out the words through stiff lips.

"I don't plan to spend the rest of my life as a monk. I'd expect my wife to provide the necessary comfort on cold winter nights."

Desiree flushed as his eyes boldly assessed her body. She found the man she had selected to be her husband quite handsome. But she had learned from bitter experience that a man became a beast when satisfying his sexual needs. She dreaded what he might expect of her. She was certain she had nothing to offer him.

But it would humiliate her to have her husband going to some other woman for his needs. In their small ranch community the talk would be bad enough if he married her. She didn't want to give her neighbors any more reason to gossip.

"I'm willing to compromise," she said at last.

"There is no compromise on this," he said. "Either you're willing to be my wife or you're not."

"I'm willing to be a real wife," she assured him. "But not until we know each other better."

Carter's lips twisted. "How long do you expect that to take?"

"I don't know." Desiree looked him in the eye and watched as he stared back, careful not to let his eyes drop to her scar.

"All right," he said at last. "I accept your proposal."

CHAPTER THREE

THEY DECIDED TO BE married a week later in a civil ceremony in Casper. Desiree offered Carter the guest bedroom, but he decided to stay in a hotel in town until the wedding so he could take care of some unfinished business.

"I'd like Nicole to be present at the wedding," Desiree said as she stood holding his shearling coat for him at the kitchen door.

"Is that really necessary?"

"Once we're married, you'll be her father. I think it would help her to adjust better if she saw us take our vows."

"From what I've heard, she'll probably think I'm a gift from Santa Claus," he muttered.

Desiree couldn't help smiling. Chances were, Nicole would.

THE DAY OF THE wedding dawned clear and crisp. Most of the snow had blown away or into drifts, revealing a vast expanse of golden grass. Desiree woke with a feeling of trepidation. Was marriage the right solution to her problem? Would she and Nicole achieve safety by bringing Carter Prescott into the house? Was that alone enough? She considered buying a gun to protect them, but realized that she wouldn't be able to use it, so it would only become one more danger.

Desiree was still snuggled under the warm covers

when she heard the patter of bare feet on the hardwood floor. Her door opened and Nicole came trotting over to the four-poster.

"Where are your slippers, young lady?" Desiree chastised as she hauled Nicole up and under the covers with her.

Nicole promptly put her icy feet on Desiree's thigh.

"Your feet are freezing!"

Nicole giggled.

Desiree took her daughter's feet in her hands and rubbed them to warm them up. "Today's the day Mr. Carter and I are getting married," she reminded Nicole.

"Is he going to be my daddy now?"

"Uh-huh." Desiree hadn't asked how Carter felt about being called Daddy. Surely he wouldn't mind. After all, being called Daddy didn't require any effort on his part.

One of her major concerns over the past week had been how well Carter would get along with Nicole. During his visits he was brusque if forced to speak at all, but mostly he held himself aloof from Nicole. She supposed that was only natural for a man who apparently hadn't spent time around children. And a man his age—he must be thirty-three or thirty-four—probably didn't remember what it was like to be a child. Obviously he would need a little time to adjust.

Desiree glanced at the clock and realized that by the time she put a roast in the oven for their post-wedding dinner, she would barely have enough time to dress herself and Nicole and get into Casper before they were due in the judge's chambers. "We'd better get moving, or we're going to be late."

Desiree took a deep breath and let it out. For better or worse, her decision had been made. Whatever price she had to pay for her own and her daughter's safety was worth it. Marriage, even the duty of the marriage bed, was not too great a sacrifice.

Carter was having second thoughts of his own. He paced the empty hallway of the courthouse in Casper, waiting for his bride. The sound of his bootsteps on the marble floors echoed off the high ceilings. The loneliness of the years he had spent wandering kept him from bolting. *Roots.* Finally he had found a place where he could belong. He would settle down on the Rimrock and be a husband and father. Again.

He paused in midstep. The sudden tightness in his chest, the breathlessness he felt, made him angry. He should have put the past behind him long ago. Beginning today he would. He wouldn't think about it anymore. He wouldn't let it hurt him anymore. It was over and done.

He looked up, and there she was.

"Hello. I'm sorry I'm late," Desiree said.

His gaze shifted quickly from the scar that twisted her smile to the first place he could think to look—his watch. "You're right on time."

"I didn't think I'd make it. We were late getting up and—"

"Are you going to be my daddy?"

"Nicole!" Desiree clapped a hand over her daughter's mouth. "She's a little excited."

"So am I," Carter admitted with a wry smile. "Shall we get on with it?" He snagged Desiree by the elbow and headed in the direction of the judge's chambers. She was wearing that moth-eaten coat again. He wondered what she had on under it. He didn't have to wait long to satisfy his curiosity. The judge's chambers were uncomfortably warm, and Desiree slipped the black wool off her shoulders and laid it over the back of a brass-studded maroon leather chair.

She smiled at Carter again, and he forced his eyes down over the flowered dress she was wearing. It was obviously the best she had, but wrong for the season, and it showed years of wear. He felt a spurt of guilt for not offering her the money for a new dress. But since she apparently didn't know about his wealth, he preferred to keep it that way. Then, if feelings developed between them, he would be sure they weren't motivated by the fact he had a deep pocket.

Desiree couldn't take her eyes off Carter. She was stunned by his appearance. In the first place, he had shaved off the shadow of beard. His blunt jaw and sharp, high cheekbones gave his face an almost savage look. His tailored Western suit should have made him look civilized, but instead it emphasized the power in his broad shoulders and his over-six-foot height. "You look…wonderful," she said.

For some reason, Carter appeared distressed by the compliment. Then she realized he hadn't said anything about how she looked. It didn't take much imagination to figure out why. She had done nothing to hide the scar on her face. She had seen how his eyes skipped away from it. But he was still here. And apparently ready to go through with the wedding.

The judge entered his chambers in a flurry of black robes. "I've only got a few minutes," he said. "Are you two ready?"

"There are three of us, Judge Carmichael," Carter said, nodding in Nicole's direction.

"So there are," the judge said. He peered over the

top of his black-rimmed bifocals at the little girl. "Hello there. What's your name?"

Nicole retreated behind her mother's skirts.

"Her name is Nicole," Desiree said.

"All right, Nicole. Let's get your mommy married, shall we? Why don't the two of you stand together in front of my desk?" the judge instructed Carter and Desiree. He called his secretary and the court bailiff to act as witnesses.

Desiree suddenly felt as shy as her daughter and wished there were a skirt she could retreat behind. Carter reached out to draw her to his side, but she quickly scooted around him so the unblemished part of her face would be toward him while they said their vows. She wished she could have been beautiful for him. It would have made all this so much easier. But she wouldn't have needed a husband if things had been different.

"Are we all ready?" the judge asked.

"Just a minute." Carter searched the room for a moment. "There they are." He crossed to a bookshelf and picked up a small bouquet of flowers. "When I arrived your secretary offered to put these in here for me."

Desiree stared at the bouquet of wildflowers garnished with beautiful white silk ribbons that Carter was holding out to her. A flush skated across her cheekbones. The thoughtfulness of his gesture made her feel more like a bride. It made everything seem more real. Her heart thumped a mile a minute, and she put a hand up as though to slow it down.

She stared at Carter, seeing wariness—not warmth—in his blue eyes as she reached out to take the flowers. "Thank you, Carter."

His features relaxed and the wariness fled, replaced

by what looked suspiciously like relief. Unfortunately, Carter's trek for the flowers had taken him across the room, and when he returned he ended up on her right side, the side with the scar. She hid her dismay, but lowered her chin so her hair fell across her face.

"Now are we ready?" the judge asked impatiently.

Desiree nodded slightly. She felt Carter's fingertips on her chin. He tipped her face upward until he was looking her in the eye.

"Are you sure you want to do this?"

"Yes," she croaked.

"Keep your chin up," he murmured. He turned to the judge and said, "We're ready."

Desiree appreciated Carter's encouraging words but had no idea how to tell him so. She heard very little of what the judge said. She was too conscious of the man standing beside her. She could smell a masculine cologne and feel the heat of him along her right side. On her other side, she was aware of Nicole's death grip on her hand.

"The ring?" the judge asked.

"Here." Carter produced a simple gold band, which he slipped on Desiree's left hand.

He turned back to the judge, who was about to continue the ceremony when Desiree said, "I have a ring for you, too."

She saw the surprise on Carter's face, but he didn't object. She fumbled in the pocket of her skirt until she found the gold band she had so painstakingly selected. She was aware of the calluses on Carter's palm and fingertips as she held his hand to slip on the ring. Desiree dared a glance at Carter's face when she saw how well it fit.

He smiled at her, and she felt her heart skip a beat:

She turned to face the judge, feeling confused and flustered.

Carter took her hand in his and waited for the judge to continue. It wasn't long before he said, "I now pronounce you man and wife."

To Desiree, the wedding ceremony was over too quickly, and it didn't feel "finished." She realized the judge hadn't suggested that Carter kiss his bride. She waited, every muscle tensed, wondering if he would act on his own. A second ticked past, another, and another.

Which was when Nicole said, "Are you going to kiss Mommy now?"

"Nicole!"

Desiree's face reddened with embarrassment. She couldn't bear to look at Carter, afraid of what she would see.

The sound of a masculine chuckle was followed by the feel of Carter's hand on her unblemished cheek. She closed her eyes, flinching when she felt his moist breath against her face. She heard him make a sound of displeasure in his throat and felt his hesitation.

Desiree forced herself to stand still, waiting for the touch of his lips against hers, but her body stiffened, rejecting before it came, this sign of masculine possession.

Soft. So soft. And gentle.

Desiree's eyes flickered open, and she stared wide-eyed at the man who had just become her husband. Her breathing was erratic, and her heart was bumping madly. It hadn't been a painful kiss. Quite the contrary. Her lips had…tingled. She raised her hand toward her mouth in wonder.

Carter was staring at her, the expression on his face inscrutable. She had no idea what he was thinking.

She had married a stranger.

It was a terrifying thought, and Desiree felt the panic welling up inside her. Carter must have sensed her feelings, because he quickly thanked the judge, shook Carmichael's hand, watched as the witnesses signed the marriage certificate, in which Desiree had once again given up her maiden name of Parrish, and hustled her and Nicole out of the courthouse.

"I've made reservations for lunch at Benham's," Carter said, naming one of the fanciest restaurants in Casper.

Desiree put a hand to her queasy stomach. The last thing she wanted right now was food.

"I'm starving," Nicole piped up.

"I guess that's settled," Carter said. "Let's go eat."

"Not in a restaurant," Desiree protested. "I put a roast in the oven before I left the ranch. Please, let's go home."

"Home," Carter said. It had a wonderful sound. "All right, then. Home. I'll follow you in my pickup."

Desiree welcomed the brief respite before they sat down to their first meal as husband and wife. Once in the truck, Nicole focused her attention on Desiree's wedding bouquet, which left Desiree free to mentally compare this wedding with her first one.

She had been only eighteen years old and desperately in love with Burley Kelton. Burley had come to work as a cowhand for her father, and she had fallen hard for his broad shoulders and his rakish smile. After a whirlwind romance they had married in the First Presbyterian Church. She had worn her mother's antique-lace wedding gown and carried a pungent bouquet of gardenias.

Desiree had been a total innocent on her wedding night, naive and frightened, but so in love with Burley that she would have done anything he asked.

Only Burley hadn't asked for anything. He had taken what he wanted. Brutally. Horribly. Painfully. She didn't dare cry out for fear her parents would hear her in their room down the hall from her bedroom. So she bore her wedding night stoically. She survived, to endure even worse in the next weeks and months of her marriage.

They lived with her parents, and Burley continued working for her father. She kept up a front, refusing to let her parents know how bad things were. Then her mom and dad were killed in a freak one-car accident, and she was left alone with Burley. It was a ghastly end to what she now realized were girlish dreams of romance.

Burley told her the pain she felt when he exercised his husbandly rights was her fault. He had to work hard to find any pleasure in her, because she was frigid. He should have married a woman who had more experience, one who knew how to satisfy a man.

Even though Burley found her wanting in bed, he was insanely jealous if she so much as said hello to another man. When she suggested they might be better off apart, he became enraged and said he had taken his vows "Till death do us part!" and that he had meant them.

It had almost come to that.

Desiree stole a glance at Carter in the rearview mirror. At least she would be spared her wifely duties for a time. Maybe if she explained that he would find no joy in her, Carter might even change his mind about wanting to take her to bed.

Carter was having similar, but contrary, thoughts. In fact, he was wondering how long it would be before his wife became his wife—in the biblical sense. He had stood next to her during the short ceremony and felt her heat, smelled the soft floral fragrance that clung to her hair and clothes and felt himself forcing back the feelings of want and need that rose within him.

He had seen her flinch when he tried to kiss her after the ceremony. It wasn't the first time she had recoiled from him, either. She must have been badly treated by some man, somewhere along the line. Her father? Her husband? So what were the chances she was going to let him get anywhere near her, anytime soon? Not good, he admitted. She had said they would have to wait until they knew each other better, and she had no idea when that would be. He was willing to be patient—for a while. He couldn't help comparing this wedding with his first one.

Carter hadn't been able to keep his hands off Jeanine, and she had been equally enamored of him. They had anticipated their wedding night by about a year, and knowing what he could expect in bed had kept him aroused through most of the ceremony and reception. He had been so much in love with Jeanine that it had been difficult to force the vows past his constricted throat. Knowing the reason they were marrying had been an extra bonus as far as he was concerned.

Looking back, he realized that the tears in Jeanine's eyes hadn't been tears of joy, as she had professed. His trembling bride had been trembling for entirely different reasons than the ones he had supposed. Now he knew why she had been so miserable. If only...

Carter swore under his breath. Wishing wouldn't change the past. He was crazy to be reliving that nightmare, especially when he had just promised himself he wouldn't look back anymore. He would do better to look forward to the future with Desiree Parrish—no, now Desiree Prescott.

Carter quashed the awful thought that arose like a

many-headed hydra: *This woman can't betray me. Her scarred face will keep her from tempting another man.* It wasn't the first time he had thought it, and he couldn't truly say whether the scar on her face had been a consideration when he agreed to marry her. But he was ashamed for what he was thinking and grateful that Desiree couldn't read his mind. She deserved better from the man who had just become her husband.

Carter pulled his truck up beside Desiree's pickup in back of the house. His wife and new daughter were already inside the house before he could catch up to them. If he hadn't known better, he would have said Desiree was fleeing from him. If she was, she was wasting her time. Now that they were married, there was no place for her to run.

Desiree hurried to make herself busy before Carter came inside. She turned up the furnace and slipped off her coat and Nicole's and sent her daughter upstairs to play.

Then she returned to the kitchen and waited beside the stove, her arms crossed over her chest. Carter didn't bother to knock before he opened the door and stepped inside. He didn't bother to close the door, either, just headed straight for her, his stride determined. A moment later he had swept her off her feet and into his arms.

Desiree grabbed hold of his neck, afraid for a moment he might drop her. His arms tightened around her, and she knew there was no danger of that. He headed right back outside.

"What are you doing?" she asked breathlessly, her eyes wide with trepidation.

"There's a tradition that hasn't been observed."

"What's that?"

Once he was outside, he paused long enough to glare down at her. Through clenched teeth he said, "Carrying the bride over the threshold." He turned around and marched right back into the kitchen.

Desiree was too astonished to protest. She stared up at his rigid jaw and realized again how little they knew of each other. "I'm sorry," she said. "I didn't know you felt so strongly about it, or I would have waited. But we never discussed—"

"There are a lot of things we haven't discussed. I guess it's going to take a while for us to adjust to each other."

He was still holding her in his arms. Desiree became increasingly uncomfortable, as another kind of tension began to grow between them. She recognized the signs on Carter's face. The drooping eyelids, the nostrils flared for the scent of her, the jumping pulse at his throat. She began to struggle for freedom.

"Let me go. Let me down. Now!"

His hold tightened. "What the hell's the matter with you?"

"Let me go!" she shrieked.

A moment later she was on her feet. She retreated from him several paces, until her back was against the wall. She stared at him, eyes wide, blood racing. "We agreed we would wait!" she accused.

"I only wanted a kiss," he said.

She shook her head. "No kissing, no touching, nothing until we know each other," she insisted.

Desiree watched a muscle jerk in his jaw. She knew he could force her. Burley had. She reached behind her surreptitiously with one hand, searching for a weapon on the counter. But there was nothing close by.

"What did he do to you?" Carter asked in a quiet voice.

"What makes you think—"

"Every time I move too fast you flinch like a horse that's been whipped. You're trembling like a beaten animal right now. And the look in your eyes… I've seen men facing a nest of rattlers who've looked less terrified. It doesn't take a scientist to figure out you've been mistreated. Do you want to tell me about it?"

Desiree couldn't get an answer past the lump in her throat. She lowered her eyes to avoid his searching gaze. She couldn't help jerking when he reached out a hand to her.

Carter swore under his breath. "I'm not going to hurt you," he repeated through clenched teeth.

Desiree forced herself to remain still as he reached out again for her chin and tipped it up so they were staring into each other's eyes.

"You're my wife. We'll be spending the rest of our lives together. I'm willing to wait as long as it takes for you to accept me in your bed."

"No kissing, no—"

He shook his head. "There'll be kissing, and hugging and touching. Even friends do that much."

"But—"

He cut her off by putting his lips against hers. Desiree fought the panic, reminding herself that his first kiss had been gentle. This one was no less so, just the barest touch of lips, but she felt a shock clear to her toes. It wasn't a bad feeling. Oh, no, it wasn't bad at all.

Luckily, his lips left hers just at the moment when

she felt herself ready to struggle in earnest. When she opened her eyes, she saw that he hadn't retreated very far.

"Desiree?"

"Carter, I…I'm scared," she admitted in a whisper.

He drew her slowly into his arms. As his strength enfolded her she forced herself to relax. It wasn't easy. Burley had sometimes begun gently, only to lose control later.

Carter's arms remained loose around her. In a few minutes she realized she was no longer trembling, that she was almost relaxed in his embrace.

"This is nice," he murmured in her ear. "You feel good against me."

Desiree stiffened. She knew he felt her withdrawal when he said, "It's all right, Desiree. It's just a hug, nothing more. Relax, sweetheart."

He cajoled her much as he might a reluctant mare, and she found herself responding to his warm baritone voice. She laid her head against his chest and tentatively put her hands at his trim waist.

Just as she made those gestures of concession, he stepped back from her. She raised her eyes to his in confusion. She hadn't expected him to stop. But she was glad he had.

"How soon will lunch be ready?" he asked.

Desiree turned quickly to the oven. She had completely forgotten about the roast beef during the past tension-filled minutes. "It should be done shortly."

"Anything I can do to help?"

Desiree raised startled eyes to study Carter's face. "You're willing to help in the kitchen?"

"Why not?"

Burley never had. Burley had said the kitchen was woman's work. "You could set the table if you'd like."

Carter took the initiative and started hunting through cabinets for what he wanted. "Best way to find out where everything is," he explained with a cheeky grin.

"You're probably right." Desiree found herself smiling back, even though it was unsettling to see a stranger going through everything as though he had the right.

He has the right. He's your husband.

As she peeled potatoes and put vegetables in a pot on the stove, Desiree realized she had been extraordinarily lucky in her second choice of husband. Carter wasn't like Burley. He could control his passions. It was too bad he was getting such a bad bargain. She couldn't be the wife he obviously wanted and needed. She was too bruised in spirit to respond as he wished.

Desiree had planned this dinner at home because she had feared that conversation between them would be stilted, and it would be embarrassing to sit across from each other in a restaurant in total silence. However, when the three of them sat down together, things didn't turn out at all as she had expected. Carter, bless him, wasn't the least bit taciturn. He even condescended to answer several of Nicole's questions. However, when Nicole finished eating and approached Carter, Desiree realized there were limits to his tolerance.

"Can I sit on your lap?" Nicole asked.

"You're a big girl," Carter replied.

"Not too big," Nicole said, sidling up next to him. "My friend Shirley sits in her daddy's lap."

"I'm not your—"

Desiree cut him off before he could deny any relationship to her daughter. "Carter has a full stomach right now. Why don't you go upstairs to your room and play," she said.

Nicole gave Carter a look from beneath lowered lashes. "Is your stomach really full?" she demanded suspiciously.

Desiree saw the war Carter waged, the way his hands fisted. "Nicole! Go play."

Nicole's lower lip stuck out, but she knew better than to argue when her mother used that tone of voice.

The little girl had already turned to leave when Carter grabbed her under the arms and hefted her into his lap. "I suppose you can sit here for a minute," he said grudgingly.

But Desiree caught the brief, awful look of anguish in Carter's eyes as his arms closed around the little girl.

Nicole settled back against Carter's chest and chattered happily, oblivious to the undercurrents.

Over the next five minutes, Carter's face looked more and more strained, and his jaw tightened. Desiree realized there was something very wrong.

"That's enough for now, Nicole," Desiree said. "It's time for you to go upstairs and choose a book for me to read before your nap."

Carter sighed as though relieved of a great burden as he lifted Nicole from his lap and set her on her feet.

Nicole ran upstairs without a backward glance, leaving them alone at the table. Desiree waited for Carter to explain himself. To her amazement, he pretended as though nothing out of the ordinary had happened.

"If I'd known how good you can cook, I'd have jumped at that first proposal," he said.

Desiree didn't press the issue. And she chose to accept the compliment, rather than be put off by the fact Carter hadn't wanted to marry her at first. "Thank you."

"Maybe you could give me a tour of the ranch this afternoon," Carter suggested.

"Nicole usually takes a nap after lunch. I should be up there getting her settled right now. You're welcome to take a look on your own."

Carter saw the relief in Desiree's eyes at the thought they wouldn't have to spend the rest of the day together. He could see she was going to use the child as an excuse to keep them apart. It was funny, because he had planned to use ranch business with her as a way to avoid the child.

"I can wait until Nicole wakes up. We'll go then," he said.

"She'll have to come with us."

As a chaperon, Carter thought wryly. But the little girl obviously couldn't be left alone, and there was no one else around to take care of her. One or the other of them would always have to be with her. Which led him to ask, "How on earth have you managed to do the chores around the ranch and take care of Nicole at the same time?"

"Sometimes it isn't easy," Desiree admitted.

Carter thought that was probably the understatement of the century.

"All right," he said. "While Nicole's napping you can show me around the house."

She gave him a disconcerted look. Was he looking for an opportunity to get her alone in the bedroom? "There isn't much to see."

"You can show me what needs fixing. I couldn't help noticing that the faucet drips in the kitchen, and the newel post on the stairs wobbles."

Two pink spots of color appeared on her cheeks. She

was thinking of bed, while he was thinking of dripping faucets! It would be funny if it weren't so humiliating. "I didn't marry you to get a handyman."

He grinned. "But isn't it lucky that I am one? Come on, Desiree, every house needs a few repairs now and then."

Her lips flattened grimly. "I'm afraid this one needs more than that."

"Oh?"

She recited a long list of problems with the house that ended, "And I'm not sure the furnace will make it through the winter."

He stared at her, stunned by the enormity of what she had been coping with on her own. No wonder she had wanted—needed—a husband. Strange as it seemed, he felt better knowing how much work the ranch needed. It was a rational explanation for why she had married him, even if she had done it in a damned havy cavy way.

He could have used his money and had repairmen do everything that needed to be done in a matter of weeks. But he didn't want her to know yet about his wealth. He wanted a chance to be needed—loved?—for himself alone. Later would be soon enough to reveal the rest.

"I guess I'll start on those repairs while Nicole is napping," he conceded finally.

"I usually do something quiet, so I won't disturb her."

"And repairing the newel post is hardly quiet." He said it as a statement, not a question.

She shook her head. He was pleased to see just the hint of a smile tease the corners of her mouth. The scar didn't pucker so badly with the smaller smile. He forced his eyes away from the mark on her face.

"All right," he said with a gusty sigh. "You can show

me the ranch books this afternoon. If you don't think that would be too noisy a proposition?"

Desiree giggled. She didn't know where the sound had come from, and it certainly wasn't anything she could remember doing recently. But the look of surrender to the inevitable on Carter's face struck her as funny.

"Just let me get Nicole settled, and I'll be back to do the dishes."

"I'll do them," Carter volunteered.

"That's not necessary, I—"

"The sooner the dishes are done, the sooner we can get to those ranch books."

What Desiree heard in his voice, what she saw in his eyes was *The sooner we can be alone.*

"Maybe you'd rather take that tour of the ranch," she suggested.

Carter shook his head no. "I'd rather wait and go with you."

Desiree stood rooted where she was, pierced by a look in his blue eyes that held a wealth of promises. She wanted to warn him that she couldn't fulfill those promises. But something kept her silent. The longer it took him to figure out the truth about her sexually, the better. She dreaded the disgust she was sure would be her lot when he realized what a failure she was in bed.

Desiree took one last look over her shoulder at Carter before she left the kitchen. He was already clearing the table. Her grandmother's silver-rimmed china looked fragile in his big hands, but he moved with easy grace between the table and sink. The thought of Nicole waiting anxiously for her upstairs pulled her from the mesmerizing sight of her husband doing the dishes on their wedding day.

To Nicole's delight, Desiree read two stories. The first because she always did, the second because she was putting off the moment when she would have to rejoin Carter in the parlor, which also served as the ranch office.

When Nicole's eyelids drifted shut and her tiny rosebud mouth fell slack, Desiree realized the inevitable could be avoided no longer.

She rose and squared her shoulders like an aristocrat headed for the guillotine. It was time to begin the process of becoming a wife and partner to the stranger downstairs.

Desiree felt her legs trembling and told herself she was being foolish. There was no need to fear Carter. He was not like Burley.

Not yet. But what happens when you disappoint him in bed?

That won't be for a while yet. Carter promised—

You saw the look in his eyes when he carried you over the threshold. Was that the look of a patient man?

So he desires me. That isn't a bad thing. Especially since we're married.

Are you ready to submit to him? To trust him with the secrets of your body?

Desiree shuddered. Not yet. *Not yet.* She ignored her trembling limbs and headed downstairs to join her husband. She would just have to be firm with Carter.

Sex would have to wait.

CHAPTER FOUR

DESIREE WALKED DOWN the stairs, knees trembling—and found Carter sound asleep on the couch. An awkward feeling of tenderness washed over her as she stared at the sleeping man. Apparently he had needed a nap as much as Nicole. She sat down across from him in the comfortable armchair that faced the fireplace in the parlor and searched his features.

The rugged planes of his face were less fearsome in repose. The blue shadows under his eyes suggested that he had put in some long hours the week before they were married. What had he been doing? The fact that she had no idea pointed to how much a stranger he was to her. A boyish lock of chestnut hair fell across his forehead, and she had to resist the urge to reach over and brush it back into place.

Desiree breathed a sigh of relief that her fears about confronting Carter hadn't been realized. At least, not yet. She knew she ought to get up and go do some chores, but the fire made the room seem so cozy that she settled deeper into the overstuffed chair. The house was quiet, with only the sound of the furnace doing its level best to keep up with the cold. She scooched down in the chair, put her feet up on an equally overstuffed footstool, and let her eyelids droop closed.

Desiree wasn't sure what woke her, but she had the

distinct feeling she was being watched. It was a feeling she recognized, and one that caused her heart to pound so hard she could almost hear it. She took a deep breath and let it out, forcing herself to relax. Then she opened her eyes.

Carter was sitting on the couch, staring at her. At some point while she was asleep, he had changed his clothes and was now wearing jeans and a red and blue plaid shirt with his work boots.

She watched him through wary eyes without moving.

"I didn't mean to wake you," he said.

She sat up carefully. "You didn't."

"If you say so." He yawned and stretched. She was impressed again by the breadth of his chest, by the play of muscles in his shoulders and arms. He caught her looking at him and grinned. "I had hoped we'd spend some part of the day sleeping together, but I had something a little different in mind."

Desiree tensed, waiting for him to make some move to close the distance between them. But he relaxed with one arm settled along the back of the couch and hung one booted ankle across the opposite knee.

"I don't suppose we'll have time now to look at the books before Nicole is awake."

Desiree looked at her watch. "We've slept away the afternoon!"

Carter thrust all ten fingers through his hair, leaving it standing in all directions. "I guess I was more tired than I thought. It's been a tough week."

"Oh?" Desiree arched a questioning brow. "What kept you so busy?"

Carter cleared his throat. "Just some business I

needed to clear up before the wedding. Nothing worth mentioning."

He was lying. Desiree didn't know why she was so sure about it, except that one moment he had been looking at her—well, not at her face, but in her direction—and the next, his gaze was focused intently on the leafy design sewn into his worn leather boots. She didn't believe in keeping secrets. It spawned distrust. But considering the fact she hadn't been totally honest with Carter, Desiree could hardly challenge him on the matter.

"What shall we do with the time until supper?" Carter asked.

Desiree was thinking in terms of chores that could be finished, when Carter suggested, "Why don't you tell me a little bit about what you've been doing in the years since we last met?"

"I wouldn't know where to start. Besides, what matters is the present and the future, not the past."

Carter pursed his lips and muttered, "If only that were true."

Desiree met Carter's gaze. His eyes held the same despairing look she had seen when he held Nicole at the dinner table. What had happened, she wondered, that had caused him so much pain? "Are you all right?"

The vulnerability in his eyes was gone as quickly as it had appeared, replaced by icy orbs that didn't invite questioning. Desiree welcomed the sight of her daughter in the doorway. "Did you have a good nap, sweetheart?"

"Uh-huh. Are we going for a ride now?" Nicole bounced over to Carter and laid her hands on his thigh, as though she had known him forever.

Desiree held her breath waiting for his reaction. It came in the form of a puff of breath Carter expelled so softly it could barely be heard. He stared at the spot where Nicole's tiny hands rested so confidently against him. He stood without touching her, and her hands of necessity fell away.

Nicole reached up to tug on the sleeve of his flannel shirt. "Can we go see Matilda first?"

"Who's Matilda?" Carter asked.

"She's my calf. She's black."

"Matilda's mother didn't survive the birth," Desiree explained quietly. "I've been keeping the calf in the barn and feeding her by hand." Desiree saw the look of incredulity on Carter's face and hurried to explain, "I—we—can't afford to lose a single head of stock."

"I had no idea things were so bad," Carter said.

"There's no danger of losing the ranch," she reassured him. "I've just been extra busy because my hired hand broke his leg and has been out of commission for nearly two months."

For reasons Desiree didn't want to explain to Carter, she hadn't been able to bring herself to hire a stranger to work for her. Which made no sense at all, considering the fact she had married one.

Nicole grabbed Carter's hand and began tugging him from the room. Desiree watched to see if he would free himself. He did, quickly shoving his hands in his back pockets. But he followed where Nicole led. She trailed the two of them from the parlor through the house to the kitchen, where they retrieved their coats, hats and gloves and headed out the kitchen door.

As usual in Wyoming, the wind was blowing. Desiree hurried to catch up to Nicole so she could pull her daughter's parka hood up over her head. Before she reached Nicole, Carter did it for her.

Desiree found his behavior with Nicole confusing, to say the least. He clearly didn't want anything to do with the little girl, but he stopped short of ignoring her. What had him so leery of children?

Desiree heard Nicole chattering and hurried to catch up. Carter had been doing fine tolerating the five-year-old, but she saw no reason to test his patience.

Thanks to the body heat of the animals inside, the barn felt almost warm in comparison with the frigid outdoors. Nicole let go of Carter's hand and raced to a stall halfway down the barn. She unlatched it and stepped inside. The tiny Black Angus calf made a bleating sound of welcome and hurried up to her.

"Matilda is hungry, Mommy," Nicole said.

"I'll fix her something right now." Desiree went to the refrigerator, where she kept the milk for the calf. She poured some out into a nursing bottle and set it in a pot of water on a hot plate nearby to warm. When she returned to the stall she found Carter down on one knee beside the calf.

"Matilda's mommy is dead," Nicole explained. "So Mommy and I have to take care of her."

"It looks like you're doing a fine job," Carter conceded gruffly.

The calf bawled piteously, and Nicole circled the calf's neck with her arms to calm it. "Mommy's getting your bottle, Matilda. Moooommy!" she yelled. "Matilda's starving!"

Desiree hustled back to the hot plate, unplugged it and retrieved the bottle. A moment later she dropped onto her knees beside the calf. Nicole took the heavy bottle from her mother and held it while the calf sucked loudly and hungrily.

Desiree met Carter's eyes over the calf's head. There was a smile on his face that had made its way to his eyes.

"This is turning out to be a great honeymoon," he said with a chuckle.

Desiree laughed. "I suppose it is a little unconventional."

"That's putting it mildly."

There was a warmth in his eyes that said he would be happy to put the train back on the rails. Desiree was amazed to find herself relaxed in his presence. However, her feelings for Carter were anything but comfortable. Her fear of men hadn't disappeared. Yet she was forced to admit that Carter evoked more than fear in her breast. She hadn't expected to be physically attracted to him. She hadn't expected to want to touch him and to want him to touch her. She hadn't expected to regret her inability to respond to him—or any man—as a woman.

Her expression sobered.

"What's wrong?" Carter asked.

She wondered how he could be so perceptive. "What makes you think anything's wrong?"

He reached out a hand and smoothed the furrows on her brow. His callused fingertips slid across her unmarked cheek and along the line of her jaw.

Desiree edged away from his touch. Her heart had slipped up to lodge in her throat, making speech impossible.

"Matilda is done, Mommy," Nicole said as she extended the empty bottle toward her mother.

Desiree lurched to her feet. "That's—" She cleared her throat and tried again. "That's good, darling." She took the bottle and Nicole's hand and hurried out of the stall. She headed for the sink in the barn and rinsed out the bottle.

Carter had started after her, but when she turned around she realized he had stopped at the stall and was examining the hinges.

"This is hanging lopsided. Do you have a pair of pliers?"

Desiree would rather have headed right back to the house, but forced herself to respond naturally. "Sure. Let me get them."

Desiree watched as Carter made a few adjustments to the stall door, tightening the bolts that held the frame in place.

"That ought to do it."

Desiree thought of the months the door had been hanging like that, when neither she nor her hired hand, Sandy, had taken the time to fix it. In a matter of minutes Carter had resolved the problem.

"Thanks," she said.

"No need to thank me. It was my pleasure."

Desiree searched his face and saw the look of satisfaction there. He was telling the truth. He had enjoyed himself. "Fortunately for you there are lots of things that need fixing around here," she said sardonically.

He headed down the aisle of the barn to return the pliers to the toolbox. "I think that's enough for today, though. After all, I am still on my honeymoon."

"What's a honeymoon?" Nicole asked.

Desiree saw the smirk that came and went on Carter's face. She found the question embarrassing, especially with Carter listening to everything she was about to say. But she had made it a habit to answer any question Nicole asked as honestly as possible.

"It's the time a husband and wife spend together getting to know each other when they're first married," Desiree explained.

"Like you and Mr. Prescott," Nicole said.

Desiree brushed Nicole's bangs out of her eyes. "Yes." Desiree looked up and found Carter watching her, his eyes hooded with desire. A glance downward showed her he was hard and ready. A frisson of alarm skittered down her spine. She rose abruptly and took her daughter's hand. "I'm going to start supper," she said.

"I'll be in shortly," Carter replied in a raspy voice. "I see a few more things I can do out here, after all."

The atmosphere at supper was strained. Not that she and Carter conversed much more or less than at lunchtime, but Nicole never stopped chattering. Carter never initiated contact with Nicole, but he didn't rebuff her when she climbed into his lap after supper. If the threat of danger hadn't been hanging over her, she might actually have let herself feel optimistic about the future.

She and Carter did the dishes together, while Nicole colored with crayons at the kitchen table. It was so much a picture of a natural, normal family that Desiree wanted to cry. Her feelings of guilt for marrying Carter without telling him the whole truth forced her to excuse herself and take Nicole up to bed early the night of her wedding.

"I'll see you in the morning," she said to Carter.

She didn't know what to make of the look on his face—part desire, part regret, part something else she couldn't identify—but fled upstairs as quickly as she could.

Once in bed, she couldn't sleep. She heard Carter come upstairs, heard the shower, heard him brush his teeth, heard the toilet flush. His footsteps were soft in the hall, so she supposed he must be barefoot. She knew how cold the floor was, even with the worn runner, and wondered if his feet would end up as icy as Nicole's always did. She hoped she wouldn't be finding out too soon. As far as she was concerned, the longer it took Carter to end up in her bed, the better. Because he wasn't going to be happy with what he discovered when he got there.

Then there was silence. Desiree heard the house creak as it settled. The wind howled and whistled and rattled her windowpanes. The furnace kicked on. She closed her eyes and willed herself to sleep.

Two sleepless hours later Desiree sat bolt upright, shoved the covers off and lowered her feet over the side of the bed, searching for her slippers in the glow from the tiny night-light that burned beside her bed.

"Damn!" she muttered. "Damn!"

She had spent two hours lying there pretending to sleep. Maybe a cup of hot chocolate would help. She opened the door to her bedroom and swore again. Apparently Carter had turned off the light she always left burning in the living room. It was her own fault, because she hadn't told him to leave it on. But that meant she either had to brave the dark or turn on a light upstairs in order to see and take the risk of waking Carter.

Frankly, the darkness was less terrifying than the thought of facing a rudely awakened Carter when she was wearing a frayed silk nightgown, a chenille robe and tufted terry-cloth slippers. Desiree knew her naturally curly hair was a tumble of gnarled tresses worthy of a Medusa, and since she had washed off her makeup, her scar would be even more vivid.

She knew the spots on the stairs that would groan when stepped on. She had learned them as a child so she wouldn't awaken her parents when she snuck down to shake her Christmas presents and try to determine what they were. She slid her hand down the smooth banister, walking quietly, carefully. When she reached the bottom of the stairs, she turned on the tiny light that was usually always lit.

With the light, it was easy to make her way to the kitchen. The old refrigerator hummed as she opened it, and there was a slight clink as the bottles of ketchup and pickles on the door shifted. Even though she was careful, the copper-bottomed pot she planned to use to heat the milk clanked as she freed it from the stack in the cabinet beside the sink.

She was standing at the stove with her back to the kitchen door, when she heard footsteps in the hallway. *Someone was in the house!*

Her heart galloped as she searched frantically for somewhere to hide, a place to escape. Then she realized Nicole was trapped upstairs. In order to get to her daughter she would have to confront whoever was in the house. She was halfway to the kitchen threshold, when she halted. Her hand gripped her robe and pulled it closed at the neck. She stared, wild-eyed, at the man in the doorway.

When she realized it was only Carter, bare-chested, barefoot, wearing a half-buttoned pair of frayed jeans that hung low on his hips, she almost sobbed with relief.

"Desiree? It's the middle of the night. What are you doing down here? Are you all right?"

"I couldn't sleep. I—"

He didn't wait for her explanation, just crossed the distance between them and enfolded her in his arms.

Desiree stood rigid. She was aware of the heat of him, the male scent of him. She was appalled by the way her nipples peaked when they came in contact with his naked chest. She became certain that he must be able to feel her arousal, even through the layers of cloth that covered her, when she felt the hard ridge growing in his low-slung jeans.

"Desiree," he murmured.

As his arms tightened around her, memories of the past rose up to choke her. And she panicked.

"No! Don't touch me! Let me go!" Desiree struggled to be free of Carter's constraining hold. She slapped at his face, beat at him with her fists, shoved and writhed to be free. But his hold, although gentle, was inexorable.

Desiree didn't scream. She had learned not to scream. There was no one who would come to her rescue; she would have to save herself. She continued fighting until she finally realized through her panic that although he refused to release her, Carter wasn't hurting her. At last, exhausted, she stood quivering in his arms, like a wild animal caught in a trap it realizes it cannot escape.

"There, now. That's better," Carter crooned. "Easy now. Everything's gonna be all right now. You're fine. You're just fine."

As Desiree recovered from her dazed state, she became aware that Carter was speaking in a low, husky voice. She was being held loosely in his arms, and his hands were rubbing her back as though she were a small child. She looked up and saw the beginning of a bruise on his chin and the bloody scratches on his face and froze.

"I hurt you," she said.

"You've got a wicked right," he agreed with a smile. He winced as the smile teased a small cut in his lip.

"I'm so sorry."

He looked at her warily. "Would you like to explain what that commotion was all about?"

"No."

His blue eyes narrowed. "No?"

"No." For a moment she thought he wasn't going to let her evade his question.

Then he sniffed and said, "Something's burning."

"My hot chocolate!" When she pulled away, he let her go. Desiree hurried to the stove, where the milk had burned black in the bottom of the pan. "Oh, no. Look at this mess!" She retrieved a pot holder and lifted the pot off the stove and settled it in the sink.

"You can make some more."

"I don't think I could sleep now if I drank a dozen cups of hot chocolate," Desiree said in disgust.

"I heard a noise, and I came down to check it out," Carter said in a crisp voice. "You're the one who went crazy."

"I didn't—" Desiree cut herself off. Although she didn't like the description, it fit her irrational behavior. She shoved a hand through her long brown hair and crossed the room to slump into one of the kitchen chairs. "Good Lord! I can't imagine what you must think of me."

Carter joined her at the table, turning a chair around and straddling it so he was facing her. "Do you think it would help to talk about it?"

Desiree wondered how much she should tell him.

And how little he would settle for knowing. "My first marriage was a disappointment," she admitted.

"I guessed something of the sort. How long were you married?"

"Two years. Then we divorced."

"I was married for five years."

"You were married?" Desiree didn't know why she was so surprised. But she was. Suddenly she had a thought. Perhaps there was a good reason, after all, for Carter's strange, distant behavior toward Nicole.

"Do you have children?"

"I have…had a five-year-old daughter. She died along with my wife in a car accident six years ago."

"I'm so sorry." No wonder he didn't want to be around Nicole! Her daughter must be an awful reminder of his loss. Desiree knew there really was no comfort she could offer, except to share with him her own grievous loss. "My parents died the same way."

"I'm sorry," he said.

A tense silence fell between them. Both wanted to ask more questions. But to ask questions was to suggest a willingness to answer them in return. And neither was ready to share with the other the secrets of their past.

It was Carter who finally broke the silence between them, his voice quiet, his tone as gentle as Desiree had ever heard it.

"If I'm going to get anything accomplished tomorrow I ought to get some sleep. But I don't feel comfortable leaving you down here alone. Is there any chance you could sleep now?"

Quite honestly, Desiree thought she would spend the rest of the night staring at the ceiling. But she could see that Carter wasn't going to go back to bed until she was settled. "I guess I am a little tired."

"I'll follow you upstairs," he said.

Desiree rose and headed for the kitchen door. Before she had taken two steps, Carter blocked her way.

"I don't know what to do to make you believe that I'd never hurt you," he said.

"I…I believe you."

Nevertheless, she flinched as he raised a hand to brush the hair away from her face.

His lips flattened. "Yeah. Sure."

Desiree cringed at the sarcasm in his voice and fled up the stairs as fast as she could. Behind her she heard the steady barefoot tread of her husband. She hurried into her bedroom and shut the door behind her. She leaned back against the door and covered her face with her hands.

I hate you, Burley. I hate what you did to me. I hate the way you made me feel. And I hate the fact that I can never be a woman to the man I married today.

Hating didn't help. Desiree had learned that lesson over the six long years since she had divorced Burley and gone on with her life. But she hadn't been able to let go of the hate—or the fear.

Because she knew that when he got out of prison in two weeks, Burley would be coming back.

CHAPTER FIVE

CHRISTMAS WAS A bittersweet event. They went to the candlelight service on Christmas Eve as a family and received the warm wishes and congratulations of the congregation on their marriage. Some of the women with whom Desiree had worked on the Christmas pageant over the past couple of years knew that Burley was due to be released from prison soon. Desiree saw the knowledge in their eyes of why she had so hurriedly married a man she barely knew. She was grateful that none of them mentioned the fact to Carter.

Nicole fell asleep on the ride home, and Desiree carried her right upstairs to bed. Carter didn't offer to help her, and Desiree didn't bother to ask. She had seen how uncomfortable he was in church, and from the moment they left the service he had been uncommonly silent. She knew he must be remembering his family—his first wife and his daughter.

While she dressed Nicole for bed and slipped her daughter under the covers, Desiree debated whether to join Carter downstairs. She pictured his face as it had looked when lit solely by candlelight during the church service. He must have loved his wife very much to still be so sad six years after her death. Of course, Desiree could identify with his despair at the loss of his daugh-

ter. After all, hadn't she been willing to make any sacrifice to ensure Nicole's safety?

By the time she had finished her musings she was
already at the bottom of the stairs. She took the few
steps farther to the parlor, where the wonderful-smell-
ing spruce Christmas tree forced an acknowledgment
of the season, expecting to see Carter there. But the
room was empty.

Desiree went in search of her husband. It amazed her
to realize that she had been so wrapped up in her own
agony over the past six years that she hadn't focused on
the fact that there must be others in similar straits. In
fact, she had seen with her own eyes that Carter Prescott
was fighting demons of the past equally as ferocious
as her own. Her heart went out to him. Comfort was
something she could offer in repayment for the security she hoped this marriage would provide for her and
her daughter.

She found Carter in the kitchen. Desiree couldn't
help the bubble of laughter that escaped when she realized he was fixing the dripping faucet.

"What's so funny?" Carter demanded.

"You. It's Christmas Eve. What on earth are you doing?"

"Fixing the faucet."

"I can see that," Desiree said as she approached him.
"What I want to know is why now?"

Carter shrugged. "You were busy. There was nothing else to do."

"You could have sat down in the living room and
relaxed."

"I don't like sitting still. It leaves me with too much
time to think."

"About your wife and daughter?" When Desiree saw

the way his shoulders stiffened she wished she had kept her thoughts to herself.

"They were killed on Christmas Eve," Carter said in a quiet voice. "They were on the way to church. I…I wasn't with them. I was at my office when I heard what had happened." He gave a shuddering sigh. "I don't think I'll ever forget that night."

Desiree followed the impulse to comfort that had brought her seeking Carter in the first place. She put a hand on his arm and felt the muscles tighten beneath her fingertips. "I don't know what to say."

He threw the wrench he was using on the counter and turned to face her. "I'd rather not talk about it," he said brusquely.

"You aren't the first man to put business before family," she replied. "It wasn't your fault the accident happened."

"I said I don't want to talk about it."

His voice was harsh and his face savage. Instead of fleeing him, Desiree stepped forward and circled his waist with her arms. She laid her head against his chest, where she could hear the furious pounding of his heart. "I'm glad you came to Wyoming," she said. "I'm glad you agreed to marry me. I'm glad you're here."

She could feel his hesitation and knew he was trying to decide whether to thrust her away or accept the comfort she was offering. She had her answer when his arms circled her shoulders, and he pulled her snug against him.

Desiree forced herself to relax. There was nothing loverlike in his demeanor or in hers. She was simply one human being offering comfort on Christmas Eve to another.

Only it wasn't that simple.

She should have known it wouldn't be. He was a man. She was a woman. As much as she tried to ignore the fact, as much as she was appalled by it, her body responded to the closeness of his.

Desiree had believed, after her experience with Burley, that there was something wrong with her, that she was defective somehow, that she didn't have whatever was necessary to make her physically responsive to a man. But ever since she had met Carter, she had been discovering that her body was more than responsive. Her blood pumped, her body ached deep inside, her breasts felt heavy and her nipples peaked whenever she was close to him. All the signs of arousal were there.

She was simply too terrified of what might—or might not—happen to allow anything to go forward. What if she was wrong? What if she couldn't respond?

"Thank you, Desiree," Carter murmured. "I didn't know how much I needed a hug."

The feel of his warm breath in her ear made her shiver. "I guess I know a little of what you're feeling," she murmured back.

He chuckled. "If you knew what I'm feeling right now you'd run up those stairs and lock your bedroom door behind you."

Desiree took a tremulous breath. "Carter?"

"What?"

"You can kiss me, if you want."

She heard him catch his breath, felt the tenseness in the muscles of his back where her hands rested. He lifted his head to look at her, but she lowered her gaze so he couldn't see that there was as much fear as anticipation lurking in her brown eyes.

"What brought this on?"

"I don't know," she mumbled. "I just thought—"

"I guess I shouldn't look a gift horse in the mouth."

Before Desiree had a chance to change her mind, his fingertip caught her chin and tipped her mouth up so it could meet his.

As with each of their two previous kisses, his mouth was gentle on hers. He cherished her with his touch. There was none of the pain she had come to expect from Burley.

"Desiree?"

She looked up at him through lids that were heavy with desire. "Yes, Carter?"

He smiled. "I keep waiting for the scratching tiger to show her claws. Are you sure you want to do this?"

"Could we just kiss, Carter? Without the touching, without anything else? I think I would like that."

She could see the rigid control in his body as he considered the scrap she had offered him in place of a Christmas feast. She wanted to offer more, but it was taking every ounce of courage she had to stand still within his embrace.

"All right, Desiree. Just kisses."

She expected him to focus on her mouth, but his lips dropped to her throat, instead.

"Ohhh." She shivered at the warmth and wetness of his lips and tongue against the tender flesh beneath her ear. He sucked just a little, and she felt her insides draw up tight. "Ohhh."

He chuckled as his mouth wandered up the slender column of her throat toward her ears. "You sound so surprised. What were you expecting?"

"Nothing like this," Desiree assured him with a gasp. "It feels…I never…"

She felt him pause. She was afraid her confession might make him stop, so she quickly said, "I like what you're doing. Very much."

His teeth caught the lobe of her ear and nibbled gently.

Desiree thought her knees were going to buckle right then and there. She laughed in delight and grabbed handfuls of Carter's shirt. One of his arms slipped around her waist and tightened, while the other remained around her shoulders. Instead of feeling imprisoned, she merely felt supported.

Now his tongue was tracing the shell of her ear, then dipping inside, before his teeth found her earlobe again. She shivered once more and realized it was becoming harder to catch her breath.

"Shouldn't I be kissing you, too?" she asked.

"In a minute," Carter rasped.

Desiree wanted to reciprocate in some way, and if he wasn't going to let her kiss him back, that left her with the option of caressing him with her hands. She felt at a distinct disadvantage. Burley hadn't been much interested in foreplay, so she didn't have any experience in arousing her partner. She wasn't sure what would please Carter. If she'd had more nerve, she would have asked him. But that was more than she could handle. She decided to experiment.

Desiree began by letting her hands slide up his back, feeling the play of muscle and sinew as she went. The sound of pleasure he made deep in his throat was all she needed to assure her that he enjoyed her touch. To her relief, although his grip on her tightened, his hands remained where they were.

His lips kissed their way across her unblemished cheek toward her mouth. He kissed one edge, then the other, then pressed his mouth lightly against hers. His tongue slid along the crease, which tickled and tingled at the same time.

"Desiree, open your mouth for me."

She felt his lips moving against hers as he spoke. She opened her mouth to answer him, but he must have thought she was responding to his request, because the instant her lips parted, his tongue slipped inside.

Desiree jerked her head away. She was panting, as though she had run a long race. And ashamed, because she had let her past fears rule once again. When Burley had kissed her like that, his tongue had thrust so hard and deep into her mouth that it had nearly gagged her.

Because she still had her hands on Carter's waist, she could feel the rigid displeasure in his body at her retreat. "I…I don't like to be kissed like that," she explained.

"What is it you don't like?"

Desiree's eyes flashed to his. She hadn't expected to be asked for details. It was too humiliating to tell the truth. "I…I just don't like it."

"All right," Carter said. "I can accept that you don't like being kissed openmouthed."

Desiree sagged with relief in his arms.

That is, until he continued, "But I do like it. So, if I can't kiss you like that, you'll have to kiss me."

"Like that?" Desiree asked. "You mean putting my tongue in your mouth?"

He laugh ruefully. "Not all at once. A little bit at a time."

Desiree cocked her head skeptically. "Are you sure you'll like it?"

His husky laugh was infectious. "I'm sure."

"What if I do it wrong?"

"There isn't any right or wrong. Just what feels good to you."

"If I just concentrate on my own feelings, how will I know you're enjoying yourself?" she asked with asperity.

"Don't worry," he assured her. "I'm sure I'll manage fine."

Desiree knew there was a catch somewhere in his reasoning, but she was so intrigued by the idea of being the one in control of the kiss that she was willing to go along with his plan. Her hand crept up to circle his neck and angle his head down for her kiss. He bent to her, and she pressed her lips against his. To her surprise, he kept his lips sealed.

She settled back on her heels and looked at him in consternation. "I thought you wanted me to kiss you."

"I do."

"Then why didn't you open your mouth?"

"You didn't open yours."

"How do you know that?"

"Well, did you?"

She grimaced. "All right. Let's try this again." Desiree put her hands flat against Carter's chest and rose on her toes to reach his mouth, careful to keep her lips parted. When they touched, she let her tongue slip into his mouth. A shiver shot down her spine. She retreated and looked up at him through lowered lashes. His lips were damp where they had kissed.

"Again?" she asked.

He nodded.

This time, she leaned her body into his so her breasts brushed against his chest. She threaded both hands into his hair and used her hold to tug his head down so she could reach his mouth. His lips were sealed again. She ran her tongue along the seam of his lips, as he had done with her. His lips parted. Tentatively she slipped her tongue into his mouth.

He groaned, a purely male sound of satisfaction.

She waited for him to take control of the kiss from her, to thrust his tongue in her mouth. But he held himself still. He left the seduction to her.

Heady with a sense of feminine power, she used her tongue to taste him, to feel his teeth and the roof of his mouth and his rough tongue. She heard his ragged breathing and knew he was aroused by what she was doing to him. What amazed her was the fact that she was equally aroused by the intimate kisses.

She withdrew her tongue and nibbled on his lower lip. His hands clutched her more tightly, but he didn't make a move toward her breasts or bottom. He exercised a rigid control on himself that gave her the confidence to continue her experiment.

"Desiree."

"What, Carter?"

"You're killing me."

"You want me to stop?"

"Hell, no! But let me kiss you back. Please."

Desiree thought about it a moment. "No. Not yet."

She watched his Adam's apple bob as he swallowed hard.

"All right," he said. "I'm putty in your hands."

Desiree grinned. The rock hard muscles in his shoulders were anything but malleable. But his mouth, as she touched it with her own, was as soft as she could wish.

As she practiced kissing him, using her tongue to tease and taste him, she was able to think less about what she was doing and more about what she was feeling. Soon her breathing was as ragged as his, her body hot and achy with need. She had kept herself separated from Carter from the waist down, not wishing to incite him to anything more than the kisses she had promised. But the instinctive need to arch her body into his became too hard to resist.

She knew the instant her belly brushed against the ridge in his jeans that she had made a mistake. The harsh, ragged sound he made was as wild as anything she had ever heard. She knew she should withdraw, but the teasing heat of him drew her back, and she rubbed herself against him, liking the feeling that streaked from her belly to her breasts to her brain.

It took her a moment to realize that his tongue was in her mouth. And that she craved having it there. He withdrew and penetrated again, mimicking the sexual act with his mouth and tongue.

Desiree had never felt anything so erotic in her entire life. She heard a guttural sound and realized it had come from her own throat. It was a sound of primitive animal need. It scared the hell out of her.

She tore herself from Carter's arms and stumbled back a step or two. She stared at him wide-eyed, panting to catch her breath, her body shuddering with unfulfilled need, her breasts swollen and aching to be touched.

"Desiree?"

Just that one word, said in a voice that demanded her attention like pebbles thrown at a windowpane. It was a plea. It was a prayer. It was an invitation she found hard to resist.

She knew, deep in her soul, that with Carter things were going to be different. After all, she had never felt anything with Burley like she had just experienced with Carter. But what if, when he bedded her, she stiffened and froze? What if she was dry inside as she had been with Burley? What if sex with Carter hurt her and disappointed him?

The risks were too great, and the rewards too uncertain. She had offered a kiss, and he had accepted. It wasn't her fault things had gotten out of hand. Well, not *all* her fault.

"I think that's enough for now." She waited with her weight balanced on the balls of her feet, her hands clenched into fists, ready to flee—or fight—if he sought more from her.

"All right, Desiree. I guess I'll be heading off to bed. It's bound to be an early morning if Nicole is anything like…"

"Like your daughter?"

He swallowed hard and nodded.

"Good night, Carter."

He didn't say anything more, just whirled on his boot heels and left the kitchen. She heard his heavy tread on the stairs and his muffled steps as he headed down the carpeted hall to his bedroom.

Desiree heaved a sigh of relief, followed by a groan of dissatisfaction. If only she had been able to follow through on what she had started, she might be lying in Carter's arms right now. She was certain the experience would be nothing like it had been with Burley. The little bit of kissing she had done with Carter had been a mistake, because now she would want more. And so would he.

She didn't want to admit it, but anything that tied her more closely to Carter was important because of the confrontation she knew was coming. That might mean swallowing her fear and submitting to Carter's desire—although even that thought did not seem so horrid as it once had.

It took Desiree a long time to fall asleep that night. Her dreams were all of a chestnut-haired man with broad shoulders and narrow hips who held her close and made tempestuous, passionate—but always gentle—love to her.

Desiree was still half-aroused when she awoke to the sound of her daughter's laughter drifting up the stairs. It was followed by a masculine rumble. She hurried to throw on her robe and stuff her feet into her slippers. She practically ran down the stairs and moments later entered the parlor, where she found Carter and Nicole sitting cross-legged beside the Christmas tree.

A fire crackled in the fireplace, and snowflakes drifted lazily down outside the picture window. The decorative lights on the tree sparkled, and there were dozens of presents under the tree—many more than had been there when she had gone to bed last night.

"Mommy! Santa Claus came!" Nicole scrambled up and headed toward her on the run.

Desiree caught her daughter and swung her up into her arms. She carried Nicole back to where Carter still sat beside the tree. "Where did all these presents come from?"

"Santa Claus!" Nicole said. "He came! He came!"

Desiree tried to get Carter to meet her gaze, but he was already reaching for a present. Nicole struggled to be put down, and Desiree slid her down until her feet hit the floor. Nicole reached Carter in three hops and bounced down into his lap.

Desiree saw him stiffen only slightly before he accepted Nicole's closeness.

"Can we open presents now, Mommy?"

"I guess so."

Desiree started to sit on the couch, but Carter patted the braided rug beside him and said, "You don't want to be way over there. Come sit beside us."

"Yeah, Mommy. Come sit beside us."

Desiree raised a brow at the "us" but couldn't resist the invitation. "Sure." She settled cross-legged beside them and waited with as much excitement as Nicole while her daughter picked up one of the presents that had miraculously appeared under the tree overnight and shook it.

"Legos, Mommy! Legos!"

"How do you know?" Desiree asked with a grin.

By then Nicole had torn the paper off, revealing the Legos she had identified by sound.

While Nicole oohed and aahed over her present, Carter handed Desiree a box with a big red bow. "Here's one for you."

"Look at all these presents! Carter, you shouldn't have!"

"What shouldn't Carter have done, Mommy?" Nicole asked.

Desiree had maintained the illusion of Santa Claus for her daughter because she believed it was a harmless fiction. So she hesitated before chastising Carter for buying so many gifts that as far as her daughter knew had all come from Santa Claus. Carter must have spent a fortune! Desiree was certain it was money he didn't have, which made his gesture all the more touching.

"Uh…Carter shouldn't have given me a present to open before you finished opening yours," Desiree said, improvising.

"I'm done now, Mommy. Open yours!"

From the look on his face, Carter was enjoying himself. After the things he had told her about his daughter, Desiree was glad he was able to bring himself to share this Christmas morning with them. It would be churlish for her to diminish what he had done by making an issue of the money he must have spent. She gave Carter a timid smile and began ripping the paper off her gift.

Her mouth split wide in a grin of delight. "How did you know I wanted this?" She held up the bulky knit sweater against herself and ran her hands over the sections of the bodice where different textures—leather and fur and feathers—had been woven into the sandy beige garment to give it an earthy look.

"I have to confess I asked my grandmother."

"How did Maddy know? I'm sure I never said anything to her about this sweater."

"I believe she heard about it from one of the ladies at church."

"Thank you," Desiree said with a shy smile.

Nicole had already helped herself to another present. "Look, Mommy!" It was a furry stuffed animal, a black cat with white paws that looked remarkably like Boots. "My very own kitten."

Nicole hugged the cat. "You open one, Daddy."

The color bleached from Carter's face. His smile disappeared, and a muscle jerked in his cheek as he clenched his teeth.

"Daddy?"

Desiree quickly scooped Nicole out of Carter's lap and into hers. She wasn't sure what to say. Apparently Nicole's innocent slip had reminded him of his child. She recognized his distress but was helpless to ease it.

"Carter?"

An instant later he was on his feet. "I need a cup of coffee. You two go on without me." He was gone from the room before Desiree had a chance to ask him to stay.

"What's the matter with Daddy?" Nicole asked.

Trust the child to know that all wasn't as it should be. Desiree was left with the unpleasant task of providing an answer that would appease her daughter. "I guess he just needs a cup of coffee."

"But we're opening presents!" Nicole protested. "He should be here." She rose with the evident intent of following Carter into the kitchen. Before she got very far they heard the back door open and close. Nicole ran into the kitchen. Desiree followed her.

"Where is Daddy going?" Nicole asked.

"I don't know, darling."

"When is he coming back?"

"I don't know."

"I want to open my presents," Nicole said. "Do we have to wait for Daddy to come back?"

Desiree felt a surge of anger that Carter should have left so abruptly without a word of explanation, and on Christmas morning! Running away wouldn't ease his pain, only postpone it. She and Nicole would still be here when he came back. If he came back. Desiree shoved a hand through her hair in frustration. She had been as much caught off guard as Carter was by Nicole's ready acceptance of him as her father. They should have realized what Nicole's reaction was likely to be. Nicole knew nothing about Burley, so there was no male figure to whom she had previously given her affection.

And after all, Nicole *had* asked for a daddy for Christmas, and Carter *had* conveniently appeared.

Nicole tugged at her sleeve. "Mommy?"

"I don't think Carter will mind if we go ahead without him. We can show him all our gifts when he comes back. How does that sound?"

"Okay!" Nicole said. She raced back to the parlor.

Desiree stared out the kitchen window and saw the tread marks left in the snow by Carter's pickup. "He will come back," she murmured to herself.

Meanwhile, Carter had driven hell-for-leather several miles from the ranch before he calmed down enough to realize how badly he had acted. He pulled to the side of the road and stopped the truck. His head fell forward to the steering wheel, and he groaned.

"What have I done? What am I doing here?"

He had only been fooling himself to think he would be able to ignore having a five-year-old child in the house. From the very first day, Nicole had made it plain she expected him to be a father to her.

What amazed and appalled him was how quickly she had slipped past the walls he had set up to keep himself from caring—to keep himself from being hurt again. When Nicole had called him "Daddy," it had set off all those painful memories of Christmases with his daughter, along with a feeling of bitter regret that his child was dead. Far worse, it had brought a lump of feeling to his throat to find himself adopted by the fatherless little girl in his arms.

He had glanced at Desiree and seen the pity—and sympathy—in her eyes. And felt ashamed that he wasn't able to handle the situation better. After all, she was willing to try marriage—and intimacy—again even though it was clear she had suffered at her husband's hands. She was dealing with her demons. Could he do less?

His feelings were complicated by the fact he had always wanted children, and Nicole was an adorable child. Nevertheless, it wouldn't be easy to play the role of father. He grimaced. It was no more difficult for him to be a father, than for Desiree to play the role of wife.

Carter didn't choose to examine his feelings for Desiree too closely. For now it was enough that he desired her, that he admired her courage and that she was the mother of the child who wanted him to be her father. Putting down roots meant having a family. He had the start of that family with Desiree and Nicole. He would be a fool not to embrace them both.

He twisted the key and turned the truck around.

They were still opening presents twenty minutes later when Carter reappeared. He stood in the parlor doorway with what could only be described as a sheepish look on his face.

"Did I miss anything?"

Desiree was too astonished that he had returned so quickly to speak. Nicole more than made up for her silence.

"Daddy! Daddy! Look what I got!"

Desiree thought for a moment he was going to run again. Though his face blanched and his jaw tightened, he stood his ground as Nicole came barreling toward him. He scooped her up and balanced her in the crook of his arm as she babbled on about the Raggedy Ann doll and the Teenage Mutant Ninja Turtle puzzle and the game of Chutes and Ladders she had gotten from Santa Claus.

"You'll never guess what Santa Claus brought Mommy!" she exclaimed.

"What?" Carter asked.

"A teeny tiny nightgown! And you can see right through it!"

Carter grinned. "You don't say!"

Desiree felt herself flush to the roots of her hair. She hadn't realized how revealing the negligee was until she held it up to look at it. She had quickly stuffed it back into the box, but not before Nicole had gotten a look at it.

"Are you going to open your presents now, Daddy?"

Desiree saw the mixed feelings that flashed across his face.

"There are presents for me?"

"Uh-huh." Nicole held up three fingers, then put one down. "Two of them."

"Guess I'd better open them and see what I got."

He carried Nicole back over to the tree. He held on to her when he sat down cross-legged, so she was once more sitting in his lap. Desiree couldn't help but wonder what had caused Carter's acceptance of a situation she knew was painful for him.

She watched with bated breath as Carter opened the present she had bought for him. She breathed a sigh of relief when she saw the pleasure on his face as he caught sight of the Western leather boots.

"These are beautiful," he said as he reverently ran his fingers across the tooled brown leather. "You shouldn't have. I can imagine these set you back a pretty penny."

"I wanted to get them for you," Desiree said to keep him from focusing on the cost of the boots. They were expensive, but she had seen how the heels and toes, not to mention the soles, were worn on his boots. If he could have afforded to replace them, she knew he would have. She didn't want him focusing on the difference in their financial situations. She knew he hadn't married her for her money. Her land, yes. But not her money.

"Open the other one," Nicole urged as she handed it to him. "This one's from me," she confided. "For my new daddy."

Desiree saw Carter's hesitation. He slowly unwrapped the gift.

Before he had the paper half off Nicole blurted, "It's a book. So you can read stories to me at bedtime."

Carter finished unwrapping the present and fingered the embossed illustration on the cover. "It's a wonderful gift, Nicky."

"My name isn't Nicky. It's Nicole."

"Would you mind if I shortened it, sort of like a special nickname?" Carter asked.

Nicole wrinkled her nose, then eyed Carter sideways. "Will that make me your little girl for real and always?"

A sudden thickness appeared in Desiree's throat. Tears blurred her eyes and made her nose burn. She waited to hear what Carter would answer.

"It makes you mine, Nicky. Now and always."

"All right," Nicole said. "You can call me Nicky." She turned to her mother. "Daddy's going to call me Nicky. You can call me Nicky, too."

"All right, Nico—Nicky. If that's what you want." Desiree fought back the sudden spurt of jealousy she felt. She had wanted Nicole to have a father, but she hadn't realized at the time what that would mean. She no longer had her daughter all to herself.

Nicole was looking at Carter with what could only be described as worship. It remained to be seen how long her daughter's adoration would last.

Desiree stood and reached over to grasp Nicole's

hands and pull her to her feet. "Now that all the presents are opened, I'd like some time to talk to Carter alone. Why don't you take a few of your things upstairs and play for a while?"

"All right, Mommy. Will you come read to me later, Daddy?"

"Sure, Nicky."

When the little girl was gone, Desiree paced away from Carter to stare out the window at the snow, which was now blowing sideways. "Where did you go?"

She was startled when his voice came from right behind her.

"Five miles down the road. It took me that long to realize it was foolish to run away from what I've been searching for all my life."

Desiree whirled to face him. She probed his blue eyes, looking for some kind of proof that she and Nicole were that important to him. "I know it must have been hard to have Nicole call you Daddy."

He nodded.

"Thank you for giving her the chance to have a father."

"I want us to be a family," Carter said in a fierce voice. "I want us to be happy together. I want to forget the past."

But it was clear from the agitation in his voice that though he might choose not to remember the past, he hadn't forgotten it. Not by a long shot.

Desiree knew she ought to take advantage of this moment to tell him the secret she had been keeping from him. But she didn't want to spoil the moment. He was offering to start over with her. She so much wanted this marriage to work!

"I want what you want, Carter," she admitted.

But her arms remained folded defensively across her chest.

He reached for her wrists and pulled her arms around his waist. He circled her shoulders so she found herself captured in his strong embrace. She waited for the fear to rise. It was marvelously absent. But she wasn't entirely comfortable, either. There was a tension, an expectation, an awareness that arced between them. She waited for Carter to act on it, to make a sexual overture.

Instead he stepped back from her and took her hands in his. She looked up at him and found his lips curled into a smile, his blue eyes twinkling with amusement.

"So you can see right through that nightgown. I can hardly wait!"

Desiree yanked her hands from his and perched them on her hips. "How could you give me a gift like that and not warn me about it? I was never so embarrassed in my life as when Nicole started asking me questions about it."

"What did you tell her, I wonder?" Carter said as his smile broadened to a grin.

Desiree felt the heat in her face. "That it was meant to be worn with a robe," she snapped.

Carter laughed, a sound that came up from his belly and rumbled past his chest. "When am I going to get to see it?"

"In your dreams, Prescott," she said. "In your dreams!"

"I'm sure they'll be sweet ones," he called to her retreating back.

CHAPTER SIX

"Do you want to go?" Carter asked.

"I'm not sure we can," Desiree replied across the breakfast table. "I don't know whether I can get a babysitter on such short notice. Especially when tonight is New Year's Eve."

Desiree knew she was being contrary, but she couldn't help it. Ever since Carter had walked out on Christmas morning, she had worried that he would do it again. Even though he had returned, the trust she had been willing to give him without question when they married was qualified now. Her anxiety wasn't unjustified.

Carter hadn't disappeared without a word over the past week, but he had begun making forays around the ranch by himself, getting the lay of the land and looking the place over. He hadn't reissued the invitation he had made the day they were married to survey the ranch together.

Desiree suspected he needed the time alone to come to terms with his new responsibilities as husband and father—although they were more *father* than *husband* so far. To her chagrin, Desiree realized she very much wanted to make the effort to become Carter's wife in every sense of the word. Only she wasn't sure how to let him know.

Attending a New Year's Eve party at Faron and Belinda Whitelaw's home would be their first outing as husband and wife. The truth was, she wanted to go. But she was worried about leaving Nicole home alone with a baby-sitter. Burley was due to be released from prison today. There was no reason to believe he would head straight for Casper—except the threats he had made six years ago.

I'm coming back, Desiree. Then I'll finish what I started.

Desiree felt cold all over. She hadn't forgotten the last night she had spent with Burley in this house. It was something she had been trying to forget. Maybe it wasn't such a bad idea to be gone from here tonight. But she wanted Nicole where she could keep an eye on her.

"I suppose we could take Nicole with us," Desiree mused. "She could sleep upstairs at The Castle. I've done that in the past when I couldn't find a sitter."

"Great!" Carter said.

"Why are you so anxious to go to this party?" Desiree asked.

"I thought it was about time we did some socializing with our neighbors. Besides, it's a wedding celebration for my half brother, Faron. He and Belinda were married at home on Christmas, with just their families present."

"You're family. Why weren't you invited to the wedding?"

He shrugged. "I was, but I decided not to go."

"Were you worried that they might be upset at how quickly you married me?"

"Not at all. It's just that Faron and I may be related, but really, we don't know each other."

Desiree's lips curled into a wry smile. "The same thing could be said about us."

"Yeah, but I'm planning to spend the rest of my life with you."

Desiree hoped so. But she had her doubts about what Carter would do when he knew the truth about why she had married him.

When she had ruthlessly sought out a man to marry, she had done so because when Burley got out of prison and came hunting her she wanted her ex-husband to see that she had committed herself to someone else, that there was no sense in his pursuing her any longer. Now she admitted to herself that she had expected to get something else out of the bargain: actual physical protection if Burley got violent.

Desiree could see how her fear and desperation had led her to expect unrealistic things from marriage to Carter. Instead of being put off by the presence of another man, Burley was just as likely to become insanely jealous. It had happened before. And she knew that instead of being around to protect her, Carter might very well be off on one of his lonely jaunts around the ranch.

Which meant she had to be ready to protect herself and her daughter. She couldn't get a protective order to keep Burley away from her until he had actually done something that constituted a crime under the law. She would have to wait for Burley to make the first move. And hope she was still alive to apply to the court for succor.

There was another option.

She could confess the whole situation to Carter and ask for his help in confronting Burley when he showed up. She felt certain Carter would offer his assistance if he knew the situation she was in. But she had her own reasons for wanting to keep her secret as long as she could.

Ever since Christmas Eve, when she had stood in Carter's arms kissing him, the belief had been growing that maybe she wasn't as frigid as Burley had always accused her of being. She had thought and thought about her reaction to Carter's kisses, about her feelings when kissing him, and she had come to the conclusion that however much a failure she had been with Burley in bed, the same thing wouldn't happen with Carter.

Desiree wasn't sure what made the difference with Carter. She didn't think it was a simple matter of her feelings toward the two men. After all, she had been head over heels in love with Burley and sex with him had been a disaster. She wasn't sure exactly what she felt for Carter, but she knew it couldn't be love. Respect, maybe, and liking, but no more than that. After all, they were still virtual strangers.

Once the idea of making love to Carter caught hold, however, she couldn't let it go. She fantasized about what it would be like to touch him, to have him touch her, for the two of them to be joined as one. Since she couldn't be sure what Carter's reaction would be when he found out the truth about why she had married him, she had to act soon or perhaps lose the chance of knowing what it meant to make love to a man.

Maybe it wasn't fair to use Carter like that, but Desiree had gotten the distinct impression that he wouldn't find making love to her a hardship. They would both benefit, and she couldn't see the harm to either of them in her plan.

Only…time was running out. If she was going to

seduce Carter, there could be no better opportunity than after the party tonight. It would be the beginning of a new year, a nostalgic time, to say the least. She would make sure Carter had a drink or two to relax him and would stay very close when they danced. And she would wear the silky black negligee he had given her for Christmas. Further than that, her thoughts would not go.

"So we're agreed?" Carter said. "We'll go to the party?"

Desiree nodded. "I'll call Belinda so she can arrange a guest bedroom for Nicole."

Desiree wasn't sure what to expect from her friends and neighbors at the Whitelaws' New Year's Eve party, but she was pleased by how cordially they greeted Carter when she introduced him as her husband.

Carter's grandmother, Madelyn, made a special point of introducing one young woman to Carter. "This is Belinda's sister, Fiona Conner," she said. "I'm disappointed you two didn't get a chance to meet sooner."

Unspoken were the words *Before you married Desiree.*

Desiree felt an unwelcome stab of jealousy as the petite blonde gave Carter an assessing look. She immediately forgave Fiona when the young woman grinned at her and said, "Maddy tells me she had Carter all picked out for me, so I'm glad you two found each other. You've saved me from Maddy's matchmaking."

"It was my pleasure," Desiree said, linking her arm possessively through Carter's. She was aware of how lovely the young woman was. There was no scar to mar her beautiful face.

Carter put his hand over hers where it rested on his arm. "I'm happy with the choice I made," he told his grandmother. "Although I can't say that if things had turned out differently, I wouldn't have enjoyed getting a chance to know you," he gallantly said to Fiona.

"It wouldn't have worked out between you and Fiona, anyway," Madelyn said with a sigh.

"Why not?" Desiree asked, her curiosity piqued.

"Fiona has a cat."

Desiree exchanged a look with Carter, and they burst out laughing.

"If you ladies will excuse us, I'd like to dance with my wife," Carter said. "I'm not bad at matchmaking myself," he said with a wink at Madelyn.

Desiree was flustered but pleased by Carter's obvious preference for her company. She was delighted to be dancing with him because it fit into her plans of seduction so well.

A half hour later, Desiree wondered who was seducing whom. She had started by letting her fingers thread into the curls at Carter's nape and gotten all the response she could have hoped for when he drew her closer into his arms. He had let his hand drift down past her waist to the dimpled area above her buttocks and slipped his leg between hers, so she could feel his arousal. It was enough to make her weak in the knees.

His cheek was pressed close to hers—the unblemished one, of course—and his teeth nibbled on her earlobe.

"I've had a wonderful time meeting all your neighbors," he said as he backed away to look at her.

"They like you," she replied.

Desiree was warmed by the desire in Carter's eyes— even though his gaze avoided her scar. She could forgive him that. It wasn't easy to face herself in the mirror each morning, so she knew what it must be like for him. At least there was no obvious distaste apparent on his face when he looked at her.

She mentally pledged to be a good wife to Carter, to trust him and—after the night was through—to reveal the secret she had kept from him.

"Listen up, everybody!" Faron said. When those gathered for the party were quiet, he said, "It's time to count down the last seconds to the new year. Ten. Nine. Eight."

"Seven. Six. Five," everyone chanted.

Desiree looked into Carter's eyes as she counted with him, "Four. Three. Two."

"One," Carter said. "Happy New Year, Desiree."

"Happy New Year, Carter."

"I think this is where we're supposed to kiss," he said as he looked around the room at the couples caught up in the celebration of the moment.

"I guess it is. Shall we join them?"

Apparently her invitation was the only thing holding Carter back, because he tightened his arms around her and sought out her lips with his. She felt the pressure of his mouth against hers and realized it wasn't enough. Her tongue slipped out and teased the seam of his lips. She felt his smile as he opened his mouth to her. Then she was opening her mouth to him, and the thrust and parry that followed was as erotic a dance as anything Salome might have managed with all her seven veils.

When they broke the kiss at last, they stared, stunned, into each other's eyes.

He was panting.

So was she.

"Let's go home," Carter said. "I'd like to start the new year together—with you in my bed."

Desiree blushed at his forthrightness. But his wishes were very much in accord with her own. "I'll go upstairs and get Nicole."

He put out a hand to stop her. "I asked Maddy if she would keep Nicky overnight. She told me Nicky had stayed with her before, and that she'd be glad to have her."

"But—"

"I told her I'd have to check with you first to make sure it was all right."

Desiree debated only a second before she said, "Tell Maddy I'm thankful for the offer. I'd like to check on Nicole before we go."

"I'll wait down here for you," Carter said.

During the ride home, Desiree chattered like Nicole, talking about how much fun the party had been and how she hoped they could invite some of their neighbors over for supper soon. Carter was silent except for a grunt of assent every so often to let her know he was listening.

Deep down, Desiree harbored the fear that Burley might somehow have already made his way to the Rimrock. So it was with a tremendous sense of relief that she observed when they entered the house that everything appeared untouched. She toed off her fur-lined boots and left them in the pantry along with her coat. Then she stepped into the terry-cloth slippers she had left there when she put on her boots. Carter followed suit, leaving his boots and shearling coat beside hers and heading upstairs in his stocking feet.

"Everything looks exactly as we left it," she said as they passed through the kitchen and into the hall.

Carter gave her a look askance. "You were expecting Santa's elves to come through and change things around?"

Desiree laughed nervously. "Of course not. I just… Never mind."

Carter grasped her hand and started upstairs with her. "Let's go to bed."

There was a wealth of meaning in those words. He stopped upstairs outside her closed bedroom door. "Your room or mine?"

"Yours," Desiree said. Her bedroom held too many awful memories.

Once she arrived at Carter's door she stopped. Even though she had made up her mind to make love to him, she couldn't help feeling afraid.

It was a sign of how attuned Carter was to her in just the little time they had been married that he asked, "Are you sure you want to go through with this?"

"Yes," Desiree said. But the word came out as a hoarse croak. She stared into Carter's eyes, warmed by the glow of desire burning there. In the next instant, he had swept her off her feet and into his arms. She laughed nervously.

"You're safe with me, Desiree," he said as he stepped through the doorway and into his bedroom.

Desiree couldn't have asked for more than that.

Carter had left the lamp burning beside the bed, and it cast the room in shadows. He had already shoved the door closed behind them with his foot, when she realized she had forgotten something. "I wanted to wear my new negligee for you."

Carter grinned. "I'm not saying I don't want to see

you in it sometime, but I think it would be wasted to-night."

Desiree stood uncomfortably by the door where he had set her down, as he left her and crossed to the bed to pull down the quilt and sheet. Then he crossed back to stand before her.

"Does this feel as awkward to you as it does to me?" Desiree asked with a shy smile.

"I don't know how you feel," Carter replied, "but this has been the longest three weeks of my life."

Desiree gave a startled laugh. "We've only been married for two."

"I've wanted you since the night I met you, since the moment you came downstairs and I saw you for the first time without that awful moth-eaten coat."

"But my face—"

"Has a terrible scar. I know." He gently removed her hand from where it had crept to cover her cheek. "There's more to you than your face, Desiree. You're a beautiful woman."

But even as he said the words, he was avoiding her scar with his eyes.

Desiree noticed there had been no words of love spoken. But, then, she hadn't expected them. They had met and married under unusual circumstances and had known each other too briefly for stronger feelings to grow between them. The desires of the flesh did not need love or commitment to flourish. The animal instinct to couple and reproduce was bred deep. They could want without loving.

And she did want Carter. Her need grew as his fingertips followed where his eyes led, across the shoulders of her knit dress and lower where the flesh was exposed along her collarbone, then down along the line of buttons between her breasts to her belly, before they fanned out to circle her hips.

"Come here," he murmured as he pulled her toward him. A moment later their bodies were flush from waist to thigh.

Desiree stiffened reflexively at the intimate contact. She closed her eyes, caught her lower lip in her teeth and forced herself to relax. This wasn't Burley. This was Carter. When she opened her eyes, Carter was staring down at her.

Carter realized suddenly how important it was for him to keep a firm grip on his desire. He didn't want to frighten Desiree. And yet he did not feel in control when he was near her. The scent of her, the taste of her, had him hard and ready. He took a deep breath and slowly let it out in an attempt to steady his pounding pulse.

"I can stop anytime you want," he said. "Anytime."

Desiree lifted a disbelieving brow. "Anytime?"

"Anytime. There's no such thing as a point of no return," Carter said. "That's an old wives' tale. A man can stop. It might not be pleasant. But he can stop."

Desiree felt tears welling in her eyes. "I wish—"

"Shh." He put a callused fingertip to her lips. "No looking backward. There's only tonight. Just you and me. I don't want anyone else in this bedroom with us."

She nodded.

He kissed her eyes closed, then let his lips drift downward toward her mouth. Desiree could feel the tension in his back and arms, the raging passion leashed by consideration for her fear. It wasn't fair, Desiree thought, that the man she had loved should have been so brutal, and this stranger so tender.

"Desiree?"

"Don't stop," she whispered.

Slowly, one at a time, he undid the buttons of her navy knit dress. She heard his murmur of approval as he revealed the black lace camisole she had worn, contemplating just such a moment. He slid the dress over her shoulders and freed her arms before shoving it down over her hips until it landed in a circle around her feet. She was left wearing only her camisole and tap pants.

Goose bumps rose on her skin.

"You're cold," he said as he enfolded her in his arms.

"You have on too many clothes," she replied, forcing him away far enough that she could reach the buttons on his shirt. Her hands were trembling, but it wasn't from the cold. Carter smiled and made short work of his buttons, letting the shirt slide down his arms. She pushed his long john shirt up and he pulled it off over his head.

At the sight of his bare chest she paused. He was so different from Burley. There was a small triangle of black curls at the center of his chest and a thin line of black down that headed past his navel. He took her hands and laid them on his chest.

"Touch me, Desiree."

It was easier than she had thought it would be to let her hands roam at will over the firm muscles of his chest. To her amazement, his nipples hardened into peaks as her fingertips brushed across them.

Carter's hands were moving in a mirror image of her own and she felt a corresponding response in her body.

"That feels wonderful," Desiree said breathlessly.

"You can say that again," Carter muttered as Desiree's hands tensed down across his belly. He slid his hands down to cup the warmth between her legs.

"That feels wonderful." Desiree was in a state of euphoria, reveling in the powerful feelings he evoked.

Carter lowered the straps on the camisole. It caught for an instant on the tips of her breasts before slipping to her waist. He shoved it down along with her tap pants.

She immediately crossed her arms over her breasts and belly to cover her nakedness.

He laughed. "What are you hiding?"

She resisted momentarily when he grasped her wrists to remove her hands, but realized she was only postponing the inevitable.

He gasped when he saw what she had been trying to conceal from him. "What the hell?"

His eyes sought hers, asking questions, demanding answers. "I wasn't going to ask how your face got cut," he said in a voice roughened by emotion. "But I don't think I can keep quiet about the rest of these scars."

She flinched when his hand reached out to the faint, criss-cross scars on her breasts. She hissed in a breath as his fingertips followed the long slash that arced down her belly.

"I was attacked," she said.

"By a man," he concluded. "Which explains why you jump every time I come up behind you. Lord, Desiree, why didn't you tell me?"

She hung her head, knowing she should tell him now about Burley. He had given her the perfect opening to do so. But she couldn't. He would be disgusted with her. And this evening would be at an end. If it wasn't already.

"I know they're ugly to look at," she began.

"Nothing about you is ugly," Carter retorted fiercely.

Not even my face? she wanted to ask. She looked up

to find out whether he was telling the truth. His eyes touched her body like hands, searching out her secrets. She kept waiting for his disgust—or her fear—to rise and spoil what was happening between them, but it never came. All she saw in his eyes was admiration, adoration.

"Come to bed, Desiree." Carter took her hand and drew her toward the bed. She knew he could feel her reluctance, because he paused.

"Have you changed your mind?"

She shook her head. "Unless you have."

He shook his head. "Is there something else you need?"

"I want to leave the light on." That would mean he would have to face her scars, but she hoped maybe she wouldn't encounter so many demons of the past if she kept the dark at bay.

He smiled. "That's fine with me."

Carter picked her up again and laid her on the bed, then rid himself of his trousers, long underwear and socks and joined her there. Desiree had already pulled the sheets up to her neck because she felt so self-conscious about her scars.

Carter slipped right under the covers with her and drew her into his arms so their bodies were aligned. They fit as though they were meant to be together, breast and thigh and belly. She could feel his heat and the hardness of his shaft against her thigh.

Her greatest fear was that now that they were in bed together he would satisfy his need and leave her wanting, as Burley had done so often.

She couldn't have been more wrong.

He went back to kissing her, concentrating on her

mouth and neck and shoulders until she was undulating beneath him. His hands sought out places on her body she hadn't guessed could be so sensitive, making her arch toward his touch.

But she knew it was taking too long for her to become aroused. She could feel the rigid tension in his shoulders, the hard muscles of his thighs. She knew he was ready. He must be impatient to get it over with.

"I…I'm ready now," she told him. She wanted to please him. She wanted him to want to do this again. So she was willing to end her own pleasure so he could find his.

Carter's hand slid down her belly to the nest of curls between her legs. He slid a finger inside, but it didn't penetrate easily.

"I don't think so," he said. "I think maybe you need some more of this." His mouth slid down from her shoulder to her breast, where he circled her nipple with his tongue.

Desiree gasped. "What are you doing?"

"Kissing you."

"There?"

She saw the moment of shock on his face before he asked, "Your husband never kissed your breasts?"

Desiree was totally mortified. Her face turned pink. She shook her head. "No," she breathed. "He… he couldn't wait for…for the other."

Carter swore under his breath.

She shrank back against the bedding.

"Desiree, honey, I'm not angry with you. Honey, please…let me love you."

Desiree eyed him warily. "You…you want to kiss my breasts?"

A roguish grin tilted his lips. "Uh-huh."

"It did feel…kind of nice," she admitted shyly. She lay back against the pillow, but her whole body was tensed.

"Relax," he crooned. His mouth caught hers in a swift kiss, and while she was still enjoying its effects, he swept lower and captured her nipple with his mouth. He teased, he sucked, he nipped. Desiree felt things she hadn't even imagined were possible.

"I feel…I feel…"

"What do you feel?" Carter rasped.

"Everything. I can feel *everything!*" Desiree exulted. She wasn't even close to frigid. Far from it. With Carter, her whole body was burning with sensual desire.

Carter's tenderness soon gave way to ardor and became an unquenchable hunger.

"Carter," she begged. "Now!"

Once again, his hand slid down her belly, into the nest of curls, finding another spot she hadn't even been aware existed.

"Oh! Oh, my!" The pleasure was so intense she felt the urge to escape as much as the urge to lie still so he could keep on with whatever it was he was doing. She had done some reading since her divorce from Burley, but words in a book couldn't do justice to what she was experiencing.

"So you think you're ready now," he said in a husky voice.

"Yesss," she hissed.

He pressed a finger inside her, and it slid easily into the moist passage. She recognized the difference between this time and the last, and realized Carter had taken the time to be sure she was aroused.

She knew he had recognized her readiness when he used his knees to spread her legs and placed himself above her. She put her hands at his waist and looked into his eyes.

"It's all right, Desiree. We have all the time in the world."

She clenched her muscles in readiness for the pain she expected. But Carter didn't thrust himself inside her as Burley had. Instead he probed slowly at the entrance to her womb, pushing a little way inside her and then backing off before intruding again. Until finally, without any pain to her—and with a great deal of self-control on his part—he was fully inside her.

It didn't hurt at all! In fact, it felt decidedly good. Her body instinctively arched upward into his.

Carter gave a grunt of pleasure.

Desiree lowered her bottom and thrust again.

Carter groaned.

"Am I hurting you, Carter?"

"You're killing me," Carter said with a husky laugh. "Just please don't stop!"

Desiree was delighted with the reversal of roles, but it wasn't long before Carter was doing his part to help.

With the joining of their bodies, Desiree found herself reaching out to Carter with body and soul, seeking the satisfaction that she had been denied for so long. When it happened, when her body violently convulsed, she tried to fight it.

"Come with me, love. Ride it out. Let it happen," Carter urged.

She looked up and saw the sheen of sweat that beaded his brow, the hank of damp hair that hung over his forehead, the light burning fiercely in his eyes. She could see the leashed passion waiting to erupt, held on a fraying tether. He was keeping his promise to her. Even now, she was in control.

That knowledge freed her to give rein to the passions that threatened to overwhelm her. Her body spasmed, her muscles tightening in exquisite pleasure as a groan forced its way past her throat. Carter thrust once more, arching his head back as he spilled his seed.

The best was yet to come. When they were both sated, instead of abandoning her, Carter reached out to pull her snugly into his arms, with one of his legs thrown over hers in a continuing embrace.

Desiree was breathless, embarrassed and exhilarated all at once. "That was…wonderful," she said with a shaky laugh.

"That word seems to be getting a lot of use tonight," Carter said with chuckle.

"I don't think anything else quite describes how I'm feeling right now," she admitted.

She was afraid to ask him how he felt, but she didn't believe he was dissatisfied, and certainly not disgusted. She didn't want to do anything to spoil the mood. It was hard to believe this sort of ecstasy could be repeated again and again all the years of their married life.

Desiree found solace for her bruised heart in Carter's arms. All the loving, all the gentle care she would have given to Burley, she bestowed on Carter. Tonight held a promise of the future, a hope for the new year. They would be good partners—in bed and out. Unfortunately, the depth of her feelings for Carter were too treacherous to admit or even to acknowledge.

Suddenly Desiree had to escape. The embrace that had felt so comforting now made her feel captive.

"I want to get up," she said in a harsh voice.

Carter was already half-asleep. "What? What's going on?" He was irritable at being woken. "Lie down."

"I'm going back to my own room."

He came fully awake and stared into her eyes. She knew the fear was back, but couldn't explain that this was different from her fear of physical harm. Burley had only beaten and terrified and humiliated her. She had given Carter the power to destroy her heart and soul.

"I need to be alone," she offered by way of explanation.

Carter's lips curled in disgust. "I'm not going to turn into some kind of beast in the middle of the night. But if you want to go, go."

Desiree yanked on a flannel shirt that Carter had left tossed over a ladderback chair and fled the room.

Carter slumped back against the pillow, then smacked it with his fist. All the love he would have given to Jeanine he had bequeathed to the woman he had lain with tonight. The emotions he had experienced as Desiree climaxed beneath him were too dangerous to explore. He hadn't been ready to let her go when she abandoned him. He felt…a loss. But what could he have done to stop her? After all, it wasn't as though they were in love. They were only married lovers.

He reached over to turn out the light. He hoped she spent a miserable night alone. He hoped she tossed and turned the way he was sure he would himself. He hoped she had bags under her eyes in the morning the size of suitcases. He hoped—

Desiree screamed. "Carter! Come Quick!"

Carter's blood ran cold at the terror in her voice. A second later he was on his way to her.

CHAPTER SEVEN

CARTER GRABBED A pair of jeans, stuck his legs in them and dragged them on as he headed on the run toward Desiree. He found her standing in the doorway to her room, her eyes so wide he could see the whites of them, the back of her hand across her mouth to stifle the awful, tearing sobs that erupted from her throat.

"Desiree, are you all right? Are you hurt? What happened?"

At the sound of his voice she turned and flung herself into his arms, which tightened around her. Over the top of her head he had a view of the chaos in her bedroom.

It had been ransacked. There wasn't an object left upright or unbroken. There were feathers everywhere from the destruction of the pillows, and even her mattress had been slashed. This wasn't the work of a thief. It was the devastation of a psychopath.

"This is crazy," Carter muttered. "Why so much destruction? And why only your bedroom?"

Desiree sobbed harder in his arms. He felt a fierce need to protect her, to crush the fiend who had threatened the woman he held so tightly.

"I'll call the police."

She grabbed him around the neck. "No!"

"Why not? They'll want to investigate. Anybody crazy enough to do something like this belongs in a cage where he can't hurt people. They'll want to find him fast."

Desiree dragged herself free of his embrace. "I know who did this," she said. "But it won't do any good to confront him. He'll just deny everything. Unless I can catch him in the act, they can't do a thing. I have to have evidence," she said bitterly, "before they'll interfere."

Carter felt his stomach turn over. "Who did this, Desiree?"

Her shoulders slumped, and she turned to lean her forehead against the cool wood framing the door. "He said he would come back."

"Who said he would come back?" Carter demanded, his voice laced with the irritation he was feeling at his helplessness.

"Burley Kelton." Desiree turned to look Carter in the eye. "My former husband. I should have told you," she said in an anguished voice. "He's been in prison for attempting to murder me, but he got out today. He warned me he was coming back. I hoped—"

"You hoped that if you had a husband he would keep his distance," Carter said in a voice like a rusty gate.

What a fool he had been! She had used him.

And weren't you using her to get the roots you wanted?

That was different.

How? You both wanted something from each other. So she wasn't totally honest about her motives. Have you been totally honest with her?

The truth was, he had married for his own reasons, not thinking much about hers. The band around his chest loosened enough that he could breathe again.

"Stay here while I check the house to make sure he's gone," Carter said.

Desiree's eyes rounded again in fear. "You don't believe he could still be here, do you?"

"I'm going to find out." Carter ushered her back to his bedroom door. He turned on the light and drew her inside. "Stay here. Close the door behind me and lock it."

Carter had no weapon handy, and wondered what he would do if he encountered the other man armed with a knife. Or a gun.

But the house had an empty feeling. A quiet, thorough search revealed no signs of an intruder. The broken lock on the front door explained how Burley had gotten in.

When Carter returned to his room he knocked and said, "It's me. Let me in."

Desiree stood hesitantly across from him until he opened his arms. Then she flew into them once more.

"Did you find anything?" she asked.

"Nothing. Except a broken lock on the front door."

She gave a shuddering sigh. "Oh, Carter. What am I going to do?"

"You mean, what are *we* going to do? First, we're going to call the police." Before she could protest, he added, "He might have left some fingerprints or some other evidence."

"Do we have to do it now?"

Carter grimaced. "I suppose tomorrow morning is soon enough."

"I'm so sorry I got you involved in all this," she said, her cheek against his chest. "I thought if he knew I was married again, he would leave me alone."

"I guess not," Carter muttered. "So Burley is the one who mistreated you?"

She nodded. She tried to talk but couldn't manage any sound past the knot in her throat.

Carter put an arm around her shoulders and walked over to the bed with her. He sat down with his back against the headboard and pulled her onto his lap. "I want to hear about it," he said.

Desiree realized Carter was almost quivering with fury. But it was all directed at the man who had harmed her.

"I was too young when I married him, and very naive. I…I put up with…everything…as long as I could. While my parents were alive, it wasn't so bad. After they were gone, his abuse got worse."

"That explains all that flinching around me, I suppose."

She nodded, her hair tickling his chin.

"One night after dinner, I got up the courage to ask him for a divorce. He went crazy. He accused me of seeing another man. He told me he'd make sure no other man would want to have anything to do with me. He told me he'd married me 'till death do us part,' and if he couldn't have me no one could.

"We were in the kitchen, and he grabbed a butcher knife. He cut my face first." Her hand protectively covered the scar. "Then he raped me."

"Desiree—"

"Let me finish!" she said. "He laughed while he was carving designs on my breasts. Said he was branding me so any other man I tried to sleep with would know I belonged to him. The wound in the belly came when I told him I would never belong to him, that I was going to leave him if it was the last thing I ever did. He assured me that leaving him would be the end of me.

"If one of the ranch hands hadn't heard my screams and come running, Burley would have killed me. As it was, he escaped the house and ran. Before he left, he promised me he would come back some dark night and finish what he had started. It took six weeks before he was caught. During that time I lived in fear for my life. I left the lights on because I was afraid of the dark. I still am," she admitted in a whisper.

"Desiree—"

"Nine months after he raped me, Nicole was born."

"Oh, my God," Carter said. "Does Burley know about the child?"

Desiree shook her head. "I don't know if he'll figure it out. But he has friends who could tell him I've been living here alone until recently." Desiree's hands snuck up around Carter's neck, where she clung for support. "I've been so afraid he'll do something to hurt Nicole. I know I've been dishonest with you. All I can say is, I'm sorry."

In that instant, Carter was tempted to tell her the truth about himself, that he had also married under false pretenses. But he knew now that his money wasn't what Desiree had been after when she married him. Unfortunately, over the past three weeks he had discovered that he wanted—needed—much more from her than the pleasure to be had from her body. Telling her the truth would only complicate matters right now.

"He'll be back," Desiree said in a whisper.

"How can you be so sure?"

"I've been through this before," she said. "I was in the hospital for a short while following Burley's attack. After I came home, in the six weeks before Burley was caught, he used to leave signs that he had been around—to terrorize me, I think. Or he would call me on the phone and just breathe. He was always careful not to leave anything that could be used as evidence against him in court."

"The police can question Burley—"

"The police have to catch Burley before they can question him," Desiree said with asperity. "Burley knows this place like the back of his hand, where to hide, all the back roads."

"So you're just going to sit here and wait for him to finish what he's started?" Carter demanded.

"What do you suggest?" Desiree retorted.

"Do you have a gun?"

"No! And I don't intend to get one."

"Then how do you propose to protect yourself?"

There was a pause before she replied, "I was counting on you for that."

There was another pause before he answered, "What, exactly, did you have in mind?"

"There's the chance that your presence here will be enough to deter anything like this from happening again."

"Do you really believe that?"

"I believe Burley will keep his distance so long as you're around." Burley only preyed on things weaker than himself.

"That's going to make it a little difficult for things to get done around here—I mean, if we have to do everything in tandem. And what about Nicole?"

"She would have to be with us, too."

Carter shook his head. "It won't work."

Desiree gripped his shoulders. "It could. What other choice do we have?"

Carter tried to come up with some other solution to the problem. But until Burley made a move, there was nothing he could do. "All right," he said. "We'll call the police and report this intrusion tomorrow morning. If they don't find anything—"

"They won't."

"I'll go along with your plan."

She hesitated only an instant before she said, "Thanks, Carter. I won't be a burden, I promise."

Nevertheless, Carter felt a tremendous burden of responsibility. She had put her safety, and Nicole's, in his hands. Once before a woman had asked him to protect her. And he had failed her...and their daughter.

"You can sleep here," Carter said. "I'll be comfortable on the couch."

"Or we could sleep here together," Desiree suggested tentatively.

"You sure?" Carter asked.

"As long as I can have the right side of the bed," she said with a shy smile.

Carter laughed. "Fine."

Desiree settled on her side of the bed as Carter turned out the light. She tossed and turned for several minutes trying to get comfortable. At last, he couldn't stand it any longer. He put an arm around her waist and dragged her back against him, so her bottom spooned into his groin and his knees were tucked behind hers. Her head fit just under his chin, and her flyaway hair tickled his nose.

"Go to sleep," he said gruffly.

He didn't know whether it was because he ordered

it or because she was comfortable at last, but the sound of her steady breathing told him sometime later that she was asleep.

Meanwhile, he lay for hours staring into the darkness, confronting the memories he had been running from for six long years.

He had thought himself the happiest of men when he married Jeanine. He was in love, and they had a child on the way. Only years later had he discovered that things were not as they had seemed. By the time Jeanine had come to him with the truth, a tragedy had already been set in motion.

Carter had greeted his wife with surprise and pleasure when she appeared at his forty-third-floor corporate office in downtown Denver. "What are you doing here, Jeanine?"

"We have to talk, Carter."

"I was just going out to lunch," he said. "Join me."

"I think it would be best if we spoke here. In private."

It was then he had noticed the redness around her eyes and the bruise on her cheek, barely hidden by makeup.

He led her over to the black leather sofa in the steel-and-glass office. "Sit down," he said. "Tell me what's going on."

She fidgeted with the gold chain on her purse, refusing to meet his gaze. "I have a confession to make."

Carter's heart was in his throat. There was only one kind of confession a woman made to a man. She was having an affair. He felt a murderous rage toward the unknown man who had seduced his wife.

"I had an affair."

Even though he had been expecting it, hearing the

words was like getting punched in the gut. All the air whooshed out of his lungs.

She looked up at him, her gray eyes liquid, as beautiful as she had ever been. "It was while we were engaged."

Furrows appeared on his brow. "That was years ago. Why are you telling me about it now?"

She left her purse on the couch and paced across the plush carpeting. "Because he won't leave me alone!"

Carter rose and followed her to the window overlooking the street below. He actually felt the hairs bristling on his neck when he asked, "Is he the one responsible for that bruise on your cheek?"

She lifted her hand to the revealing mark and winced in pain at even that slight touch. "Yes."

His hands fisted. "I'll take care of it. Tell me where to find him."

"It isn't that simple," she said. The tears began to fall, leaving tracks across her perfect makeup. "You see, he's Alisa's father."

Carter's heart skipped a beat. His face blanched. He couldn't have heard what he had thought he'd heard. "Some other man is the father of my child?"

She nodded.

"Alisa isn't mine?"

"No, she's not."

Carter's stomach churned. His heart was pounding so hard it felt as though he had been running a race. A race he was losing. "Why are you telling me this now?" he asked in a harsh voice.

"Because I need your help," she said. "I realized my affair with Jack—"

"Is that his name?"

"Yes. Jack Taggert. I realized my affair with him was a mistake, but by then I was pregnant. I told him it was over, but he wouldn't take no for an answer. Business took him overseas for five years after you and I were married, but now he's back. He wants to pick up where we left off. And he wants to see Alisa."

"How the hell does he know Alisa is his?" Carter demanded.

"She has a birthmark. It's something all the Taggerts have. He saw it, and he knew."

"Dammit, Jeanine, why the hell didn't you tell me about this *before* we were married?"

"Because I was afraid you wouldn't understand."

"You're damn right I don't!" He paced angrily away from her. "Now what?" he demanded.

"I love you, Carter."

"Sure you do!" he said sarcastically. "That's why you've been passing off some other man's kid as mine!"

"Carter, I—"

"I don't want to hear any more of your lies, Jeanine. Just get the hell out of here."

"Carter, I'm afraid of Jack. He's—"

"He's your problem, not mine," Carter said ruthlessly. "You deal with him."

"You don't understand."

"I sure as hell don't! Why did you marry me, Jeanine? Why didn't you marry the father of your child?"

"You had more money," she snapped back at him.

Carter's lips flattened. "Thanks for that bit of honesty."

"I was being sarcastic!" she cried. "I love you, Carter. I need your help. Please!"

He went to the door and held it open for her. "I need to think, Jeanine. Go home."

"You don't seem to understand," she said as she stood on the threshold. "Jack has been stalking me, Carter. He's threatened to kill me if I don't come back to him."

"You expect me to believe that?" he said with a sneer.

"It's the truth."

"I'll call you when I make up my mind what I'm going to do," he said. "Don't let that bastard near Alisa until you hear from me."

He had closed the door quietly behind her, then sunk down along the wall and dropped his head onto his knees. His whole world had been ripped apart. He was furious with his wife for betraying him, hated her for lying to him. It had been a crushing blow to learn that the woman he had loved, and whom he believed had loved him, had really married him because he had more money than the man who had fathered her child.

But most of all, he was devastated by the discovery that his daughter was not his daughter. Alisa, the delight of his life, was not even his own flesh and blood!

Carter thought of the doll he had bought Alisa for Christmas, the one that could talk and drink and wet. Alisa had sat in his lap and played with his tie and told him all about it. He had brushed the blond hair from her eyes and told her she should be sure to write Santa and ask for one. Then he had rushed right out to buy one for her.

Later that fateful day he had asked his secretary to call his wife and tell her he was going on a business trip that would take him out of town for a week. Maybe by the end of that time he could figure out what he was going to do with his life.

But he hadn't been given a week. Three days later, on Christmas Eve, his wife and daughter had been on the way to the Christmas pageant, when they were run off the road in a fiery crash that had completely destroyed both cars. The police had identified the driver of the second vehicle as Jack Taggert.

It wasn't until he heard that his wife and daughter were dead that Carter realized the mistake he had made. Biology wasn't what had made Alisa his daughter. And even if Jeanine had not loved him, he had loved her. As his wife, he had owed her his trust and his protection. He had betrayed her every bit as badly as she had betrayed him. Only he was never going to get the chance to make things right.

Here in Wyoming he had found another daughter who was not his own, another woman who was threatened by a man from her past.

This time he wouldn't fail them.

Carter tightened his hold on Desiree, which was when he realized she wasn't asleep, after all.

"What are you thinking?" she whispered in the dark.

"How did you know I was thinking?"

"You kept making little noises in your throat."

Carter made a little sound in his throat.

"Just like that," she said as she snuggled back into the curve of his hips. "What were you thinking about, Carter?"

"About my wife and daughter." He felt her stiffen.

"About how much you miss them?"

"My wife was being stalked by an old boyfriend when she was killed along with our daughter," Carter said. "She asked me to protect her, but I didn't. I didn't realize how serious the danger was. And we had fought...."

Desiree reached for the light on her side of the bed and turned it on. She saw the pain of his loss etched in his blunt features. She reached out a hand to cradle his bristly cheek. "How awful," she said in a quiet voice. "Why didn't you tell me about this before?"

Carter lifted himself up on his elbow. "It isn't something I'm very proud about. In fact, I've felt guilty about it for years."

"And now you have a chance to atone," Desiree said as she brushed her thumb across his cheek, "by taking care of me and Nicole."

"Something like that," Carter admitted.

Desiree dropped her hand, then reached over and turned out the light. She lay down on the edge of the bed with her back to him and remained very still.

After a few minutes, Carter asked, "What are you thinking, Desiree?"

"How do you know I'm thinking?"

"Because you're so quiet."

At first he thought she wasn't going to answer him. Then she said, "I'm not sure marrying you was the right thing to do."

"Oh?"

"I had hoped that if I was married, Burley would accept the fact that I'm not ever going to let him back into my life. What happened tonight proves that either he hasn't seen you, or he doesn't care. I'm sorry for using you like that, Carter. But I was desperate."

"Why didn't you just sell the Rimrock and go somewhere Burley would never find you?"

"This house was built generations ago by my forebears. Do you understand what I'm saying?"

"Yes. I think so. You have deep roots that tie you

to the land." Like the roots he was beginning to grow himself.

"Besides," she said, "if I had run away, Burley would only have followed me. I'd rather stand and fight."

"You didn't do so well the last time you tangled with Burley."

"Last time I didn't have you on my side."

Carter grunted an acknowledgment of her point. Apparently, she thought his presence was going to make a difference. He hoped she was right.

"I'm glad I found you, Carter."

"I'm glad you found me, too. I promise I'll take care of you, Desiree. You and Nicky both."

"Thanks, Carter. I'm kind of tired. I think I'll go to sleep now."

She was curled up on the edge of the bed, as far as she could get from him. He could have left her there. It was clear that after his confession she was having second thoughts about her marriage to him. But Carter didn't want them to start the new year on opposite sides of the bed.

He scooted over to the middle of the bed, reached for Desiree and dragged her back against him.

"Carter—"

"I need you close to me, Desiree."

She lay stiff in his arms a moment longer, then pressed herself close to him. "Happy New Year, Carter."

"Happy New Year, Desiree."

CHAPTER EIGHT

DESIREE KNEW CARTER meant the promise he had made to protect her. But it was depressing to think that the care he took of her over the next weeks and months was motivated by guilt, rather than feelings of love. She wanted more. She wanted him to love her. Because, God help her, she had fallen in love with him. However, she wasn't about to tell him how she felt, because that wasn't part of their bargain. A marriage of convenience shouldn't have emotional strings attached.

Their call to the police on the morning after Burley's rampage through her bedroom had yielded exactly the result Desiree had expected. There were no fingerprints, no solid evidence to connect Burley to the crime. The officers were sorry, they would keep a lookout, but unless they had some proof that Burley was the culprit, there was nothing they could do.

Carter hadn't been satisfied with that. "I'm going to hire a couple of extra hands to help out around here," he said.

"I—we—can't afford it."

"I've seen the books," Carter said. "We can afford it if we cut costs somewhere else. I want some people here, so I'll know you're safe if I'm not around."

"But—"

"No buts."

She had given in. Not graciously. She had argued for a day and a half. But she had seen he was determined, so she had agreed.

Gradually winter had loosened its grip on the land. The buffalo grass and wheatgrass and grama grass had put up sprouts of green. Desiree spent more and more time outside with Nicole, working in her vegetable garden behind the house. She always had one eye on the rolling prairie, waiting for Burley to show up. But he seemed to have disappeared.

Ordinarily she stayed close to the house. But on one unusually warm and beautiful March day, when Nicole was with Carter in the barn, her eyes strayed to the horizon. She caught sight of a patch of colorful wildflowers on the hillside that begged to be picked.

Even though the flowers were within easy calling distance of the house and barn, she debated the wisdom of leaving the area of the house to go pick them. As she dug with her trowel, weeding the carrots and squash and watermelon, she got angrier and angrier over the fact that Burley had made her so much a prisoner that she couldn't even walk a couple of hundred yards to pick wildflowers.

She dropped her trowel, yanked off her gloves and started marching up the hill. She picked wildflowers almost defiantly, breaking the stems and dropping them into her shirt, which she held out like a basket. Once she had picked the patch she had seen from the garden, she whirled to return to the house, which was when she spied another, even more beautiful, patch.

She looked around her, and there was nothing visible in any direction. She wasn't far from the house, still within easy shouting distance.

"He's *not* going to make me a prisoner," she said aloud. She started marching toward the next hill. She did that twice more, and was startled, when she glanced up, to realize she could no longer see the house.

He appeared out of nowhere.

Desiree realized she had been lured into a false sense of security by the extra men Carter had hired, and by the fact Burley hadn't shown his face in the twelve weeks since he had ransacked her bedroom.

"What are you doing here?" she demanded when he rose up to block her way.

"I was just taking a little look around the place. You've made some improvements while I've been away, Ice."

Desiree shuddered at the name he called her. It had hurt when he used it before, because she had believed it was true. Thanks to Carter, the word had lost its power to wound her. If she had ever been like ice in bed, that was no longer true. She lifted her chin and stared into Burley's dark brown eyes.

She wondered what she had found so attractive about him once upon a time. He wore his long hair combed back in front, in an old-fashioned bouffant that reminded her of Elvis. He had gained a bit of weight in prison, so now he was not only tall, but heavyset. A grizzled black stubble coated his cheeks and chin. The twinkling brown eyes that had courted her, that had flirted with lazy winks, were puffy, the color of dull brown mud.

His clothes were dirty and wrinkled, as though he had been sleeping in them. She realized it was entirely possible that he was camped somewhere on the Rimrock.

"You'd better leave," she said. "Or I'll call the police and have you arrested for trespassing."

"Oooh, I'm scared," he said in a singsong voice. "Where did you find the man?"

"What man?"

He grabbed her arms in a grip so tight she knew there would be bruises there tomorrow.

"Don't play games," he snarled.

"His name is Carter Prescott. He's my husband."

"I heard something like that," Burley said. "You can kiss him goodbye. Better yet, kiss me hello."

Desiree kept her teeth clenched as Burley forced a kiss on her. His breath was fetid, and she gagged.

"You've gotten awful high and mighty since I've been gone," he said, angrily shoving her an arm's distance away.

"Carter will kill you," she retorted.

"Not if I kill him first."

Desiree gasped at his threat. "I don't love you anymore, Burley. I don't want to be with you. I want you to leave me alone. And I want you to leave Carter alone."

"What about the kid?"

Desiree's heart missed a beat. "What about her?"

"Who's her father, Desiree?"

"Carter Prescott."

He shook his head. "Uh-uh. Prescott didn't show his face around here till this past Christmas. The kid is what? Five? Six? She's mine, isn't she?"

"No. There was another man—"

"I want to see her," Burley interrupted.

Desiree felt panic clawing at her insides, but she kept her voice calm and firm. "No."

"I'll bet one of those newfangled blood tests would

prove she's mine," Burley said in a silky voice. "Then I could get a court to let me see her, don't you think?"

"Don't do this, Burley. You never wanted children. You told me so every time we—" Desiree cut herself off. She couldn't bring herself to identify intercourse with Burley as making love, not after she had experienced what lovemaking really was.

"I'd be willing to forget about the kid if you paid a little attention to me."

Desiree gritted her teeth to keep the disgust she felt from showing on her face. She should have known Burley was only using Nicole to blackmail her. She was determined not to be a victim again. She decided to promise him anything now. And make sure she was never anywhere he could catch her alone again.

At the sound of approaching hoofbeats, Burley jerked his head around and searched the hillside. "You're expecting company?"

"Carter was planning to join me," Desiree lied.

Burley pulled out a switchblade and snapped it open. "Don't go doing anything stupid," he said. "I'll be back to see you another time. So long, Ice."

Once he was gone, Desiree whirled and ran toward the man approaching on horseback. To her relief, it was Carter. He dismounted on the run, and she met him halfway, sobbing with relief by the time she threw herself into his arms.

"Are you all right?" he asked, clutching her tightly against him.

"I'm fine. I wanted to pick some wildflowers, and I guess I wandered too far and got frightened."

She saw him eyeing the wildflowers strewn carelessly across the ground, flowers she hadn't been holding when they had first spied each other.

"What happened here, Desiree?"

"Nothing."

"Don't tell me that!" Carter said in a harsh voice. "He was here, wasn't he?"

Desiree nodded jerkily. She clung to Carter to keep him from going after Burley. "He has a knife! Let him go."

"How did he get here?"

They heard the roar of a motorcycle, which answered his question.

"I was so scared," Desiree said as she clutched Carter around the waist. "I'm so glad you came. How did you know he was here?"

"I didn't," Carter admitted. "I stepped out of the barn for a minute and looked for you in the garden. When I didn't see you, I thought…I thought maybe something had happened to you." His grip tightened so she could barely breathe. "I don't know what I would do if anything happened to you."

Desiree knew it wasn't love that made him say such things. It was guilt. Carter wouldn't be able to live with himself if he lost another wife to a stalker. Whatever the source, she was grateful for the concern that had sent him hunting for her.

She looked up into Carter's eyes, trusting him enough to let him see her desperation and her fear. "Burley said he wants to see Nicole. He knows she's his."

"Nicky isn't going anywhere with that man," Carter said. "You don't have to worry about that."

"He is her father."

"Only biologically. I'm Nicky's father now."

Desiree stared up at Carter in surprise. Even though Nicky had been referring to Carter as her daddy for the past three months, it was the first time he had acknowledged himself in that role.

"You want to adopt her?" Desiree asked.

Now it was Carter who looked surprised. "I hadn't thought that far ahead, but I suppose so. Yes."

Desiree laid her head on his shoulder. "Thank you, Carter."

"This time we've got that bastard cold," he said. "He was trespassing on Rimrock land."

"Did you actually see him?"

"No. But I know he was here."

She shook her head, her brown hair whipping her cheeks. "It wouldn't do any good. It's his word against mine."

"Dammit, Desiree! That man should be put away in a cage where he can't hurt you or Nicky."

"I won't go beyond sight of the house again unless someone is with me," she promised. "He won't come near the house as long as there are people around." Her lips twisted ruefully. "He's too smart—and too much of a coward—for that."

"I hate living like this," Carter said.

"And you think I don't?" Desiree responded tartly. "But there's nothing either of us can do about it."

"There's something I can do," Carter said.

Desiree framed his beard-roughened cheeks with her palms and forced him to look at her. "You aren't going to confront him, are you? Because all that would accomplish would be to get one or the other of you killed. I don't want to lose you, Carter. Promise me you'll stay away from him."

His lids dropped to conceal the feral look in his blue eyes. His lashes fanned out like coal crescents across his weathered face. When he opened his eyes again, he had hidden his feelings behind a wall of inscrutability. "I'll stay away from him. But I'm not making any guarantees if he comes back to the Rimrock."

"All right." She let her hands drop to her sides, but kept her eyes on Carter. Now that her fear had dissipated, there was another kind of tension building. She couldn't be around Carter without feeling it. The need. The desire. This time she was the one who let her lids drop to hide her avid expression.

"Desiree?"

Her body trembled at the sound of her name in that husky voice he used when he wanted her. His body almost quivered with animal excitement. The blunt ridge in his jeans was proof of his need. The wind carried with it the musky scent of aroused male. Desiree lifted her lids and stared up into blue eyes lambent with passion.

It was a sign of how far they had come over the past three months that there was no longer any question whether she was ready for him. She was always as ready for him as he was for her. What was more, she trusted him not to hurt her—no matter how uninhibited their lovemaking became.

So when he grabbed the front of her blouse and jerked, sending buttons flying, she responded by pulling the snaps free on his shirt and forcing it down off his shoulders. His mouth clamped onto her breast and sucked through the lace bra she was wearing. She followed him down onto the soft shoots of new grass, their tangled bodies rolling once or twice until they came to rest with her beneath him.

While he unsnapped her jeans and pulled down the zipper, she did the same to him. He shoved her jeans down, while she released him from his. With a single thrust he was inside her. Carter claimed her as she claimed him, their bodies moving urgently, seeking satisfaction.

"You're mine," Carter said as he climaxed within her.

"Yours," Desiree confirmed. "Only yours."

When it was over, they lay beside each other in the cool grass, staring up into a sky as wide and blue as any on earth.

"Do you ever wonder where you would be now if I hadn't proposed to you in the church parking lot?" Desiree asked.

Carter pulled up some clover and twirled it between his fingers. He leaned over to hold it under Desiree's nose so she could smell the sweet scent. "I'd still be looking, I guess."

"For a wife?"

"For a place to settle down."

"Are you happy, Carter?"

"Are you?" he countered.

Desiree thought about it a moment. "Most of the time."

"And the rest of the time?"

She hedged against admitting that what would make her really happy was to know that he loved her. Instead she said, "I don't think we've seen the last of Burley."

"If he comes back, I'll be ready for him."

As the days turned to weeks, and the weeks to a month, Desiree began wishing that Burley would just return so they could get the confrontation over with. The waiting was driving her crazy. Especially since there were signs—ominous things, but nothing she ever dared mention to Carter—that he hadn't gone away.

She found the laundry she had hung on the line in the backyard pulled down into the dirt. The heads of her marigolds were all cut off. A birdhouse was destroyed. And Nicole's Black Angus calf, which had never been sick, not even when it was first born, mysteriously died.

Desiree had been with Nicole when they found the calf. Nicole had let herself into the stall and dropped to her knees beside the calf, which was lying on its side with its tongue hanging out.

"Mommy, what's wrong with Matilda? She isn't moving."

Desiree entered the stall and lowered herself to the hay beside Nicole. "Let's see what the problem is."

She knew the instant she touched the stiff, cold body that the calf was dead. One of the basic laws of farm life was not to make pets of the animals. It was likely they would have to be sold, or killed and eaten. She had broken that rule when she had allowed Nicole to name the calf. Nicole would have to suffer now for her folly.

"Matilda's dead, Nicky," Desiree said.

Her daughter looked up at her in shock, then looked back at the motionless calf. She put a finger on its nose, seeking for breath that wasn't there, and felt the unnatural texture of its skin. Her face scrunched up and tears flowed freely down her cheeks.

Desiree enfolded her daughter in her arms and did her best to console the inconsolable child.

"What happened to her, Mommy? Why did she die?"

Until Nicole mentioned it, Desiree hadn't focused

on what might have killed the calf. She looked around her suspiciously. "I don't know. Let's check and see if we can find out what happened."

Having something to do helped both of them. Desiree examined the calf, but there was no obvious wound. Nor was there anything in the feedbox that appeared different or unusual. Desiree did find a white dusting of powder that had sifted through the feed box onto the stall floor.

Poison. Strychnine or arsenic, most likely, she realized.

Which meant that Burley had been there. Desiree was furious that Burley had chosen to kill the calf. She was terrified at the thought that he had been so close, that if Nicole had come in here alone, her innocent daughter might have been confronted by a man fully capable of brutalizing her, perhaps even killing her. Suddenly Desiree no longer felt safe in the barn.

"Come on," she said to Nicole, "let's go tell your daddy what happened."

Grim-lipped, Carter listened to Nicole's tale of woe. He lifted her into his arms and carried her upstairs, where he sat with her until she fell asleep for her afternoon nap.

Desiree waited downstairs for the showdown she knew was coming. Carter didn't keep her waiting long.

"Burley did this." He said it as a fact, or rather, snarled it through his teeth.

"I found some white powder on the floor of the stall that I think might have been poison."

"You don't expect me to keep this from the police, do you?" he asked through tight jaws.

She sighed and lay back in the chair where she was

ensconced. "No. I think this should be reported. But I don't think you'll get any satisfaction."

"I want it on the record that someone's been making mischief around here."

"All right."

"You aren't arguing with me."

She sighed again. "It isn't the first time Burley's come onto the Rimrock over the past month."

"What?" He crossed to her and stood with his legs spread and his hands fisted on his hips.

"I didn't want to worry you, but he's done a few things to let me know he's still around."

"Like what?"

"Pulling down the laundry, trampling my flowers, wrecking the birdhouse. Stuff like that."

"And you never said anything to me?"

Desiree could see that Carter was hurt, by the fact that she hadn't shared her problems with him. She shoved herself up out of the chair until she was sitting on the back with her feet on the seat. "There was nothing you could do."

"I could have shared what you were feeling."

"I didn't know you wanted to," she said simply.

"We're husband and wife—"

"Because you wanted the Rimrock," Desiree said, being brutally frank.

She saw him open his mouth to deny it, then snap it shut again. She dropped her head into her hands. "If I'd thought you could help, I would have said something," Desiree admitted. "But there was no way any of those things that happened could be connected with Burley. It would have been a waste of time confronting him."

And dangerous. But she wasn't going to say that to

Carter. He was already too anxious to go hunting for Burley Kelton.

Abruptly Carter left the room.

Desiree felt a despair such as she hadn't experienced since the time she was married to Burley and had been bullied by him day and night. She was as much Burley's prisoner now as she had ever been as his wife. And it seemed there was no escape from her nightmare.

She had thought things couldn't get worse, but later that afternoon a police car drove up behind the house. Desiree was on her feet in an instant and running toward it. Carter had been gone all afternoon, and she was deathly afraid that something might have happened to him.

Something had.

When Carter stepped out of the backseat of the police car, Desiree barely recognized him. His face was a mass of cuts and bruises. Both his eyes were black and his lip was swollen. She didn't ask what had happened to him. She knew.

"The doc said to keep some ice on those bruises, Mizz Prescott," the young patrolman said. He turned to Carter and grinned. "That's some right cross you've got. Never saw a man go down so hard as Burley did."

Desiree stared in vexation as Carter tried to return the grin. His face was too battered to manage it.

"When you two are through exchanging compliments I'd like to follow the doctor's orders and put some ice on Carter's face," she said in a frigid voice.

The patrolman tipped his hat. "Sure, Mizz Prescott. The judge'll be expecting you on Monday," he reminded Carter.

Desiree didn't wait to see if Carter followed her. She

marched into the kitchen and began pulling ice from the freezer and wrapping it in a dish towel. When she turned, he was standing in the doorway.

"Sit down and shut the door," she snapped.

"He looks worse than I do," Carter said as he dropped with a groan into a kitchen chair.

"That's comforting," Desiree said sarcastically.

"It had to be done."

"I don't know why men think everything can be settled with violence. What have you accomplished except to give Burley another reason to want revenge?"

"He won't be doing anything anytime soon," Carter said with satisfaction.

"Are you going to end up spending time in jail because of this?" Desiree asked with asperity.

Carter started to grin again, put a hand to his puffy lip and thought better of it. "You may not believe this, but Burley started it. I was only defending myself."

"Where did you find him?" Desiree asked.

"There's a bar in Casper where he hangs out."

"Where's Burley now?"

"In jail. Or the hospital."

"Oh, Carter," Desiree said as she eyed his battered face. "You foolish, foolish man. You didn't have to do this for me."

His features hardened, his eyes narrowed. "I didn't do it for you," he said. "I did it for Nicky."

Desiree turned away so he wouldn't see how hurt she was. Carter didn't—couldn't—love her, but he had given his affection to her daughter. She tried to be happy that Nicky had found such a protector. It was hard not to wish that he could love her just a little bit, too.

"Desiree?"

Carter took her hand and pulled her onto his lap. She laid her head on his shoulder and felt him stroking her back, playing with her hair.

"I have a confession to make," he said in a quiet voice.

"What?"

"I've wanted to get my hands on Burley Kelton ever since I first realized he was responsible for the scar on your face." He paused and added, "What he did to the calf…it was just an excuse to go after him."

Desiree let her hands slip into the hair at Carter's nape. "You foolish, foolish man," she whispered. "I'd rather have a hundred scars than see one bruise on this face of yours."

Carter's arms tightened around her. They sat there for a long time. Wishing things were different.

She wished that he loved her.

He wished that she could love him.

Neither spoke their wishes, both being too grown-up to believe that dreams do come true.

CHAPTER NINE

As SPRING PASSED into summer, Burley kept his distance. Maybe Carter had beat some sense into him after all, Desiree mused. She began to hope that perhaps Burley had changed his mind about wanting her, that he had gotten over his unhealthy obsession. Maybe he had found someone else and that was why she hadn't seen hide nor hair of him—or any sign that he had been watching her. She began to relax her vigil, to make occasional forays from the house on her own.

Carter was not so sanguine about Burley's intentions. When he caught Desiree hunting for four-leaf clovers up in the hills behind the house one afternoon during Nicole's nap, he lashed into her. "Are you crazy?" he demanded. "Or do you have a death wish?"

"What's the matter with you?" Desiree demanded, her fists perched on her hips.

"I happen to care what happens to you," he retorted.

His comment smacked too much of the guilt she knew he felt, and not enough of the love she wished for in vain. "Don't worry," she snapped back at him. "I won't get myself murdered by a stalker. Lord knows how you would survive it a second time!"

His face bleached white and his mouth flattened into a thin line. "If you don't care whether you live or die, I don't suppose it makes much difference what I think."

Desiree was still too angry to be sorry for the wound she had inflicted on Carter. She had flung the accusation at him hoping he would deny that guilt was what motivated his care for her, hoping he would contradict her with protestations of love. Instead he had responded to her wound with a wound of his own.

"Faron has a bull I want to take a look at," Carter said through clenched teeth. "I was going to ask you to come with me, but I can see you've got other plans." He turned and marched down the hill.

She watched him speak to one of the men he had hired to watch over her. The two appeared to argue for a moment before Carter got into his pickup and gunned the engine, raising a cloud of dust as he peeled out of the backyard.

Desiree sank down onto her haunches and dropped her head on her knees. How could she expect Carter to mention love, when she was so careful not to speak the word herself? She couldn't go on this way. When Carter returned, she was going to have to tell him how she really felt. The mere fact he didn't love her back wasn't going to change anything.

Desiree wasn't aware how long she had been sitting there, until she realized she wasn't alone anymore.

"Carter?"

"Guess again."

A shiver of terror raced down Desiree's spine. She lurched to her feet and started to run. She didn't get far before Burley caught the tails of her shirt and hauled her to a stop.

She turned and fought him like a wildcat, her nails raking his face, her fists beating at him. She screamed, knowing there was help not far away.

"Don't waste your breath," Burley said with a laugh. "The man your husband left to watch over you drove away five minutes ago."

Desiree paused to stare in horror at Burley's malicious smile of triumph. "If you touch a hair on my head Carter will hunt you down," she threatened.

"Carter will be dead before you are," Burley retorted. "Come on." He began hauling her down the hill toward the house.

"Where are we going?"

"I want to see my kid," Burley said.

"No," Desiree begged. "Please, do whatever you want with me, but leave Nicky alone."

He ignored her, tightening his hold and yanking her after him.

Desiree kicked at him and caught him behind the knee, causing his leg to buckle. Instead of losing his hold, he dragged her down with him. Burley was good and angry by the time he got back on his feet. He slapped her once, hard enough to split her lip and make it bleed. ·

"Don't do that again, Ice," he warned. "Or I might have to get mean."

Desiree dug in her heels as Burley dragged her down the hill. She had no doubt of the fate that awaited her when they reached the house. What terrified her was the thought of what Burley might do to Nicole. She had to find some way to escape him, or to render him helpless. Carter was gone. She would have to protect Nicole herself.

Think, Desiree! Think!

By the time they reached the kitchen door, Desiree still had no idea how she was going to save herself and her daughter. By the time they reached the foot of the stairs, she was frantic.

Think, Desiree, think!

But her wits had been scattered by terror. No plan of action came to mind.

Fight, Desiree. Don't give up without a fight.

But he was so much stronger! If only words could kill, she thought. She knew they could wound. She had hurt Carter easily enough.

Words. Use words against Burley!

They had reached the top of the stairs and were heading down the hall to Nicole's room.

"You really ought to stop calling me Ice, you know," Desiree blurted.

"If the shoe fits," Burley said with a sneering glance.

"But it doesn't," she protested. "It wasn't me who had the problem in bed, Burley. It was you."

He stopped so abruptly she ran into his back. He whirled around to face her. "Who says?"

"I'm not cold in bed with Carter," she taunted. "I'm hot. Steamy. He's a better lover than you could ever think of being."

"We'll just see about that," Burley said.

Desiree had accomplished her purpose. Burley was no longer headed for Nicole's room. He was dragging her back down the hall in the other direction, toward her bedroom. She didn't want to imagine what was going to happen when they got there.

As they crossed the threshold into her bedroom, Desiree was very much afraid she might have jumped right from the frying pan into the fire. She only knew that she had to stay alive. For Carter's sake.

What on earth was she going to do now?

CARTER WAS FURIOUS WITH Desiree and even angrier with himself. Why hadn't he just told her he was in love with her? So what if she hadn't even mentioned the word? So what if she had married him just to have someone to protect her from Burley Kelton? The fact he loved her wasn't going to change, even if she didn't love him back.

He wished he could be sure that hired man wouldn't take off before he got back. He had promised Jubal Friar that he could have the afternoon off, but that was when he thought he was going to have Desiree and Nicole with him. Jubal had been upset that Carter had gone back on the agreement. Carter had threatened that if Jubal didn't stay, he was fired.

He hadn't waited for an answer from Jubal before he had jumped into his pickup and taken off. What if Jubal had just walked away? That would mean Desiree and Nicole were alone on the Rimrock right now. Burley would find no one to say nay if he decided to go after the two people who meant everything to Carter.

Carter turned the wheel of the truck so sharply that it skidded as he made the U-turn to take him back to the Rimrock. He knew he was going to feel like a tom-fool when he got back and found everything just as he had left it. But a gnawing in his gut told him he would be forever sorry if he didn't make sure.

His heart leaped to his throat when he drove up behind the house and realized Jubal's truck was gone.

"Damn him! And damn me for a stubborn fool!" he railed to himself.

He looked up on the hillside, but there was no sign of Desiree where he had left her. He checked the garden, but she wasn't there. He gave the barn a glance, but realized it was far more likely she was in the house. It wasn't long before Nicole would be up from her nap.

He entered the house quietly, listening for the voice of his wife, the laughter of his daughter. Everything was deathly silent. He was on the stairs when he heard the murmur of voices. A woman's. And a man's. Burley Kelton was upstairs! Judging from the sound, he was in Desiree's bedroom. And Desiree was in there with him.

Carter felt the contradictory urges to race up the stairs and to remain as silent as a shadow. He couldn't do both. He opted for silence. If he could surprise Burley, the situation might be resolved with a minimum of bloodshed. Not that he minded shedding Burley's blood. But he didn't want to see Desiree hurt. Not before he told her he loved her. Not before they had a chance to explore their feelings for each other.

He bit his lip to remain silent when he heard Desiree taunting Burley about his prowess as a man. Did the fool woman think she was invincible? By the time she was through pricking Burley's pride, the ex-convict was going to attack her like the maniac he was.

He could hear the snaps coming undone on Burley's shirt, the rasp of his zipper and the rustle of cloth as his jeans came off. One more second, another second and the man would be naked and vulnerable. Then Carter would attack.

It didn't take another second before he heard a scuffle in Desiree's room.

"Give me my knife, you bitch!" Burley shouted. "If I have to take it from you, I'll break your arm."

Carter's heart shot to his throat as he charged into the bedroom. When the door crashed open, he saw that Burley was still dressed in his long johns. The huge man wrenched the knife from Desiree's fist and backhanded her, sending her flying against the wall.

Carter saw red. "How would you like to try that on someone your own size?" he said with a low growl of menace.

Burley ignored Desiree and turned to face this new foe. "Well, well, well. If it isn't the husband. Desiree and I were just renewing our acquaintance, so to speak." He waved the knife in front of him. "Come on in and join the fun."

With his eyes, Carter warned Desiree to stay put. Then he gestured Burley forward with his hands. "Come on, big man. Let's finish this once and for all."

"Fine by me," Burley said.

Carter had taken a step toward Burley when he heard a small noise behind him. At the same instant he turned to investigate, Desiree screamed, "Nicole, call 911!" and Burley charged.

The little girl turned and fled downstairs.

"Carter!" Desiree cried. "Look out!"

Carter arched his body, so the knife that would have cut him deep merely left a bloody arc across his chest.

"I'm going to kill you," Burley said.

Carter said nothing, merely watched his adversary with intent blue eyes, waiting for the next attack, looking for any chance to get in under Burley's guard.

Both men had forgotten about Desiree, who hadn't been idle. The only thing she had found to use as a weapon was an antique pitcher and bowl that sat on her chest. She grabbed the pitcher and swung it at Burley.

Because he was so tall, the pitcher's effect was lessened. Instead of being knocked out by the blow, Burley was merely irritated and distracted by it.

Desiree's distraction was exactly what Carter had been waiting for. He shot forward and grabbed the wrist that held the knife and began applying pressure to make Burley release it.

Unfortunately, Desiree hadn't retreated quickly enough after hitting Burley, and he managed to grasp her hair and pull her toward him. When she was close enough, he caught her head in the crook of his other arm.

Burley smiled a feral grin and turned to Carter. "Let go of my wrist, or I'll crush her head like a walnut."

"Don't do it," Desiree said. "He'll only kill you, too, before he kills me."

Carter wavered, uncertain what he should do.

Desiree saw that Carter would let Burley kill him rather than watch her be killed before his eyes. She did the only thing she could think of to do.

She pretended to faint.

Unready for so much deadweight, Burley watched in dismay as Desiree slid through his arm and onto the floor at his feet. He tried to take a step forward, but stumbled over her. As he fell, the knife the two men had been struggling over imbedded itself deep in his chest.

Carter waited a moment to see whether the big man would get up. But the knife had done its work.

Carter went down on one knee and pulled Desiree into his arms. "Desiree? Darling, are you all right? Are you hurt? Please say something!"

"I...I..." Three simple words, *I love you,* and she didn't have the courage to say them. Desiree slowly opened her eyes and beheld the worried, beloved face hovering over her.

"What is it you're trying to say, darling?"

"Oh, Carter, I…I…I'm glad you're all right."

He kissed her. A deep, possessive kiss, that claimed and captivated her. Then he lifted her into his arms, stepped over Burley and turned to pull the door closed behind him.

The sound of sirens in the distance announced that help was on the way. And reminded Desiree of her daughter. She struggled to be set down. Once on her feet, she clambered down the stairs, with Carter right behind her.

"Nicky? Where are you?"

She found her daughter sitting at the kitchen table, with the phone at her ear, still talking to the 911 operator. "I have a mommy and a daddy," she was saying, "just like my friend Shirley."

Desiree picked up her daughter and hugged her tight, while Carter took the phone and explained to the operator that the situation was under control. When he hung up the phone he turned to embrace his wife and daughter.

"Who was that mean man, Mommy? Why did he want to hurt Daddy?"

Desiree met Carter's eyes and begged him for an explanation that a five-year-old could understand.

"He was just a man who got lost and scared," Carter said.

"Where is he now?" Nicole asked.

"He's in your mother's room. He had an accident."

"Is he all right?"

Carter reached out a hand to smooth Nicole's bangs from her eyes. "No, Nicky. He's dead."

"Oh. Can we still go see Maddy this afternoon?"

Carter and Desiree exchanged a look that expressed

their gratefulness that Nicole was too young to understand the horror of what had happened.

"Maybe we'll have time to go see Maddy after the police are gone," Carter replied.

But it was well after dark before the police had finished their investigation, collected Burley's body and warned Carter not to leave the neighborhood. Desiree's room was cordoned off, and she had instructions to stay out of it until the police had another chance to look around in the morning.

Desiree had retreated to the kitchen and prepared a meal that she was loath to eat. She pushed the food around her plate, washed the dishes after dinner, then headed upstairs to bathe Nicole and put her to bed. She couldn't help shuddering as she passed the closed door to her bedroom.

It was over. The years of horror, of dread, were finished at last. She was free.

Carter joined her at Nicole's bedside and put his arm around her as she read her daughter a story from the book Nicole had given Carter for Christmas. It had only been a few short months, but it felt as though she had known the man sitting beside her for a lifetime.

When the story was done, Carter leaned over and kissed Nicole on the forehead. She threw her arms around him and hugged him. "I love you, Daddy," she said.

Desiree saw the moistness in Carter's eyes, and fought to keep from crying herself.

"I love you, too, Nicky," he said.

Abruptly Desiree rose and left the room, heading for the deep, comfortable chair in the parlor. She sank into it wearily and waited. It wasn't long before Carter joined her.

"We have to talk," she said as he sat down on the sofa across from her.

"Yes, we do," Carter agreed.

"The reason I married you no longer exists," she said tentatively. "As for the reasons you married me—"

"I married you to have a place where I belong. That holds as true now as it did the day we married."

Desiree felt her heart sink to her toes. She had known he only wanted roots. She had confirmation of it now. She couldn't bear staying married to him, when all he really wanted was the ranch. "Now that I'm no longer in danger, there's no reason for us to stay married. We could just be business partners," she suggested.

"Is that so?"

Carter realized that he had to reach for happiness with both hands, or he was going to lose it. "There are a few things you might like to know before we change things around here," he said.

Desiree cocked her head. "Such as?"

"I've found everything I've been searching for my whole life right here on the Rimrock," he said.

"You mean you've put down roots."

"Yes, I have. Only what I've discovered is that roots aren't a particular place or a thing that can be bought. All the money in the world—" He paused and flushed before he continued. "And I have quite a bit—won't buy roots."

"You're rich?"

He ignored her and went on, "Roots are a sense of belonging. Roots grow wherever the people you love are. This is where you are, Desiree. And Nicky. I could never give you up now."

Desiree lifted her eyes to meet Carter's intense gaze. She discovered that he was looking right back at her, and that his loving gaze didn't avoid the scar on her cheek, but encompassed it. She suddenly realized that her terrible scar no longer existed for him, except as a beloved part of her. Desiree launched herself from the chair into Carter's open arms.

"I love you, Carter. I have for so long!"

"I love you, too, Desiree, but I was too damned scared to admit it."

They headed upstairs together, smiling. Actually, they were grinning like idiots. Once in Carter's bedroom, they undressed each other slowly and carefully. His lips found the teardrops of joy at the corners of her eyes and followed them down her scarred cheek to her mouth, where his tongue joined hers in a passionate exchange.

They spent the night loving each other, reveling in the knowledge that their lovemaking was an extension of the feelings they had for each other. They were still twined in each other's arms the next morning—like the gnarled roots of a very old oak—when Nicole joined them there.

She climbed under the covers and stuck her feet on Desiree's thigh, only it turned out to be Carter's, instead.

Carter yelped. "How can your feet be so cold in the middle of summer?" He grabbed for them to warm them with his hands.

Nicole giggled as she snuggled down under the covers. "My friend Shirley has a sister," she said. "Do you think if I asked Santa, he would bring me a sister for Christmas?"

Carter chuckled.

Desiree laughed.

"It is entirely possible," Carter said.

"Entirely," Desiree agreed with a knowing smile.

Birds sang outside the window as the sun rose on a new day. They were a family, Carter thought, with roots and branches and little buds. It was a great beginning for a solid family tree.

* * * * *

THE UNFORGIVING BRIDE

PROLOGUE

FALCON NOTICED THE WOMAN right away, even though she was standing in the middle of a crowded sidewalk in downtown Dallas. She was not the sort of female who usually attracted his attention, being boyishly slim and merely pretty, rather than beautiful. But there was something about her that drew his eyes and held him spellbound.

He had barely begun to admire her assets—long, silky black hair whipped by the hot summer breeze, spectacular blue eyes and a tall, supple body—when he spotted the little girl at her side. The woman was joined a moment later by a man who slipped his arm around her slender waist and captured her mouth in a hard, possessive kiss. The little girl quickly claimed the man's attention, and he leaned down to listen to her excited chatter.

Falcon felt a sharp stab of envy that he wasn't the man in the quaint family picture. Not that he wanted kids, or wanted to be married, for that matter, but he would have given anything to be on the receiving end of the warm, approving look the woman gave the man as he attended to the little girl.

He was startled to realize that he knew the man. Which meant he could easily wrangle an introduction to the woman.

She's married.

Falcon didn't dally with married women. At least, he never had in the past. He pursed his lips thoughtfully. There was no reason why he couldn't meet her. Without stopping to think, he approached the trio.

"Grant? Grant Ainsworth?" Falcon inquired, though he knew he wasn't mistaken.

"Falcon Whitelaw!" the man exclaimed. "I haven't seen you in—it must be ten years!"

"Nearly that. Guess we lost touch after graduation from Tech," Falcon said with a smile as he extended his hand to meet the one that had been thrust at him. He forced himself to keep his eyes on his old football teammate from Texas Tech. But he wanted to meet the woman. He wanted to feast his eyes on her face at close range. He wanted to figure out what it was that made her so alluring.

"What have you been doing with yourself, Grant?" Falcon asked.

"Got married," Grant replied with a smug grin. "This is my wife, Mara, and my daughter, Susannah."

Falcon turned to greet Mara Ainsworth. He was sorry she wasn't one of those progressive women who shook hands with a man. He would have liked to touch her. She nodded her head and smiled at him, and he felt his stomach do a queer turn. He lifted a finger to his Stetson in acknowledgement of her. "Ma'am."

Because he knew it was expected of him, he lowered his eyes to the little girl. She was hiding half behind her mother's full skirt. Susannah had Mara's black hair, but her eyes were hazel, rather than blue. "Howdy," he said. "You're a pretty little miss. Almost as pretty as your mother."

The little girl giggled and hid her face completely.

From the corner of his eye, Falcon caught the flush of pleasure on Mara's face. He wanted to touch her cheek, to feel the heat beneath the skin.

"How old is your daughter?" he asked Mara. He needed a reason to look at her. His eyes lingered, cataloging each exquisite feature.

"Susannah's seven," Mara replied.

Falcon heard Grant talking, but he couldn't take his eyes off Mara. For a moment he thought he saw something in her open gaze, an attraction to him as strong as the one he felt for her. But he knew that was only wishful thinking.

Her lids lowered demurely so her lashes created two coal crescents on milky white skin. Whatever she was feeling, it was hidden from him now. Her lips parted slightly, and he could just see the edges of her teeth. He had to restrain a harsh intake of breath at the overpowering desire he felt to claim her mouth with his. He had never felt a need so strong or so demanding.

Falcon was aware that Grant was asking him something, but he only caught the last half of the sentence.

"...so if you're staying the night in Dallas, maybe we could get together and have a few drinks for old times' sake," Grant finished.

Falcon saw the quick flash of annoyance on Mara's face. Obviously she would rather have Grant to herself than share him with an old friend. Falcon started to give her what she wanted but realized that if he had a few drinks with Grant he could find out more about Mara, more about the state of their marriage. It looked happy from the outside, but if there were problems, maybe there was a chance Mara would welcome his attention.

Falcon hated what he was thinking. It wasn't like him to go after some other man's woman. But there was something about Mara Ainsworth that struck a chord deep inside him. If he had found her unattached, he might even have contemplated giving up his bachelor freedom. But it was folly to let himself even think about her so long as she was another man's wife.

By the time Falcon had come to the conclusion he ought to just get the hell away from the Ainsworths, he realized he had already invited Grant to have drinks with him at a bar near the stockyards.

"What brings you to town, anyway?" Grant asked.

"I'm here to buy cattle for my ranch."

"Didn't know you had a ranch of your own," Grant said.

"I inherited the B-Bar from my grandfather, my mother's father, about five years ago," Falcon replied.

Grant whistled in appreciation. "If I remember rightly, that's quite a spread."

Falcon hadn't done anything to earn the B-Bar, but he was proud of owning it. It *was* a big spread. He glanced at Mara to see if she was impressed. Most women were. But she was watching Grant. She had caught her lower lip with her teeth and was chewing on it. She looked worried about something. Was his rendezvous with Grant going to interrupt some previously made plans?

Falcon had grown up in a family where strong wills were the norm. He had learned that with determination and a little charm, he could usually get what he wanted. As a result, he wasn't used to denying himself anything. That had worked out fine, because there hadn't been anyone but himself to please for the past five years since he had inherited his grandfather's ranch. Suddenly he found himself wanting to take the worry from Mara's brow, even if it meant giving up the opportunity to quiz Grant about her while they were having drinks.

"Look," Falcon said, "if you all have other plans for the evening, I don't want to intrude."

Mara had opened her mouth to respond when Grant said, "No plans. I'll meet you at eight. See you then."

Falcon watched the gentle sway of Mara's hips as Grant led her away. She glanced back at Falcon over her shoulder and caught him staring at her. He felt himself flush, something he couldn't remember doing for a long, long time. He tipped his Stetson to her one more time. It looked like she wanted to say something to him, but Grant kept walking, his arm around her, and the moment was lost.

When the three of them were gone from sight, Falcon exhaled a long, loud sigh of regret. The woman of his dreams had just walked out of his life. He debated whether he ought to do something else tonight and leave a message at the bar for Grant that he couldn't make it. His feelings for Mara Ainsworth were dangerous. If he pursued the matter, he was asking for trouble.

But when eight o'clock came, Falcon was waiting at the Longhorn Bar. Five minutes later, Grant Ainsworth came in. There was a bond between teammates that extended beyond ordinary friendship, and Falcon was reminded of all the times he and Grant had tipped a brew after winning a difficult football game. He knew nothing of what had happened to Grant after college, but he intended to find out.

A country band with a wailing violin was playing up front near the dance floor, but Falcon had settled in one of the booths near the back, where the noise wasn't quite so loud nor the smoke so bad.

"What are you drinking?" he asked as Grant slid in across from him.

"I'll have a whiskey, neat," Grant replied.

Falcon gestured to a waitress wearing skintight jeans and a peasant blouse and ordered the drink Grant had asked for and another Pearl beer for himself.

When the drinks arrived, Grant held up his glass and said, "To pretty women."

Falcon grinned. "I'll drink to that." He took a sip of beer; Grant had finished his whiskey in a few swallows.

Grant slammed his glass onto the table and said, "That went down pretty damn smooth. I think I'll have another." Grant gestured and had the waitress bring him another whiskey.

"You need any ranch hands for that place of yours?" Grant asked after he had taken a sip of the second drink.

Falcon was startled by the question. "You need work?"

Grant shrugged. "Been laid off recently. Could use work if you've got it."

Actually, Falcon was sure he had all the help he needed. But he thought of Mara and Susannah without food on the table and said, "Sure. There's always room for another hand."

Grant's shoulders visibly relaxed. He finished off the second whiskey and called for another. "You don't know what a relief that is. Mara was beginning to think I would never... But I've got a job, after all, so everything will be fine."

It was plain from the look on Grant's face that he and his wife must have argued over the matter. Falcon was happy to change the subject to what he wanted to talk about most.

"Where did you meet Mara?"

"Her father was foreman on a ranch in west Texas where I worked right after college. I took one look at her and knew she was the one for me. It took a little convincing to get her to say yes. But she did. We've been married for eight years now."

"Where have you been living?"

Grant looked sheepish. "Here and there around Texas. We've moved every year or so. Last job I had was in Victoria. We came to Dallas because I heard some ranches around here were hiring help."

Falcon frowned. Most cowhands were footloose and fancy free—when they were single. A married man settled down in one place and raised his family. He wondered whether Grant had willingly left all those jobs, or whether there was something he had done to get himself fired. He had seemed steady enough in college, but college was ten years ago.

Had Grant Ainsworth become a thief? Was he a bully? Lazy? Incompetent? Cantankerous? Any of those faults would get him laid off in a hurry.

What had it been like for Mara to move around like that? Could she be happy with a man who was constantly losing his job? He recalled the adoring look on Mara's face when she had watched Grant with Susannah. Whatever Grant's shortcomings, Mara apparently still loved him.

"There are some houses on the property for hired hands. You're welcome to use one of them," he heard himself offer.

"I'd appreciate that," Grant said. Only he wasn't looking at Falcon when he answered.

Falcon was amazed and appalled when he realized that Grant was flirting with a pair of women sitting at a table across from them. He felt outraged on Mara's behalf. A man with a wife like her waiting for him at home had no business making eyes at other women. Suddenly Falcon didn't want to be where he was anymore.

"Look, I've got to be up early tomorrow. The drinks are on me—for old times' sake. I'll see you when you get to the ranch." Falcon threw a twenty on the table.

"There's no need—"

Falcon cut Grant off with a quick shake of his head. "Call it a celebration of your new job."

At the door to the bar Falcon glanced back and saw that the two women had already joined Grant in the booth. He scowled. Son of a bitch was cheating on his wife! Falcon felt a burning anger deep in his gut.

Falcon realized he just might have discovered why Grant had been let go from jobs so often. Suppose Grant played around with women wherever he went? That would certainly raise the hackles of the men he worked with and get him booted fast. Falcon grimaced. What kind of man had he just hired to work on the B-Bar?

Falcon thought of having Mara Ainsworth living on the B-Bar, in a house where he could see her every day. Knowing her husband didn't appreciate her. Knowing she loved the bastard anyway.

It was going to be hell.

FALCON HAD WANTED to see Mara Ainsworth again, but he had never dreamed it would be at her husband's funeral. He stood at the back of a crowd of mourners shrouded in black, waiting for a chance to speak to her, to tell her how sorry he was that Grant was dead. And he was sorry, for Grant's sake. No one deserved to die that young. Deep down, in places where honesty reigned, he felt that Mara was better off without him. But he wasn't going to voice those feelings. He owed Grant that, at least.

But he couldn't forgive Grant for the utter senselessness of his death: his friend had been killed in a one-car accident the same night Falcon had met him in the Longhorn Bar. Falcon bitterly regretted leaving Grant with money for several more drinks. Obviously Grant hadn't sobered up before he got behind the wheel. It was a tragedy that happened all too often, and Falcon could only be grateful that there had been no innocent victims in the accident.

If Falcon felt guilty at all, it was because he coveted Grant's widow. Mara was free now. He could have her if he wanted her—after a decent period of mourning, of course. Even he wasn't blackguard enough to go after a grieving widow.

But he wanted her. More than he ever had.

Dressed in black, Mara had an ethereal beauty. The deep circles under her eyes only made her look more hauntingly attractive. He knew she couldn't have gotten much sleep in the past week since Grant's death. Susannah stood beside her mother looking bewildered.

Falcon had tried to see Mara when he first heard about the accident, but realized he didn't know how to find her. He had read an announcement of the funeral services and made plans to attend. That way he could talk to her and extend his sympathy. And find out where she planned to go from here.

Because he wanted to know where he could find her when she had finished mourning Grant Ainsworth.

The graveside service had ended, and most of those gathered for the funeral had returned to their cars. Susannah had apparently gone with one of Mara's friends, because Mara was alone beside Grant's grave when Falcon approached her.

"Mara," he said.

It took her eyes a second to focus, but he knew the instant she recognized him, because her features twisted with loathing.

"How dare you show your face here!" she said in a harsh, bitter voice. "My husband is dead, and it's all your fault!"

Falcon was stunned at her accusation.

"You invited him to that bar! You got him drunk! And then you let him drive home!"

"I—"

"I hate you!" she said in a venomous voice. "I hope you rot in hell! I hope someone you loves dies a horrible death!"

She opened her mouth to speak, but all that came out was a low, ululating cry of pain. Her face crumpled in a mask of despair as she dropped to the grass beside her husband's newly dug grave. Her body shook with sobs of grief.

There was thickness in Falcon's throat that made it painful to swallow. He had never dreamed that she would blame him. How could she think he was responsible? He hadn't even been there when Grant left the bar. It wasn't his fault. She was wrong.

Not even in the farthest reaches of his mind had he planned to get Grant drunk and send him out to die in a fiery one-car crash. He had wanted Mara, it was true. But he had never wished Grant dead so that he could have her.

Small chance of his having her now. She hated his guts. She never wanted to see him again. She would as soon scratch out his eyes as look at him.

Falcon wanted to reach out to comfort her, to hold her in his arms and let her cry out her pain against his chest. He actually went so far as to touch her shoulder. "If there's ever anything I can do to help…"

The instant she realized who had touched her, she turned on him. He had never seen a woman's face contort in such fury and revulsion.

"Get away from me!" she hissed. "I don't need your kind of help. Go to hell, or go anywhere at all, but don't ever come near me again!"

He had backed away, stumbled over something, then turned and fled. He felt as though a tight band was constricting his chest. He couldn't breathe. He couldn't swallow. He felt like crying.

It was over. Mara was gone from his life before she had ever been a part of it. She hated him. She blamed him for Grant's death. He would never see her again.

But it would be a long time before he forgot the look of loathing toward him on Mara Ainsworth's face.

CHAPTER ONE

One year later

MARA HAD TRIED every other alternative, and there was only one left. She had to swallow her pride and approach Falcon Whitelaw for the help he had once offered. Although, she couldn't imagine him even giving her a chance to open her mouth before he shut the door in her face. Mara shuddered when she remembered the awful things she had said to him, even if they were true.

But Susannah was sick, very sick, and she needed treatment that would cost thousands of dollars. Mara had applied to a number of agencies for help, and it was available, but only if she and Susannah left home and traveled to another state. Life was grim enough these days without leaving behind everything that was familiar.

On Grant's death, Mara had used most of his life insurance to buy a home for herself and Susannah. She had vowed never to move again. If there was any way to stay in Dallas, where they had finally grown roots—shallow ones, but roots, nevertheless—Mara intended to pursue it. She had exhausted every other road to achieve her goal. There was only one left. She had to approach Falcon Whitelaw and ask him for money to help with Susannah's medical expenses.

Begging left a bitter taste in her mouth. But Mara was willing to humble herself in any way that was necessary to make sure Susannah got the treatment she needed. It was galling to have to approach the one man in the world she blamed for her current predicament. If Grant hadn't died in that accident, they would have had the health insurance he usually received as a part of his compensation. But Grant had been between jobs, so there was nothing. Instead Mara had been caught in every mother's nightmare. She had a sick child and no insurance to pay for medical bills.

Health insurance had been the last thing on her mind when Grant had left her widowed, and she found herself unemployed with a meager amount of life insurance and a child to raise. She had used the balance of the life insurance left after she bought the house to pay college tuition, believing that an education was the best investment for their future. It was a wise move, but had left the two of them exposed to the disaster that had occurred.

Mara hadn't even realized, at first, that Susannah was sick. In the months following Grant's death, her daughter had been tired and listless and seemed uninterested in doing the things she normally did. Mara had thought Susannah was merely grieving in her own way. Until one day Susannah didn't get out of bed at all. She had a high fever, and nothing Mara did could bring it down.

She took Susannah to the emergency room of the hospital and experienced the horror of watching her small, helpless child be hooked up to dozens of tubes and monitors. The diagnosis of Susannah's illness had come as a shock. Mara had sat stunned in the chair before Dr. Sortino's cluttered desk and listened with disbelief.

Acute lymphocytic leukemia.

"Children die of that," Mara had managed to gasp.

A pair of sympathetic brown eyes had looked out from Dr. Sortino's gaunt face. "Not as many as in the past. Nearly three-quarters of all children diagnosed with this disease today live."

"What about the rest?" Mara asked. "What about Susannah?"

"Our cure rate with chemotherapy is ninety percent. If that doesn't work, there's always a bone-marrow transplant to consider."

Mara had stared at him with unseeing eyes. *Chemotherapy.* She had never known anyone personally who had taken chemotherapy. But she had read enough, and seen enough on television, to know that chemotherapy made you vomit, and that your hair fell out. The thought of that happening to her precious daughter, the thought of all Susannah's long black hair falling out, made her feel faint.

"Mrs. Ainsworth? Are you all right?"

Dr. Sortino was on one knee beside her, keeping her from sliding out of the chair. She felt the sting of tears in her nose and eyes. "No, I'm not all right!" She fixed a blazing stare on the doctor who had been the messenger of such ill tidings.

"I'm angry," she spat. "I'm furious, in fact! Why Susannah? How did this happen? She's just a little girl. *She's only eight years old!*"

Dr. Sortino's eyes were no longer sympathetic. A look of pain and resignation had glazed his eyes after her vituperative attack. He rose and returned to his place behind the desk, putting a physical barrier between them that did little to protect him from her anger and despair.

"I'm sorry, Mrs. Ainsworth," he said. "There are as many as a dozen factors that may have been responsible for Susannah contracting the disease. We haven't done enough tests yet to make a guess on the precise reasons for her illness. But we can cure it…in most cases. You're lucky. Susannah has a tremendous chance of survival. With other diseases…"

He left her to contemplate her good fortune. But Mara didn't feel lucky. Leukemia was a serious disease. Her precious, wonderful daughter might die. "When do you start treatment?" she asked. "Will Susannah have to stay in the hospital? How will we know if it works?"

That was when kindly Dr. Sortino had started asking questions about insurance. That was when she had realized the enormity of the cost of treatment, and the hospital's inability to absorb another patient of this kind without a payment from some source.

"There are other facilities that can serve your needs better if you can't pay at least a portion of the costs up front," the doctor had said.

But those facilities were in another state.

Mara had tried buying insurance, but Susannah's illness was a preexisting condition and could not be covered.

"But I don't need insurance for anything else!" she had argued.

After the insurance companies turned a deaf ear, Mara tried the various foundations that provided assistance for children. And got the same answer. Help was available only if she was willing to go somewhere else to get it.

Mara knew she was foolish for clinging to the familiar, but she wasn't sure she could survive weeks, and maybe months, of living in a Ronald McDonald House in a strange city, all alone with only Susannah and her fears to keep her company. She needed a place that was home. She needed the support of the few friends she had made. And Susannah needed the normalcy of school and friends around her during her recuperation.

Her daughter was going to be one of the lucky seventy-three percent who were cured of the disease. Mara refused to consider any other outcome to Susannah's treatment.

But she needed money and needed it fast. Borrowing was out of the question. She had just finished her first year of college, working part-time as a cook in one of the college hangouts. She didn't qualify for the sizable loan she needed without some security, and she hadn't enough equity in the house to do the job.

On the other hand, Grant had told her before he'd gone to the bar that Falcon Whitelaw was as rich as Croesus, that he had inherited a fortune from his maternal grandfather, including the B-Bar Ranch on the outskirts of Dallas. Falcon wouldn't even miss the thousands of dollars it was going to cost for Susannah's care. Besides, she was going to offer him something in return.

Mara had grown up at her mother's side and knew everything there was to know about keeping house for a rancher. She planned to trade her services as housekeeper to Falcon in exchange for his financial assistance in paying Susannah's medical bills. She feared she would end up indentured to him for a long time. Just the initial treatment was going to cost nearly 25,000.

Which reasoning all led her to the front doorstep of Falcon Whitelaw's B-Bar Ranch. She had to admit the ranch wasn't what she had expected. The terrain was flat and grassy, but long ago someone had planted live oaks around the house. It had the look of a Spanish hacienda, with its red tile roof and thick, whitewashed adobe walls.

Her hand was poised to knock, her heart in her throat. She swallowed both heart and pride and rapped her knuckles on the arched, heavy oak panel.

No one answered.

She knocked harder, longer and louder.

At last, the door opened.

FALCON HAD BEEN out late carousing, and he had just dragged on a pair of jeans to answer the door, not even bothering to button them all the way up. They hung down on his hipbones and revealed his white briefs in the vee at the top. He scratched his belly and put one bare foot atop the other. He squinted, his eyes unable to focus in the harsh sunlight that was streaming in through the crack he had opened in the door. He thought better of trying to see and put a hand over his eyes, pressing his temples with forefinger and thumb in an attempt to stop the pounding inside his head.

"Who's there?" he muttered.

Mara stared in disbelief at the bleary-eyed, tousle-headed, unshaved face that had appeared at the door. "It's eleven o'clock," she said with asperity. "Are you just getting up?"

"Good God," Falcon said with a moan. He would

never forget that condemning voice, not in a million years. Of all the days for her to show up at the B-Bar, she had to come now. He slowly lowered his hand and squinted painfully into the sunlight until his eyes had adjusted enough to confirm what his ears had told him.

It was Mara Ainsworth, all right. She was wearing that same derisive, accusing look she had worn at Grant's funeral.

Falcon considered shutting the door in her face. He didn't owe her anything. He had offered her his help a year ago, and she had refused it in no uncertain terms.

So what is she doing here now?

From the look on her face she had come to play Puritan temperance woman. He just wasn't up for the game.

Mara's belief that Falcon was an irresponsible care-for-nobody was reaffirmed as she eyed him from head to barefoot toes. Her nose wrinkled in disgust when the smell of beer assaulted her nostrils. He was drunk! Or rather, had been. He looked hungover at the moment.

"Are you going to invite me inside?" she demanded.

Falcon was a second late responding, and Mara invited herself in, since he was obviously in no condition to do it. She pushed past Falcon and walked through the arched doorway right into the living room, leaving him standing at the open door.

The house was dark and cool. The furniture was leather and wood, large and heavy, the sort of thing the conquistadors must have brought with them from Spain. Navajo rugs were thrown on the redbrick floor, and Mara found herself facing shelves full of Hopi Indian decorations. Arches inset along the walls held ornamental vases, adding to the Spanish flavor of the room. It was beautiful. It felt like a home. Which was odd, she thought, considering a bachelor lived here.

Without turning to face Falcon she said, "I need to talk to you." Mara surreptitiously rubbed her stomach where she had brushed against him. Her belly was doing strange things. He was an animal—that was why she felt this animal magnetism toward him. She hated the man. It was absolutely ridiculous to think she could be attracted to him.

She turned to face him, willing herself not to feel anything.

But she hadn't forgotten the powerful shudders that had rippled through her when Falcon looked at her the first time they had met. Something had definitely happened that hot summer day on the street in Dallas. She despised herself for what she had felt then. And it had happened again just now.

Animal magnetism, she repeated to herself. *That's all it is.*

Falcon shut the door with a quiet click and leaned back against it. He folded his arms across his bare chest, crossed one bare ankle over the other and stared at her. "I didn't think you ever wanted to see me again."

She flushed. The color started at the edge of her square-necked blouse and shot right up her throat to her cheeks, where it sat in two bright pink spots. "I...I didn't."

His eyes narrowed. "But now you do?"

She swallowed hard and nodded once.

"Well." He paused. "Well." Falcon didn't know what else to say. This was certainly an astounding turn of events. Just when he had convinced himself he could live without her, the woman of his dreams had shown up at his door. Of course, she hadn't exactly picked a moment when he was at his best.

Falcon didn't ask her to sit. He didn't want her to be any more comfortable than he was. And he was downright miserable.

That didn't keep him from feeling the singular, consuming attraction for her that had struck him the first moment he saw her. And this time he knew he wasn't mistaken—she was feeling it, too. His lips curved in a self-satisfied smile. So, she was ready to admit the attraction she felt and had come to apologize for all those horrible things she had said to him.

Falcon gave free rein to the fierce sexual desire he felt for Mara Ainsworth. His groin tightened, and his blood began to hum. He refused to hide his arousal. Since she had invited herself in, she could just put up with the condition she found him in.

Mara was appalled at the blatant sensuality in Falcon's heavy-lidded stare. There was no hiding the bulge that was lovingly cupped by his butter-soft jeans. Even more appalling was her body's reaction to the prickly situation in which she found herself. She was dumbfounded by her gut response to Falcon's maleness. Her breasts felt heavy, and her belly tensed with expectation.

It was time to state her business and get out.

"I've come to get the help you offered a year ago. I need money. Lots of it."

Mara saw the shock on Falcon's face and hurried to finish before he could throw her out. "Susannah is very ill. She could die." She swallowed over the lump of pain that always arose when she said those words. "She has leukemia."

Falcon had dropped his lazy pose against the door

and was standing now on both feet with his hands balled at his sides.

"When Grant died he was between jobs and we didn't have any insurance and I don't have the money for chemotherapy and I've tried to get it other places but they want us to leave Dallas and Grant said you have lots of money so you wouldn't miss it and I think it would be better for both Susannah and me if we stayed where we are. So can you help us?"

Falcon had taken several steps toward Mara during this breathless speech. As he reached out to give her the comfort she so obviously needed, she took a step back away from him.

So. She wanted his money, but she didn't want him. That was blatantly clear.

"I'll work for you," she choked out. "I'll keep house, cook, clean, whatever you need. I know how to keep ranch books. I'll pay you back in service for every penny, I promise you that. I'm…I'm desperate. Please."

Falcon felt sick to his stomach. Mara, pretty Mara, had been reduced to begging. And she wasn't even asking him to give her the money. She was going to pay it all back. She didn't want to be beholden to him. Because she despised him.

It was there on her face every time she looked at him. She still blamed him for Grant's death. She was never going to forgive him.

So why should he give her the money?

Because there is a chance, just the slightest one, but a chance, that you might be responsible in part for her predicament. Falcon was shaken to the core by that possibility.

And that poor kid. He remembered Susannah's hazel

eyes peeping out from behind Mara's skirt on the day he met her and the childish giggle before she hid herself completely from his sight. It was a shame for any kid to be sick, but it caught him in the gut to imagine that engaging little girl bedridden.

"Is Susannah…will she get well?" he asked.

"There's a good chance, a three-to-one chance, she'll be cured by the chemotherapy. But the hospital won't start treatments before I assure them I can pay. Can you…will you help?"

"Give me a figure. I'll see my accountant tomorrow and cut you a check."

"Thank you," Mara said.

He watched her take a step toward him, as though to hug him, to share the joy and relief she was feeling. Then she must have remembered who he was, because she stiffened and stopped herself.

"Thank you," she said again.

But she didn't look at him. She was looking at her hands, which were threaded together and clenched so hard her knuckles were white.

"I can start work right away," she said.

"That won't be necessary," he said in a harsh voice.

Her head snapped up, and her brow furrowed. "I don't understand."

"I'd go nuts with you stomping around here all self-righteous, watching every little move I make and raking me over the coals with those big blue eyes of yours. Thanks, but no thanks. You can have the money, but I'll dispense with your services, if it's all the same to you."

Mara was stung by the image he had painted of her. She wanted to fling his money back in his face, but she had to think of Susannah. She bit her lower lip hard and kept her peace.

"Are we finished with this talk?" Falcon asked irritably. "Because I have a headache, and I'd like to get some aspirin."

"I'll pay you back," Mara said quietly. "Somehow." She hurried to the door. It meant going past Falcon. He didn't move to get out of her way, and she shivered as their bodies brushed.

"Aw, hell. You're not going to get cooties if we touch."

"I didn't—I only—" she stuttered.

"Just get the hell out of here," he said in disgust. He opened the door and held it as she rushed through, dropping a slip of paper in his hand with a breathless "My address," and then slammed it behind her.

"Women! Who the hell needs them!"

He crumpled the paper without looking at it and tossed it on the floor. He wouldn't see her to give her the check. He would have his accountant do it. There was no question, though, about his helping her. He owed it to Grant, and to the little girl who was sick. He owed Mara nothing. He hoped their paths never crossed again.

Finally, at last, he and Mara Ainsworth were quits.

CHAPTER TWO

"You don't have the money."

"What?"

"You heard me, Falcon. I said you don't have the money to be giving a blank check to some bimbo."

"Watch what you say, Aaron. Mara Ainsworth is a lady."

"My apologies. That doesn't change your situation."

"Just what, exactly, is my situation?" Falcon asked.

"To be blunt, you've damn near run through your grandfather's fortune in the past five years."

Falcon was stunned. He stopped pacing the thick carpet in his accountant's high-rise Dallas office and sank into a leather-and-chrome chair. "You're kidding, right?"

"I wish I were," Aaron said.

"Why didn't you say something sooner?" he demanded.

"I did."

Falcon remembered a conversation or two when Aaron had warned him not to make some high-risk investments. Then there were the cars. And the parties. The trips to Europe. The fancy studs and champion bulls. And the gifts he had given to his lady friends. He hadn't thought it was possible to spend a fortune in just five years.

"How much have I got left?" he asked, still a little stunned by Aaron's news.

"Enough to keep the B-Bar afloat—if you're careful and give the ranch some attention. Not enough to be loaning thousands of dollars to some woman."

"Lady," Falcon insisted. "Mara is a lady."

"Lady," Aaron conceded.

Falcon dropped his head into his hands. He could always go to his family for help; his parents and his brother and sister had assets if he really needed a loan to help Mara. And he had two uncles and an aunt. But he would be too ashamed to admit to any of them that he had squandered his inheritance. He would never live down the humiliation. And he couldn't bear to see the look on his father's face if he disappointed him. His mother would hide the pain she felt at his failure, because she knew how hard his father could be on anyone who threatened her happiness—even, or especially, her children.

Falcon was the middle child of the Three Whitelaw Brats, as they had come to be known in the vicinity around Hawk's Way, the northwest Texas ranch where he had been raised. Falcon's father, Garth, had been a hard taskmaster, demanding honesty and responsibility and accomplishment from his two sons and daughter. But Garth Whitelaw had held the leash too tight, and all three of them—his elder brother, Zachary, and his younger sister, Callen and himself—had revolted.

They had formed a secret alliance, the Fearless Threesome, and protected each other, deftly covering one another's tracks when they were caught out in some prank. Not that they had been vicious or mean in what they had done, but they had been incorrigible, unmanageable, all three of them, daring anything and often finding themselves in desperate situations that required feats of bravado to escape.

They had been punished for their recklessness, but had remained undaunted. As a child, Falcon's behavior had been as wild and untamed as his Comanche forbearers. He hadn't improved much over the years. At thirty, he was a maverick who refused to be tied down to anything or anyone.

His siblings weren't much more settled. His sister, Callen, was a black-haired, brown-eyed rebel who had defied their father's attempts to direct her life by twice accepting marriage proposals against his wishes—and breaking both engagements when the man turned out to be the cad her father had told her he was. Zach, with his coal-black hair and dark inscrutable eyes, had become a recluse, a man who rode alone and didn't seem to need or want a woman in his life.

Thanks to the Fearless Threesome, Falcon was used to escaping the consequences of his folly. Was it any wonder he had been careless and irresponsible with his fortune? Only this time, he didn't think he could ask Zach or Callen to help him out of his trouble. Maybe it was time to grow up at last. Maybe it was time to act like the dependable, reliable, trustworthy person his parents had raised him to be.

"Isn't there something I can do to help Mara and Susannah?" Falcon asked the man sitting across the desk from him.

Aaron chewed on his pencil, a habit that was apparent from the series of teeth marks that already creased the yellow stem. "There is one thing."

Falcon waited, but when Aaron didn't speak he asked, "All right, what is it?"

"You could marry her."

"What?" Falcon leapt up and slammed his palms flat on Aaron's marble-topped desk. He leaned forward intimidatingly. "What purpose would that serve?"

"Thanks to your capable accountant, you have an excellent health-care plan. You see, the insurance company wanted your business for health coverage of employees at the B-Bar. So I was able to negotiate a special clause in the contract that allows you, as the owner, to cover your dependents—even for a preexisting condition—as soon as you acquire them, in this case, by marriage."

"That's incredible."

Aaron smiled. "I thought so myself when I wrote it into the agreement with the insurance company. You can marry Mara Ainsworth and have Susannah's medical expenses one-hundred-percent covered the next day."

"I have to think about this," Falcon said as he rose and headed for the office door. He paused with the doorknob in his hand and turned back to Aaron. "Are you sure that's the only way I can help?"

Aaron shrugged. "You could always sell the B-Bar and give her the proceeds."

Falcon grimaced. "Don't be ridiculous."

"I was being frank," Aaron retorted. "Your choices are limited, Falcon. Let me know what you decide to do."

Falcon left his accountant's office in a daze. He was dealing with a lot of emotions all at once, not the least of which was shame. What would his parents say, especially his mother, when she found out how profligate he had been with her father's bequest to him? And how was he going to face Mara Ainsworth and admit the truth? That he had managed to run through a fortune in five years of dissipated living. What would happen to Mara and Susannah if he couldn't provide her with the funds she had requested?

You could marry her.

How could he marry a woman who despised him? A woman who would never forgive him for making her a widow? A woman who shrank from his touch?

Unfortunately he had no choice. And neither did she, when it came right down to it. They would just have to make the best of it. It would be one of those marriages of convenience, where they shared the same name and the same house, but nothing else.

It would be a royal pain in the rear.

But it wouldn't last forever. Just until Susannah was out of deep water. Just until the crisis was over. He could stand being close to Mara for that long without touching.

He didn't linger and let himself come up with excuses why Aaron's suggestion wouldn't work. He jumped into his Porsche and headed for the address on the paper Mara had stuffed in his hand when she had raced away from the B-Bar yesterday.

He found her house on a shady street in an old, quiet neighborhood in Dallas. There were bicycles in the driveways and tire swings in the trees. The houses were two-story wood frame structures with picture windows and big, covered front porches. There was even one house with a white picket fence. It belonged, he discovered, to Mara Ainsworth.

He didn't see a car in the driveway, so he wasn't expecting her to be home. But he knocked anyway.

She opened the door wearing very short cutoff jeans and a Dallas Cowboys T-shirt. She was barefoot. And she wasn't wearing a bra. He knew because her nipples peaked the instant she set eyes on him.

He turned her on, but she hated his guts. It was just plain crazy. He had fought the attraction he felt, knowing it could lead nowhere. But it was clear to him, if not yet to her, that some powerful magnetism still existed between the two of them.

"Hello," he managed.

"Oh! I thought you were my neighbor Sally. But, of course, you aren't."

Of course he wasn't. He stood there on the porch for a moment, waiting for her to invite him inside. When she didn't, he took a page from her book and stepped inside on his own. He heard the door close behind him.

"Where's Susannah?" he asked when she didn't immediately appear.

"She's still in the hospital."

"Oh."

Falcon looked around with a critical eye, wanting to find something about Mara's home that he could dislike as much as she disliked him. The living room was done in quiet colors and simple Western patterns that were easy on the eye. She had a green thumb, because there were lush plants everywhere, bringing the outdoors inside. Plump pillows decorated the couch, and a cozy, overstuffed chair invited him to sit down.

Only, he knew better than to make himself comfortable. Once she heard what he had to say, she might very well throw him out. He turned to face Mara.

She was leaning against the door in much the same way he had done, but there was nothing relaxed about the pose.

"I didn't bring a check," he said.

She caught her lower lip with her teeth. "You changed your mind about helping us?"

"No, I didn't change my mind," he retorted irritably. "I don't have the money."

She snorted in disbelief. "You mean you choose not to loan it to me."

He began to pace, like a tiger in a cage. "No, I mean exactly what I said. I don't have the money." He paused in front of a natural-rock fireplace and leaned both palms against the mantel with his back to her. "It seems I've already spent most of my fortune. I only have enough left to keep the B-Bar in business."

"I'm sorry," she said.

He whirled, his eyes blazing. "I don't need your pity."

"I don't pity you," she said.

No, it wasn't pity he saw in her eyes. It was disappointment. And disgust. He felt a burning rage deep inside that he should be subjected to all this.

It wasn't my fault. I wasn't the one who killed Grant Ainsworth. Why should I feel responsible for rescuing Grant's wife and child?

If not for the situation he found himself in, it wouldn't have been anyone's business but his own whether he squandered his fortune.

"You could have told me all this in a phone call," Mara said. "Why did you bother coming here?"

"Because even though I can't give you the money I promised, there is a way I can help you."

He saw hope blossom bright and beautiful in her

eyes. And dreaded the moment of disillusionment when he told her what he had to say.

"If you marry me," he announced, "Susannah will be covered by my insurance the day after we tie the knot."

"What?"

He thought she was going to faint, so he went to her, to help her. He stopped in his tracks when she backed away from him.

"I don't understand," she said.

"I thought I was very clear," he said in a harsh voice. "My insurance policy will cover any dependents of mine, even for a preexisting condition, the day after I acquire them. If you marry me, my insurance will cover Susannah's treatment."

"Marry you?"

"Yes, dammit, marry me! You don't have to sound so appalled at the idea."

"I'm not...appalled. I'm just...surprised."

Mara crossed to the overstuffed chair and sank into it. "I hadn't thought of getting married again."

"Especially not to the likes of me," Falcon finished for her.

Her brow furrowed. "I don't know what to say."

"Say yes."

She sought out his eyes with her own, and he could see the turmoil there. He knew he ought to let her refuse. Then he would be out of it, and the problem would be hers again. But the truth was, he wanted to be the one to rescue her. He wanted to redeem himself in her eyes. He wanted to earn her respect. He wanted a chance to prove he wasn't the good-for-nothing she thought he was.

"It doesn't have to be a real marriage," he said. "We'll

have to live together, of course. But that shouldn't be a problem."

"I don't want to leave my house."

"It's just a house," Falcon argued.

"It's more than that," Mara said, eyes flashing indignantly. "It's a place where I belong, where I have friends. I can't give that up, too."

She bit her lip to keep from letting the whole of her tragedy spill out at him—namely, her fear that she might soon lose Susannah, as well.

He saw the tears that filled her eyes, ready to brim over. He knew she was going to reject him again, but he had to make the effort to comfort her anyway. He pulled her up out of the chair and into his arms.

To his amazement, she clutched him around the waist and pressed her forehead against his chest and began to sob. He tightened his arms around her and crooned words of solace. He didn't know how long they stood there, but when she finally stopped crying, one of his hands was tangled in her hair and the other pressed her tightly against him.

His throat felt thick. His chest ached. He would have given anything to be worthy of her. But it was too late. He had lived a profligate, self-indulgent existence. Now, without the other two-thirds of the Fearless Threesome to rescue him, he was finally going to have to face the consequences of his behavior.

He knew when she was herself again, because she stiffened in his arms. She didn't struggle to be free, but he knew that if he didn't let her go soon, she would.

"Marry me," he whispered. "I promise I won't do anything to make you uncomfortable in my home. For Susannah's sake. Marry me."

She heaved a ragged sigh that ended in a sob that she quickly caught with her fist. She lowered her hand and raised her tear-drenched face to his. "All right," she said in a hoarse voice. "I'll marry you."

She took a step backward, and he was forced to release her.

"I'll take care of getting the license," he said. "You'll have to get a blood test—"

"I'll take care of that on my own. When?" she asked.

"As soon as possible, don't you think?"

Her face looked ravaged. Her eyes were red-rimmed. But she faced him without flinching this time. "You tell me when and where, and I'll be there."

"I'll help you move your things—"

"I'll leave the house exactly as it is," she said fiercely. "It's my home, mine and Susannah's. When this travesty of a marriage is over—" she choked back a sob "—when Susannah is *well,* we'll be coming back here to live. Now get out! I can't stand to look at you anymore."

Falcon backed away to the door, unable to take his eyes off her. Mara hated him. And he was going to marry her. He told himself it was a sacrifice that he owed her.

But as he closed her door behind him, he couldn't help feeling regret, and even despair.

How the hell were they going to get through the next year together?

CHAPTER THREE

I T WAS HER wedding day, and Mara felt trapped. This was not the perfect solution she had been searching for, not at all. But at least she didn't have to leave Dallas. She would find some way to keep Susannah in the same school, and she would be able to keep an eye on her house. But she had paid a high price for those small victories. She had to marry the man responsible for Grant's death.

Falcon had promised her it would be a marriage in name only, but in the same breath he had insisted they live together. She supposed there was some danger the insurance company could refuse to pay if they discovered it was a sham marriage, so it had to look real.

But it was a sham. A farce. A pretense. A mockery. She would be Mrs. Falcon Whitelaw. She would be married to a man she despised, a man so irresponsible he had run through a fortune in five years. She had to live in his house, make his meals, iron his clothes. *Be his wife.*

But she would never forgive him. What he had done was unforgivable. And yet, she owed him something for the help he had given her.

Mara felt torn in half. Because there were other feelings she had for Falcon Whitelaw that had nothing at all to do with hate and scorn. She felt drawn to him in a way that was disturbing, to say the least. She had tried to deceive herself, to say that there was no substance to her attraction to the handsome rogue. But her body made a liar out of her every time she got near him.

So how was she going to survive living in the same house with him, seeing him every day?

"Are you ready?"

Mara was jerked from her thoughts by the words Falcon had murmured in her ear.

"It's time," he said.

"I'm ready." She turned to Falcon. He looked as grim as she felt. "Isn't there anybody you wanted to have here? Some family?" she asked him.

"No. You?"

"No. My parents are gone, and I haven't any brothers or sisters." But she knew Falcon had family. Grant had told her about the Fearless Threesome. Falcon must be missing his brother and sister about now. She wondered how he was going to explain all this to them.

As Falcon listened to the judge reading the words legally binding him to Mara Ainsworth, he was wondering the same thing. How was he going to explain a wife and child to his family? How was he going to explain this slapdash wedding, to which none of them had been invited?

He couldn't tell them the truth. But he didn't want to lie. Better to tell them half the truth. That he had met a very special woman, and that he and Mara hadn't wanted to wait to get married. He would promise to bring his wife to meet the family soon but explain that they had to stay in Dallas for the moment because Mara's daughter was sick and needed treatment at the hospital here. That ought to keep them at bay for a little while.

Then what?

He would worry about the future when it got here, Falcon decided. Right now he had his hands full dealing with the present.

He answered "I will" at the proper moment and watched Mara's face as she said the same vow. Her complexion was pale, and she had been chewing on her lower lip so it pouted out a little. He wanted to soothe the hurt. Before the thought got much further than that, the judge was telling him he could kiss the bride.

Falcon put his hands on Mara's shoulders, because he suspected she would retreat if he gave her the chance. He was watching her face as he lowered his mouth toward hers, so he saw the moment her eyelashes fluttered down. Her body was rigid beneath his hands, but her mouth…her mouth was soft and pliant beneath his.

Falcon had kissed a lot of women, but there was no time when he had ever felt like this. It was a reverent meeting of lips, and he cherished Mara, giving himself to her and imploring her to take what he offered.

For a moment, she did.

He felt, as much as heard, her tremulous sigh. She gave herself up to the kiss, her trembling body melting into his, her mouth clinging so sweetly that he thought his heart was going to burst with the joy of it.

Then she jerked away with a cry of distress that she quickly stifled. Her eyes, wide and wounded, stared at him accusingly, as though her surrender was all his fault.

Then he was turning away to smile at the judge—or at least to bare his teeth in a semblance of one—and shake the man's hand and receive congratulations. Falcon didn't risk putting his arm around Mara to lead her from the judge's chambers, but he walked as close behind her as he dared.

The judge knew his father, but had promised to let Falcon break the news of his wedding. Even so, Falcon kept up the facade of wedded bliss until the door was closed behind him, because he didn't want any stories about the real state of his marriage getting back to his family. At least not before he had figured out how to explain things that didn't leave him in such a bad light.

Falcon opened the door of his Porsche and made sure Mara's calf-length ivory dress was inside before he closed it after her. They were on their way now to pick up Susannah, who was well enough to come home from the hospital until her induction therapy began. Funny name for it, Falcon thought, *induction therapy,* but that was what the hospital called chemotherapy used to induce remission. Susannah needed six to twelve weeks of treatment, which was scheduled to begin on Monday. With her condition stabilized, she was being allowed to spend the weekend with her family.

"How have you explained our wedding to Susannah?" he asked Mara.

A flush of color appeared on her ashen cheeks. "I told her we met and liked each other very much, so we decided to get married."

Falcon hit the brakes and almost caused an accident. "You told her *what?*"

"What did you expect me to tell her," Mara retorted. "That I was marrying you to get the money for her treatments? She's an impressionable child. I want to leave her some illusions about life."

"What's going to happen the first time she sees you cringe when I touch you?" Falcon demanded. "Or didn't you think she was going to notice?" he asked sarcastically.

"I…" Mara hadn't, in fact, thought any further than the wedding. She glared at Falcon. "I suppose I'll have to stop cringing," she announced.

"Great," Falcon muttered. "That's just great. What about our sleeping arrangements? How are you going to explain separate bedrooms to this precocious child of yours?"

"I'll be staying in a room next to Susannah," Mara said. "You'll be the understanding husband who wants me to be near my sick child."

Falcon snorted. "You've thought of everything, haven't you?"

"I wasn't able to think of a way to get out of marrying you!" she snapped.

Falcon slid the car into a parking place at Children's Hospital and cranked off the ignition. He turned to face Mara. "All right," he said, "let's get a few things straight before we go in to see Susannah."

Mara crossed her arms over her chest. "I'm listening."

Big concession, Falcon thought. "You're the one who wants Susannah to believe this marriage is real. I'm willing to go along with you."

This time Mara snorted.

Falcon ignored her and continued, "So I think we better set some ground rules. First, no more cringing, flinching or stiffening up like a board when I get near you. Can you handle that?"

Mara nodded curtly.

"Second, no more mudslinging, in either direction. Agreed?"

"That's fine with me."

He took a deep breath. "Third, you're going to have to allow me to show you some signs of affection."

"What? No! Absolutely not!"

"You're not thinking this through," Falcon said. "Won't Susannah be sure to make comparisons between the way you act toward me and the way you acted toward Grant? She'll know right away that there's something wrong if I never kiss you, if I never lay a hand on you."

Falcon watched Mara's face. He could see the struggle going on, the war she was waging. He saw the moment she conceded the battle. Her chin came up pugnaciously, and her hands balled into tight little fists.

"All right," she said through gritted teeth. "We'll do this your way." She turned to face him, eyes bright with unshed tears. "But don't push me, Falcon. Because I won't stand for it!"

There were things she had put up with in her marriage with Grant that she had decided in the year since his death she should never have tolerated. She wasn't going to make the same mistake twice. Better to lay down rules with Falcon now that would protect her later.

Falcon could have wished for more cooperation from Mara. At least she had been forced to put a door in the high walls that kept her separated from him. Falcon felt the first signs of hope he had known since he had agreed to this untenable situation. He would be able to hold Mara, to kiss her. Maybe, as she got to know him better, as he earned her respect, she would allow him to do more.

He would have a year to prove himself. Mara had told him that after Susannah had the chemotherapy treatments, her leukemia had to stay in remission for a year in order for her to be deemed past the first hurdle toward a cure. Mara and Susannah would be with him at least that long. And a year was a long time.

"I won't go beyond what I think is necessary to convince Susannah we have a normal relationship," Falcon said at last. He knew his idea of "necessary" signs of affection and hers were likely poles apart. But he wasn't about to make promises he couldn't keep. "Shall we go inside now and get Susannah?"

Falcon had forgotten how much Susannah looked like her mother. Her face had the same oval shape, the same strong cheekbones and short, straight nose. Her eyes were large and wide-set like Mara's. But he was shocked at the toll her serious illness had taken on Susannah. It was like seeing Mara pale and thin. His heart went out to the little girl the instant her eyes met his.

"How are you, Susannah?" he asked with a cheerful smile. "Do you remember me?"

Mara was sitting on the bed next to her daughter, and Susannah retreated behind her mother, peeping out at him shyly around Mara's shoulder.

"Your mother has some news for you," Falcon said.

Mara shot him a perturbed look, then smiled down at her daughter. "Yes, sweetheart. Falcon and I got married this morning."

Susannah looked curiously at Falcon. "Are you my daddy now?"

Falcon felt the floor fall out from under him. He obviously hadn't focused on all the responsibilities he was taking on. "I...suppose I am."

"Will you buy me a pony?"

"Susannah!" Mara exclaimed. "You shouldn't be asking Mr. Whitelaw to buy you things."

"Why not, if he's my daddy?" Susannah demanded. "Will you buy me a pony?"

Mara looked helplessly at Falcon, who shrugged helplessly back. Then he turned his attention to Susannah.

"Sure I will, pumpkin. What color pony did you want?"

Mara's lips pursed. "You're going to spoil her rotten."

"That's what fathers are for," Falcon replied. "Right, Susannah?" He grinned and tousled the little girl's hair affectionately.

Susannah beamed. "Right."

Falcon stopped what he was doing when it dawned on him Susannah's hair was all going to fall out when the little girl had chemotherapy. He kept the smile on his face for Susannah's sake, but he felt sick inside.

Mara saw Susannah's smile, the first one she had seen in weeks, and forgave Falcon for catering to her daughter. Nevertheless, she couldn't help resenting the fact that Falcon was able to give Susannah something that Grant wouldn't have been able to afford. She and Grant had barely been making ends meet, in fact. But she kept her mouth shut about how she felt. She had promised to curb her tongue for Susannah's sake.

Susannah had to ride a wheelchair downstairs, but the moment they reached the hospital exit, Falcon swept the little girl up into his arms. Mara didn't have time to feel left out, because Falcon slipped his other arm around her waist and pulled her close. A quick, warning glance kept her from pulling free.

Mara was glad she hadn't when Susannah reached out and grabbed her hand, so the three of them were completely connected. "Let's go home, Mommy," the little girl said.

"We're going to my house, if that's all right with you," Falcon said.

Susannah frowned.

"I live on a ranch," Falcon added.

Susannah's face brightened. "Will my pony be able to live with us?"

"Yes, he will."

"Is Mommy coming, too?"

"Wouldn't go without her," Falcon confirmed.

"All right. Let's go," Susannah said.

Mara marveled at how little effort it had taken for Falcon to convince Susannah that his ranch was a better destination than the home she had worked so hard to create for her daughter over the past year. But other than the doll Susannah had grasped tightly in her arms, and Mara herself, her daughter apparently had no attachments to the house in Dallas.

To Mara's amazement, Falcon turned out to be a totally charming companion on the trip to the B-Bar Ranch. He kept Susannah entertained with outrageous stories about himself and his siblings. The Porsche plainly needed to be replaced with a family car. Mara didn't relish confronting Falcon on the issue. Maybe he would realize the problem himself.

Falcon had just finished an anecdote when Susannah sighed and said wistfully, "I wish I had a sister. Can you and Mommy get one for me?"

Mara exchanged a horrified look with Falcon, whose lips twisted in a wry smile.

"That's entirely up to your mother," he said, throwing the ball back into her court.

"Will you, Mommy?"

"It's not quite as simple as buying a pony," Mara said as she sent a cutting glance toward Falcon. "Why don't we wait awhile, until you're well. Then we'll see."

Mara saw Falcon's eyebrow arch at the way she had caviled. But she refused to take away any of Susannah's dreams, no matter how far-fetched. Especially since there was no telling how much longer Susannah had to dream dreams.

That awful lump was back in Mara's throat, and she swallowed it down and forced a smile to her face. "Besides, you'll be too busy with your new pony to have time for a little sister right away."

"We're here," Falcon announced.

He unbuckled Susannah's seat belt and lifted her into his arms. "Come on," he said. "I want to show you your new home."

Mara followed, feeling forgotten, and though she wouldn't have admitted it, a little jealous of her daughter. Just when she thought Falcon was going to leave her behind, he stopped and set Susannah on her feet in the arch of the Spanish tiled entryway.

"There's a ritual that has to be observed," he said with a wink to Susannah.

Without warning, he swept Mara off her feet and into his arms. "I have to carry my bride over the threshold."

Susannah laughed. "Falcon picked you up, Mommy."

"He sure did!"

Mara was glad Susannah had bowed to Falcon's request in the car and was calling him by his name. It would have been sad to see Grant displaced so quickly by Falcon in her daughter's affections. But children, thank God, were resilient creatures, and Mara was glad Grant's death hadn't devastated her daughter.

"Can you get the door, Susannah?" Mara asked. "If Falcon stands here too long, he just might get tired and drop me."

Susannah laughed at the idea. "Silly Mommy," she said.

Falcon was surprised to hear the teasing quality in Mara's voice. He was enjoying holding her, and he wished he didn't have to set her down until he got her upstairs to his bed. Only it wasn't his bed anymore. He had ceded it to Mara.

Susannah pushed the door open, and he followed her inside. He managed to plant a quick, searing kiss on Mara's lips before he set her down. She shot him a warning look, but with Susannah present, there wasn't much else she could do. Falcon figured all was fair in love and war, and this marriage was sure to have a good deal of the latter.

"Welcome to your new home, Mrs. Whitelaw," he said.

The stricken look on Mara's face came and went so quickly he might have missed it if he hadn't been watching her so intently. But he did see it. He set his back teeth. So she didn't want his name, either.

Falcon had never really desired anything badly that he couldn't buy with money or have for the asking. Now he was finding out what it was like to want something that was beyond his reach. What he hadn't known about himself until this moment was how hard he was willing to strive to achieve his wants. And, though it irked him to admit it, he wanted Mara to want him with the same aching desire he felt for her.

It might take some time for him to find the right methods to win her over, but he was determined to seek them out. However, he was starting at the bottom of a very tall mountain and he didn't think he was in for an easy climb. Still, when he thought of the rewards to be had at the top, he was willing to take the first step.

If he could only figure out what it was.

Right now he had to concentrate on getting the three of them situated in his house. He took Mara and Susannah upstairs to show them the master bedroom and the guest bedroom next door to it.

"I'm in the bedroom downstairs," he said. "That way we won't get into each other's way."

Mara had moved in her and Susannah's things the previous day and had worried about whether Falcon would take one of the other two upstairs bedrooms. She managed not to sigh aloud in relief that he had relegated himself to the downstairs area.

"We'll join you in a little while," Mara said. "I want to change clothes before I start lunch."

Falcon had been dismissed. He took one last look at his wife and new daughter before heading down the stairs.

They joined him an hour later in the kitchen. Falcon took a moment to admire his wife. She was wearing jeans that molded her hips and long slender legs and a plaid Western blouse that had the first two buttons undone so he saw a hint of her rounded breasts. She had rolled up her sleeves and had tied her hair in a ponytail that made her look like a girl again. He wanted to be the teenage boy that got her alone in the backseat of an old convertible and taught her all about the birds and the bees.

"I would have been glad to fix lunch," Mara said when she saw the table set and food waiting to be served.

"It was my pleasure," Falcon said. "It's just steak and baked potatoes and a salad." He grinned roguishly. "I'm afraid that's my entire repertoire."

Mara sat down in the chair he held out for her and watched with raised brows as he poured decanted red wine into a crystal glass.

"Wine?" she said. "At lunch?"

"It's a late lunch," he quipped. "And we did just get married," he pointed out.

Mara flushed and wasn't sure whether it was chagrin or pleasure she was feeling. Maybe it was both. She could be excused for her confusion. This was, after all, a somewhat muddled situation.

Falcon poured some milk into a wineglass for Susannah. "So you can join in our toast to a happy life," he said.

Mara saw how pleased her daughter was to be included in the grown-up ritual. It appeared Falcon Whitelaw had a knack for pleasing females that she hadn't imagined.

Once they were served and Falcon had seated himself, he raised his glass for the toast he had promised. "To a long and happy life," he said.

Mara stared at him aghast. Such a toast might be appropriate for a newly wedded couple, but with Susannah sitting there, her life in the balance, it seemed particularly cruel. Falcon held his glass aloft, ignoring her wordless censure, demanding that she join him.

At last she did. "To a long and happy life," she echoed, clinking her glass against his and against Susannah's.

"To a long and happy life," her daughter said. Susannah grinned and drank some of her milk. "I'm hungry, Mommy. Let's eat."

That was a good sign. Susannah had been nauseous after the interim treatment she had received, and the doctor had given her a Benadryl injection to help counter the sickness. Apparently it was working.

"I was thinking that you might like to come see the horses in my stable after lunch," Falcon said to Susannah.

"Is my pony there?"

Falcon laughed. "Not yet. But I have a few colts and fillies that you might like to pet."

Susannah was beaming again. *How did he do it?* Mara wondered. Maybe the reason she was unable to make Susannah laugh was because she didn't feel much like laughing herself. So perhaps some good would come of staying with Falcon, after all.

"Do you want to come with us?" Falcon asked as he headed out the back door with Susannah after lunch.

Mara felt anxious letting Susannah out of her sight. But she didn't want to spend any more time with Falcon than she had to.

Misreading her indecision, Falcon said, "I'll take good care of her. I won't let her get hurt."

"Susannah's spent a lot of time around horses. She knows how to act." Her words came out sounding sharp and reproachful, and she wished them back. But it was too late. Falcon frowned and turned his back on her.

"We won't be gone long," he said as he let the screen door slam behind them.

Mara looked around at the mess in the kitchen and realized this was a way she could repay Falcon in part for the service he had rendered when he married her. There was more to be done in the kitchen than simply cleaning up after the meal. Falcon obviously hadn't had a housekeeper in a while. The floor needed scrubbing, and the cabinets were disorganized. There were other things she would be able to do when she had more time: curtains for the windows, flowers on the sill, cleaning the refrigerator and the stove. She would settle now for washing dishes and putting away leftovers.

Mara was just wiping down the front of the refrigerator when Falcon returned with Susannah. He had been gone, she suddenly realized, for most of the afternoon. Where had the time gone? She looked around her and saw a kitchen that sparkled. Her eyes shifted back to Falcon.

Mara sensed from the worried look on his face that something was wrong. Susannah had her head on his shoulder, and her arms were wrapped around his neck.

"I didn't mean to keep Susannah out so long," Falcon said. "She got a little tired. I'll take her upstairs for you."

But his eyes said, *Please don't leave me alone with her.*

In fact, Falcon was terrified. Without warning, Susannah had deflated like a balloon with a pinhole in it. One second she was patting the forehead of a pretty bay filly with four white stockings, the next she was hanging on to the leg of his jeans as though that was all that was holding her upright. Susannah had sagged into his arms when he picked her up, almost like deadweight.

He could feel her erratic breaths against his neck, and she had become unusually quiet. He was even more afraid of what Mara would say about Susannah's condition.

"We didn't do anything strenuous," he found himself saying to Mara. He waited for her to pull down the covers so he could lay Susannah on her bed. "One minute she was fine, and the next minute she was practically asleep on her feet."

"It wasn't anything you did," Mara said. "It's the disease. It saps her strength."

She took off Susannah's tennis shoes and covered her with the sheets and a quilt. The little girl was already asleep.

Mara turned to face Falcon and found herself wanting to smooth the furrow of worry from his brow. "She'll be all right again once she's rested."

When the shadows didn't leave his blue eyes, she reached out a hand to him. "It isn't your fault," she said in a quiet voice. "You didn't do anything wrong."

He seemed to notice suddenly that she was touching him. He stared at her hand, then turned his hand to thread his fingers with hers. "Come downstairs with me," he said. "We need to talk."

Mara felt the calluses on his hand, felt the strength of it and felt all kinds of other things that she had no business feeling. For a moment she resisted his gentle tug. Then she was on her feet and he was leading her downstairs.

He sat on the heavy Mediterranean couch of deep wine leather and dark wood and urged her down beside him. He slipped his arm around her and pulled her close.

Mara nestled her head under Falcon's chin and felt

the lickety-split beat of his heart and the grip of his hand on hers. She didn't try to free herself or chastise Falcon for his presumptuousness. She knew he needed comfort, and she needed it too much herself to refuse it to him. They sat there for a long time in silence.

Without fanfare, without warning, dusk fell. The light coming in through the arched windows turned pale yellow and pink and orange. It wouldn't be long before it was full dark. "I thought we were going to talk," Mara said.

"We are," he said. "I just needed this first."

"Me, too," Mara admitted.

"Is she going to die?" Falcon asked.

Mara felt the tears sting her eyes. "No."

Falcon tightened his hold on her. "Is that wishing? Or is that the truth?"

Mara told him everything she knew about acute lymphocytic leukemia. About the six to twelve weeks of chemotherapy to induce remission. About the ninety-percent cure rate for the chemotherapy. About the possibility of relapse, which could happen at any time, and which would require the entire chemotherapy treatment all over again.

"If she makes it for a year without a relapse, there's a good chance she'll be home free."

"And if the chemotherapy doesn't work?"

"There's always a bone-marrow transplant."

"And if that doesn't work?"

Mara tore herself from Falcon's embrace; it was no longer comforting. She rose and turned to face him with her hands on her hips, her feet widespread in a fighting stance. "What do you want me to say? That

Susannah may die? The possibility exists," she said. "Are you happy now?"

He rose and faced her in an equally belligerent stance. "No, I'm not. How can you stand it, knowing what may happen?"

Suddenly all the fight went out of her. "I don't have much choice," she said, her eyes bleak.

"Mara, I—"

Falcon reached for Mara, to comfort her, but she whirled and ran. He didn't go after her. He wished he hadn't let himself get involved. He wished he had borrowed the money from someone to pay for the treatments Susannah needed. Because he didn't think he could stand by and watch Susannah Ainsworth die. Most of all, he didn't think he could bear to watch Mara suffer if her daughter didn't survive.

It was too late to back out now. He wanted Mara. And he had already given a piece of his soul to Susannah. He was bound to both of them by ties he hadn't even begun to imagine existed before they came into his life.

He would make sure Susannah had the best care possible, no matter what it cost. Even if he had to humble himself before his family to get more money to pay for it.

CHAPTER FOUR

FALCON HAD BEEN married for two weeks, during which time Susannah had begun induction therapy in earnest. He made it a point to be at the house whenever Mara returned from the hospital with her daughter. He carried the child up to her bedroom from the van he had recently bought to replace his Porsche, holding her limp form in his arms while Mara arranged the bed. Then he settled her under the covers.

It was getting harder and harder to smile for the little girl. But Falcon forced himself to be cheerful. Mara's face was stark, her eyes bleak and worried. He didn't think so much solemnity could be good for Susannah.

"How are you feeling?" Falcon asked Susannah. He immediately regretted the words, but to his surprise Susannah lifted a flattened hand and tipped it back and forth like airplane wings.

"So-so," she said.

"Why ask when you know she's feeling sick?" Mara rebuked him.

"There's sick, and then there's sick," Falcon said. "Isn't that so, Susannah?" He brush her bangs away from her forehand and a hank of hair came out in his hand.

He turned stricken eyes to Mara, but found no comfort there. She looked as stunned as he felt.

Falcon sought a way to hide the scrap of hair from Susannah, but she saw it and took it from him, inspecting it carefully.

"My hair is falling out," she said matter-of-factly.

"It appears so," Falcon replied cautiously.

"Dr. Sortino says that's a good sign," she explained to Falcon. "He says that means the medicine is working. I want to get a red hat, like my new friend Patsy wears. Is that okay?"

"That's fine, pumpkin," Falcon said. "Your mom and I will see if we can find one." He started to playfully tug a curl that lay on Susannah's cheek and barely managed to stop himself in time. What if it came away in his hand? Susannah's disappearing tresses didn't seem to worry her, but he was still shaken by his recent experience.

Falcon tucked Susannah in and leaned over to kiss her on the forehead. As he did so he realized he was going to be devastated if chemotherapy didn't stop the disease. He had already started reading about bone-marrow transplants. They were horribly painful, and it was difficult to find donors. And they didn't always effect a cure. The statistics weren't encouraging. He couldn't imagine putting Susannah through it, knowing how much she suffered from the induction therapy.

When he stood up, he realized Mara had already left the room. That wasn't like her. Usually she stayed to read to Susannah after he was gone.

"I wonder what happened to your mom," he said.

"She left a minute ago," Susannah informed him. "She was crying again."

"Again?"

"She doesn't think I know, but I've seen her cry lots

of times," Susannah confided. "She thinks I'm going to die. Am I?"

Falcon was startled by such frank speaking. He wanted to reply "Of course not!" But that wouldn't have been honest. On the other hand, did an eight-year-old child deserve to hear an honest evaluation of her chances of survival?

Mara should be answering these questions, he thought.

Before he could answer Susannah, she asked, "What is it like to die?"

Falcon grinned ruefully. "You've got me there, pumpkin. I can't answer that. My suggestion is that you concentrate on getting well."

Susannah wrinkled her nose. "You never answered my first question. Am I going to die?"

Falcon didn't care if it was a lie. It was the only answer he was willing to give her. "No, pumpkin. You're going to be fine. But you have to rest and take care of yourself."

Falcon was amazed that Susannah accepted his dictum as truth. She closed her eyes and settled back against her pillow.

"Tell Mommy it's okay if she cries. I understand."

Falcon felt his throat swell with emotion. "I'll do that," he managed to say.

He got out of the room as quickly as he could, closing the door behind him.

He didn't have to search far for Mara. She was standing right there with her back against the wall, her chin on her chest, her arms crossed protectively over her breasts.

"Did you hear?" he asked quietly.

She looked up at him and nodded. Her eyes welled with tears. As he watched, one slid onto her cheek.

"I didn't know what to say," he confessed.

"You said exactly the right thing."

"I lied."

"*It was not a lie!* She's going to live!" Mara said fiercely.

Falcon slipped an arm around her shoulder and led her toward the master bedroom. "Susannah's liable to hear us," he warned.

Mara jerked herself free, and instead of going the rest of the way to her bedroom, headed downstairs. "Let's go where we can talk freely."

Falcon followed after her. It hadn't been an easy two weeks of marriage, but he and Mara had managed to remain civil to each other. He had a feeling their truce was about to end.

Mara marched all the way to the kitchen, where she found a glass and some ice and poured herself some tea. She drank half the glass and wiped her mouth with the back of her hand. "All right, let's get this over with."

"I don't want to fight with you," Falcon said.

Mara was filled with pent-up anxiety. If she didn't release it, she was going to burst. She slammed her tea glass down on the table. "You must be missing all those parties about now," she said. "All that late-night carousing…all those women—"

"Don't start," Falcon warned, grabbing her shoulders and giving her a shake. "I'll accept that you're overwrought because of Susannah's condition. That's no reason to take out your frustration on me."

Mara stared at Falcon, stunned at the accuracy of his statement. Dread and fear crowded her every waking moment, making it impossible to act normally. She shuddered at the thought of how she was behaving toward Falcon. True, she despised his irresponsible, devil-may-care attitudes. But if it hadn't been for his lighthearted teasing, his smiles and cajolery, she didn't think she could have survived the past two weeks. And there were so many more weeks to be endured!

She looked up at Falcon and let him see the remorse she felt. "I'm sorry," she whispered.

Her lips were trembling, her eyes liquid with feeling. Falcon didn't think, he acted on impulse. His mouth slanted across hers, and he thrust his tongue inside, meeting hers in a passionate duel. His hands slid from her shoulders across her breasts, and he heard her moan as he cupped their fullness.

Mara's hands slid around Falcon's waist and up his back, as she sought solace for the ache deep inside. She wanted to disappear inside him, to be absorbed into his being so there was no more Mara and Falcon, only one stronger being, more capable of surviving the awful uncertainty of the future.

"Falcon," she whispered in a ragged voice. "Please. Please."

Falcon picked her up and carried her to his bedroom. He kicked the door closed behind them and captured her mouth as he lowered her to the bed.

"Are you protected?" he asked. There was no sense bringing an innocent child into this convoluted situation. Later, if things worked out... But not now.

"Are you?" he demanded in a voice harsh with the need he was striving to control.

Mara nodded jerkily. "Hurry," she said. "Please hurry." It was a strange thing for a woman to ask a man who was about to make love to her. But Mara didn't want time to think about what she was doing. Nor did she want to give Falcon time to change his mind.

Mara wanted to touch his skin, to feel the warmth, the strength of him. She yanked the snaps free on his shirt and shoved it off his shoulders. She tested bone and sinew with her hands, then tasted with her mouth. She heard the zipper slide down on her jeans and felt Falcon pushing them down along with her panties.

Then she was naked to his touch and his hand was caressing her. His fingers slid inside her, first one and then another. She arched beneath him and bucked a little as the pleasure became too intense to bear. She bit his shoulder, hardly aware of what she was doing, only knowing that she wanted him, needed him. Now.

She reached for him and felt the hard bulge that threatened the seams of his jeans. He groaned as she cupped him in her hand and then stroked up and down. He unsnapped his jeans and shoved them down along with his briefs.

An instant later he was inside her. She moaned deep in her throat as she felt the hot, hard length of him thrust once into the welcoming warmth, then retreat and thrust again.

She lifted her hips in a primitive response to him, then reached for his mouth to mimic with her tongue his intrusion below. She gasped as she felt her body begin to convulse. Her fingernails left crescents on his flanks as she urged him deeper. She wrapped her legs around him and held him captive as he released his seed.

It was over too soon.

Mara felt the tears squeezing between her tightly

closed lids. She was panting, trying to catch her breath, and failing. She felt totally enervated. And exultant.

And horrified.

What had she done? She shoved frantically at Falcon's broad shoulders, and he rolled over onto his back. He exhaled a deep sigh of contentment. Mara scrambled to her knees, pulling up her underwear and her jeans, which she realized had caught around her ankles. She searched for her shirt, meanwhile crossing one arm across her breasts.

"Where are you going in such a hurry?" Falcon asked.

"I…I have to get out of here," Mara said.

Falcon kicked his jeans the rest of the way off. Mara was appalled to realize that they hadn't even been able to wait long enough to get their clothes off! She chanced a glance at Falcon and was sorry she had looked. He looked smugly satisfied. As well he should be. She had practically fallen on him and dragged him to the ground. What on earth had she been thinking? She had just made love—no, no—she had just *had sex* with a man she despised!

She had been seeking comfort, and he had willingly offered it. The cad. The rogue. The cur.

"Don't bother seeing me out," she snapped, shrugging her way into her shirt.

He laughed.

She glared at him. "What's so funny?"

"You are. You can't pretend nothing happened, Mara."

"Oh, yes I can!" She turned and marched out the door. At the last instant she was careful not to slam it. She didn't want to take the chance of waking Susannah.

All the way up the stairs Mara pounded her fist against the banister. "How on earth did I let that happen? I'm an idiot. I have to be out of my mind," she muttered.

But the truth was, she had never had such a devastating sexual experience with a man. She wasn't sure exactly what had happened, but she was terrified that she wouldn't be able to resist Falcon if he offered her a chance to repeat the encounter.

How the mighty had fallen.

It was time she reevaluated her relationship with Falcon Whitelaw. Maybe, if she looked hard enough, she could find enough redeeming features in him to justify a second look at the man.

IT HAD BEEN three long weeks since Falcon had made love to his wife—and he had been making love, even if she hadn't. Lately she looked sideways at him every time he got near her, as though she expected him to pounce on her and carry her off to his bedroom again. He wouldn't have minded one bit. But it was as clear as a pane of glass that she would fight him if he made the attempt. So he bided his time, waiting for the moment when she came to him.

Falcon needed to talk to someone about his feelings for Mara. Could he really want a woman this bad who went out of her way to avoid him? Was it asking for heartache to keep hoping she would forgive him— and herself—and work with him to make theirs a real marriage? Falcon had mulled the subject until he was nearly crazy but found no answers. Which was when he decided to approach his brother for advice.

Zach was the person closest to him, the person he

had always turned to in the past when he needed a sounding board. He didn't want to leave Mara and Susannah for even the couple of days it would take him to visit his brother at Hawk's Way. So he called Zach and asked him to come to Dallas.

"What's going on?" Zach asked.

"I got married," Falcon confessed.

There was a silence on the other end of the line. "Who's the woman?"

"You don't know her," he said. "She has a daughter who's very ill. There were reasons… Look, I don't want to have to explain all this on the phone. Will you come?"

"I'll be there tonight," Zach said.

Zach piloted his own jet, so airline connections weren't a problem for him. Falcon made arrangements to pick him up at Dallas/Fort Worth International Airport.

Falcon realized he would just as soon not introduce his wife to his brother, or his brother to his wife. So he took Zach to a restaurant in town for dinner.

"Where does your wife think you are tonight?" Zach inquired as he folded the menu and set it beside his plate.

"Mara and I aren't accountable to each other."

Zach's brow arched in disbelief. "That's some marriage you have, baby brother."

"There are…complications," Falcon conceded.

"And?"

Falcon found it difficult to explain his marriage of convenience to his brother. Especially when Zach interrupted him to say, "I've never heard of such an idiotic reason to get married. You should have come to me for the money. Or gotten it from Dad."

His eyes narrowed and Falcon felt his brother's sharp perusal. "Unless you didn't really marry the woman just to help her out of her financial troubles. Is that it? Are you in love with her?"

Falcon flushed. Trust Zach to put his finger on the pulse of the problem. "I have feelings for her," Falcon conceded. He wasn't going to label them love, although they felt suspiciously like it. But only a fool would admit to love under the circumstance. "Unfortunately she hates my guts," he told Zach.

Zach hissed in a breath of air. "That's too bad. Any hope she'll change her mind?"

Falcon flashed his brother a devil-may-care grin that was tremendously hard-won. "I have some hope of it."

"So why did you call me?" he asked bluntly.

"I guess I wanted someone to tell me I *wasn't* an idiot to marry her," Falcon muttered.

Zach laughed. "Sorry I couldn't oblige you. Look, once the kid is well, you can get a divorce and forget all about the woman."

Falcon's lips flattened. "I don't want to forget about her. And the *kid's* name is Susannah."

"Well, well. Baby brother has grown some sharp teeth. If you feel so strongly, why don't you act on your convictions?"

"And do what?" Falcon demanded.

"Woo her. Win her love. Make it a real marriage."

"How?" Falcon asked in an agonized voice.

Zach took a sip of his whiskey. "I have a suggestion. I don't know if you're going to like it."

"I'm desperate. What have you got in mind?"

"Give her an ultimatum."

"What?"

"Tell her you can't be expected to live like a eunuch for the next year, and if she doesn't want you looking cross-eyed at other women, she can fulfill her marital duties."

Falcon flushed. "I couldn't put her in that position."

"Why not?"

"That wasn't part of the original bargain."

"So what?"

"You can be a ruthless, coldhearted bastard, Zach." He pitied the poor woman who ever fell in love with his brother.

Zach shrugged. "You asked for my advice. I've given it. You're welcome to come up with your own solution to the problem."

Maybe it wasn't fair to demand conjugal relations, Falcon thought, but perhaps he could merely *suggest* they start sleeping together. He knew from their one experience together that he and Mara were completely compatible in bed. It wasn't much on which to base a relationship. But it was a start.

"Thanks for coming, Zach," Falcon said.

"Don't mention it. When am I going to meet this paragon?"

"Not this trip," Falcon said. He didn't think he could stand to have Zach see the way Mara flinched when he got near her. It was one thing to admit to his big brother that he had problems, it was another to allow him to witness them in person. "If Susannah's induction therapy is successful we might be able to come for the family Labor Day picnic."

"I'll count on seeing you there." Zach threw his napkin down on his clean, empty plate. "If we're finished," he said wryly, "I think I'd just as soon fly back to Hawk's Way tonight. I can catch a cab back to the airport. I think you should go home."

Falcon rose and shook his brother's hand. "Goodbye, Zach. I think I'll take you up on that."

It wasn't that he thought Mara would be worried about him. She didn't like him enough to worry about him. But he wanted to be there to say good-night to Susannah before she went to bed.

"Think about what I said," Zach called to his retreating back.

Hell, Falcon thought, it wasn't likely he was going to be thinking about much else.

CHAPTER FIVE

"IS FALCON THERE?"

Mara tensed at the sultry sound of the female voice on the other end of the line. "Yes, he is," she answered.

"Who's this?" the female asked.

"This is his wife," Mara said with relish.

"Oh. Then I don't suppose he's free to fly to New York this weekend."

"That's entirely up to him," Mara said.

"Oooohh."

Mara could tell she had created confusion at the other end of the line. But really, did she have the right to dictate when and where Falcon went? She was his wife, but it was a marriage in name only. If he wanted to go traipsing off to New York with some sexy Southern belle, who was she to say him nay. "I'll get him for you," she said as she set the phone down on the desk in Falcon's office.

She found Falcon in the kitchen with Susannah. "There's a call for you," she said.

Falcon picked up the wall phone extension in the kitchen. Mara stood there listening, her arms crossed defensively over her chest. She knew Falcon must have a lot of old girlfriends, and she wanted to know how he was going to handle this situation.

"Oh, it's you, Felicia." Falcon turned his back on Mara and lowered his voice.

"Yes, I am married," he said. "Over two months ago. It was a very small wedding, Felicia. I didn't even invite my family!" he said in exasperation. "New York? This weekend?" He turned to face Mara, an incredulous look on his face. "My wife has no objection to my going? How do you know that?"

Falcon frowned. "She told you so?"

Mara shrugged with great indifference.

"No, I can't go, Felicia. I have responsibilities here."

Even from across the room Mara could hear the other woman's laughter and see Falcon's embarrassed flush.

"I know that's never stopped me before," Falcon hissed into the phone. "Things have changed since I got myself a family.

"I have a daughter, too," Falcon said. "She's eight. As a matter of fact, we have plans of our own this weekend. We're going shopping for a pony. So, I'm afraid I can't meet you in New York. Have a good time, Felicia. Goodbye."

Falcon slammed the phone down and had rounded on Mara in a fury when he noticed Susannah's wide-eyed interest. "You finish your lunch," he said to the little girl. "I want to talk to your mother in private."

He dragged Mara all the way to his office, which was across the hall from his bedroom, and shut the door with an ominous click behind him. Then he turned to face Mara with his legs spread and his hands fisted on his hips.

"How could you dare to suggest to Felicia that I'd be willing to trot off to New York? I'm a married man!" he snarled. "I take those vows seriously."

"It's a marriage of convenience," Mara corrected. "Plain and simple."

"Have I gone out *once* without you in the two months we've been married?" he demanded. "Well, once," he conceded, recalling his meeting with Zach. "But have I spent even one night away from home?"

"No."

"Then what makes you think I'd be willing to go carousing with another woman in New York? Did you *want* me to go?"

"No," Mara admitted in a small voice. She lifted her chin and said, "I...I thought you might need to be with a woman."

"And better anyone else than you," he said in a harsh voice. "Is that it?"

Mara dropped her chin to her chest. "I thought..."

"You didn't think!" Falcon accused. "Or you would have realized there isn't any woman I want except you!"

Her head snapped up, and her eyes widened in astonishment.

Falcon let her see the desire he felt for her, let his eyes roam her body voraciously. He should have done what Zach recommended. He should have come right home and demanded his husbandly rights.

But when he had returned from meeting Zach he had found Mara with Susannah in the upstairs bathroom. The little girl had her head bent over the toilet, where it had been for an hour. He had sat down beside Mara, and the two of them had stayed with Susannah until she had finally lain her head down in Mara's lap, exhausted. Falcon had carried Susannah back to bed and told her funny stories about his childhood until she had fallen asleep at last.

He had taken one look at Mara's face, at the terror and exhaustion, and known he couldn't ask anything from her that night. Nor had an opportunity arisen over the succeeding days and weeks. Falcon had faced the fact that his needs would have to wait. It was one of the first truly unselfish acts of his life.

Now he saw that his self-sacrifice had earned him nothing in Mara's eyes. She believed he was capable of abandoning her and Susannah for a weekend on the town.

"You must not think very much of me," he said, his brow furrowed with the distress he felt.

Mara realized now the mistake she had made. And why she had made it. She had heard that other woman's voice on the phone, and she had been jealous of her, and of every woman who had ever enjoyed Falcon's attention. Because she wanted that attention for herself.

Unfortunately, for both her sake and Falcon's, she had been too much of a coward to ask for it. He had not made one move toward her since the night they had made love, had not hinted by so much as a look that he wanted to repeat the experience. Meanwhile, she ached whenever she looked at him. Her body coiled with excitement when he merely touched her hand. She couldn't look him in the face for fear her feelings, which she was certain he didn't return, would be blatantly apparent to him. Obviously she had put him in an awkward position when she sought oblivion in his arms. Obviously he hadn't enjoyed it as much as she had. Obviously he hadn't wanted to repeat the experience.

It was easy to believe that he might have contacted Felicia, or that he might have planned to have Felicia call so Mara would let him go. Now he was telling her that she had been wrong. That he would prefer a week-end with her and Susannah to a weekend with a lus-cious femme fatale in New York.

"I'm sorry," she said. "I mistook the matter. I'll un-derstand if you want to change your mind about spend-ing time with me and Susannah—"

"Sometimes I could just shake you," Falcon said. He suited word to deed and grabbed her by the shoulders. "I burn for you, woman! Can you understand what that means? I want to be inside you. There isn't a moment when I don't remember what you taste like, what you feel like. I don't want another woman. I want you!"

His mouth slanted over hers, and he told her of his desperate need with his lips and his hands. It took a mo-ment for him to realize that she was crying.

He let her go and stepped back, tunneling all ten fin-gers through his hair. "Hell, Mara. I'm sorry."

She closed her eyes and pressed the back of her hand over her mouth.

"You don't have to worry about that happening again. I can control myself. I'm not an animal."

He turned on booted heel and left the room, closing the door quietly behind himself.

Mara let out a tremulous sob. "Oh, my God. What have I done? And what am I supposed to do now?" she said to the empty room.

How could she want to make love to the man respon-sible for Grant's death? How could she let him hold her, love her, when she could not forgive what he had done?

More to the point, why was she finding it so impos-sible to let go of the anger she felt over Grant's death? It had been more than a year. Her feelings of bubbling hostility should have dissipated by now. But whenever she thought of Grant, feelings of vexation, of frustration and annoyance simmered to the surface. Until she could manage to quell those feelings, she would be better off keeping Falcon at arm's distance. For his sake, as much as hers.

DESPITE THEIR ALTERCATION, Falcon was true to his word. He announced to Mara the next time he saw her, that the trip to the auction to find a pony for Susannah was all planned.

"We'll be getting there just in time to see the ponies auctioned, so Susannah shouldn't get too tired," he said.

"Come on, Mommy!" Susannah said excitedly. "Hurry up and get ready. It's time to go!"

Mara felt her spirits lift when she saw how happy and excited her daughter was. She quickly dressed in a Western blouse, jeans and boots and joined Falcon and Susannah outside.

Falcon was sitting on the edge of a tile fountain that graced the courtyard in back of the house, with Susannah in his lap. As Mara came up behind them she saw that Falcon had given Susannah a penny and was telling her to make a wish and toss the coin into the fountain.

"Will my wish come true?" Susannah asked.

"Who knows?" Falcon said. "This may be a magical fountain."

Susannah squeezed her eyes closed and tossed the penny. It landed with a plop that sent water back up onto her face. She opened her eyes and laughed as Falcon brushed the crystal droplets away with his fingertips.

Mara was moved by his gentleness with the little girl. "I'm ready," she announced. But a moment later she realized she wasn't the least bit ready to deal with the things Falcon made her feel.

She stood frozen as his eyes roamed her body. She felt warm everywhere his eyes touched her. She wanted to surrender to him heart and soul. She gritted her teeth against her wayward feelings.

Remember Grant, she admonished herself.

But the hate wouldn't rise the way it had so easily in the past.

That's because you know who's really to blame for Grant's death, don't you, Mara? And it isn't Falcon Whitelaw. Admit it, Mara. You're to blame! You knew what would happen, and you let Grant go anyway. It's all your fault! Your fault! Your fault!

"Mara? Is something wrong?"

Falcon's interruption silenced the accusing voice in Mara's head. She pressed a hand to her temple where her pulse pounded. "I'm fine," she said. "Shall we go?"

Falcon gathered Susannah in his arms and walked toward Mara. When he reached her, he slipped an arm around her waist and guided her toward the van. Their hips bumped, and she tried to free herself, but his hold tightened. She was aware of the warmth of his hand at her ribs, of a desire to be alone with him, when he could let that hand ramble at will.

You're crazy, Mara. You're out of your mind. How can you even think about making love to Falcon Whitelaw? He killed Grant!

No, *you* killed Grant.

Mara chewed on her lower lip, wishing the awful voice would go away and leave her alone.

Falcon saw the furrow on Mara's brow and wondered what was troubling her now. Maybe he shouldn't have let her know how he felt about her. Maybe she was concerned he would try to take advantage of their situation.

It perturbed him that Mara could think he might take by force what she did not willingly offer him. He had never forced a woman into his bed. Despite Zach's advice, he wasn't about to start now. But he didn't think there was anything he could say that would ease her mind. Every time he opened his mouth he ended up with his foot in it. Better to just let sleeping dogs lie.

At the auction Falcon nodded and tipped his hat to the several ranchers he knew, but he didn't approach them as he would have if Mara and Susannah hadn't been with him. He didn't want to have to explain a year from now about his absent wife and daughter. Instead he concentrated all his attention on finding just the right pony for Susannah.

It was quickly apparent that Susannah wanted a pinto.

"I like the ones with patches," she said.

It was up to him to find an animal she liked that also had both excellent conformation and a good disposition. It wasn't until near the end of the auction that he was satisfied with an animal that Susannah also liked.

"That one!" Susannah breathed with a sigh of awe. "Oh, please, Falcon, that one!"

The pony had a white face, with a black patch that ran across his eyes. Falcon was having trouble deciding if the gelding was black with white patches, or white with black, it was so evenly divided by the two colors.

"I'm going to call him Patches," Susannah announced as she hugged the pony's neck after the auction. "You like that name, don't you, Patches?"

They were approached by one of the ranchers Falcon had seen earlier, Sam Longstreet.

"Howdy, Falcon," the tall, rangy man said, tipping his hat. "Are you going to introduce me to this little lady?"

He said "little lady," but his eyes were on Mara when he spoke, so Falcon knew it wasn't Susannah who had caught his interest.

Sam Longstreet and his father had a cattle ranch that bordered Hawk's Way. Sam was a little older than Falcon, maybe two or three years, but his face had more lines and his body was leaner, toughened by long days spent on the range. His sun-bleached chestnut hair was shaggy and needed a cut, and he hadn't shaved in the past day or so. Sam's boots were worn and his jeans frayed. Falcon wasn't sure whether that was because Sam didn't worry about appearances, or whether it meant hard times for the Longstreet ranch. Sam's father, E.J., had some business dealings with Falcon's father, although Falcon wasn't up on the exact details.

"How are you, Sam?" Falcon said. "I'd like to introduce my wife, Mara, and my daughter, Susannah. Mara, this is Sam Longstreet. Our families have been neighbors for generations."

Sam grinned. "It's a mighty big pleasure to meet you, ma'am. You're a sly one," he said to Falcon. "Haven't heard a peep out of your folks about you getting hitched."

"They don't know."

"I won't breathe a word to them," Sam said. "If that's how you want it."

"It's not a secret," Falcon said. "I just haven't found the right moment to tell them the news."

Sam grinned again. "Can I tell E.J.?"

That was sure to put the fat in the fire. Word would get back to his father through E.J. that he had gotten married. "Give me a day to call my folks, then be my guest."

So, the moment of reckoning had come. He would have to tell his parents what he had done, and try to keep them from visiting the newlyweds before he had resolved his relationship with Mara.

Sam turned his attention back to Mara. "How did you hook up with this maverick?" he asked.

Falcon saw the consternation on Mara's face and knew she was trying to decide the best way to explain things to Sam.

"We met through an old friend of mine, a former football teammate at Tech," Falcon said. That was the absolute truth, and so much less than the whole story.

"Makes me wish I'd gone to Tech," Sam said, with an admiring glance at Mara. "Didn't make it to college myself." He turned his attention to Susannah, who was rubbing her own nose against the velvety soft nose of her new pony.

He squatted down so his green eyes would be at a level with her hazel ones. "My name's Sam," he said. "What's yours?"

To Falcon's amazement, Susannah didn't run and hide behind her mother. She answered Sam with a girl-ish, "My name's Susannah. This is my pony. His name is Patches."

Sam reached out to run a big, work-worn hand along the pony's jaw. "He's a mighty fine-looking pony," Sam agreed.

Susannah was wearing her red hat, but it was plain

to anyone who looked closely that she was bald underneath it. Sam wasn't the kind of man to miss a detail like that. He exchanged a surprised look of sympathy with Falcon before he set his hands on his thighs and pushed himself back onto his feet.

He didn't ask questions about Susannah. Things hadn't changed so much in the West that a man could ask another man's business uninvited.

"Guess I'd better be getting along," Sam said. "I've got a new bull to get loaded up, and then I'm headed home."

"Be seeing you," Falcon said.

"Hope so," Sam said with a smile aimed at Mara. "Ma'am." He touched the tip of one callused finger to his battered Stetson, a mark of respect to Falcon's wife.

"What a strange man," Mara said.

"How so?" Falcon asked.

"He looks so…dangerous…and yet his eyes are so… kind. Which is the real Sam Longstreet?" she asked.

Falcon shrugged. "I don't know him very well, even though we lived close. He's older than me or Zach, and his father needed him to work on the ranch, so he never socialized much."

"Will he tell your family about us?"

"He'll tell his father, which is the same thing. But not before tomorrow. Which means I need to call them tonight."

"What do you think they'll say?"

Falcon had a pretty good idea, but he didn't want to burn Mara's tender ears. "They'll be happy for us," he lied.

"Come on," he said. "Let's get this pony home where Susannah can ride him."

But by the time they got home, Susannah's good day had gone bad. She was feeling sick and so tired that she could hardly keep her eyes open. Mara and Falcon put her to bed together with promises that she could ride Patches the moment she was feeling better.

"Are you sure the day wasn't too much for her?" Falcon asked as he and Mara left the room.

"The trip was a wonderful idea. It was only to be expected she would get tired," Mara said. "I don't think she would have missed it for anything," she said in an effort to take the guilty look off Falcon's face.

Falcon allowed himself to be assuaged by Mara's absolution. He didn't want to be responsible for making Susannah any sicker than she already was, and if Mara believed the day hadn't been too taxing for her daughter, he was willing to take her word for it.

"I'd like you with me when I make the call to my parents," Falcon said.

Mara followed him into his office and sat on the bench that ran parallel to his desk. Falcon sat down in the swivel chair in front of the oak rolltop.

"What are you going to tell them?" Mara asked.

"That I met a woman, and we got married."

"Won't they ask questions?"

"Probably."

"How will you explain…everything?"

Falcon grinned ruefully. "It depends on what they ask."

"You know what I mean," Mara said. "What will you tell them about *why* we got married?"

Falcon fiddled with his computer keyboard. "I don't know."

"Will you tell them the truth?"

"Not all of it," Falcon said. "They wouldn't understand."

"Why do you need me here?" Mara asked.

"They may want to say hello to you, to offer their best wishes," he said. They would want to do more than that, Falcon feared. They would want to know every last detail about Mara Ainsworth Whitelaw.

He dialed the phone number. It was answered on the second ring. His mother was breathless. She had apparently run to answer the phone. "Hi, Mom," he said.

"Falcon! We've been wondering what you've been up to. You haven't been in touch for *months!*"

"I've been busy," Falcon said.

"Surely not too busy to write or call your parents and reassure them you aren't lying dead in a gully somewhere," Candy Whitelaw chastised. "Now, tell me what prompted this call?"

His mother had never been one to shilly-shally around, Falcon thought. "I wanted to let you and Dad know that I got married."

"You what?" His mother called into the other room, "Garth, pick up the phone in there. It's Falcon. He's gotten married!"

Falcon heard his father's deep voice asking, "When did this happen? Do we know the bride? When are you bringing her here to meet us?"

"Is she there?" his mother asked. "Can we talk to her? What's her name?"

"Her name is Mara Ainsworth. She's standing right here. I'll put her on so you can say hello." Falcon handed the receiver to Mara, who looked at it as though it had grown fangs. At last she took it from him and held it to her ear.

"Hello?" she said tentatively.

"Hello, dear," Candy said. "I'm Falcon's mother. We're so delighted to hear the news. When did you and Falcon meet? When was the wedding? Oh, I'm so sorry we missed it!"

"Hello, Mara," Garth said. "Welcome to the family. When are we going to get to meet you?"

Mara wrinkled her nose at Falcon. She held her hand over the mouthpiece and said, "You rat! They're full of questions I think you should answer."

"It's nice 'meeting' you at last, Mr. and Mrs. Whitelaw. I—"

"Call me Candy, please," Falcon's mother said. "And Falcon's father is Garth. Now, tell us everything."

"Thank you, Mrs.—Candy," Mara said. "I don't know where to start."

"Where did you two meet?" Garth asked.

"In downtown Dallas. I was there with my husband and daughter and—"

Mara cut herself off when she heard a gasp on the other end of the line. She looked up at Falcon and saw his eyes were squeezed closed. He was shaking his head in disbelief.

"I'm a widow now," she blurted into the phone.

There was a silence and then a relieved sigh at the other end of the line.

"I'm sorry to hear that," Candy said. "Oh, this is so awkward, isn't it, because if you weren't a widow you wouldn't be married to Falcon, and of course I'm glad Falcon found you, but not under such sad circumstances."

"I feel the same way, Mrs.—Candy," Mara said in a soft voice.

"Tell us about your daughter," Garth said.

"Her name is Susannah, and she's eight years old. She's been very ill lately, but we're hoping she'll be well soon."

"Is there anything we can do?" Candy asked.

"Pray," Mara said in a quiet voice.

"It must be very serious," Candy said. "Are you sure—"

"Susannah has leukemia. She's in treatment right now. We'll know more when the therapy is completed."

Again that silence on the other end of the line, while Falcon's parents digested the newest bomb dropped in their laps.

"Let me speak to Falcon," Garth said.

Mara handed the phone to Falcon. "Your father wants to talk to you."

"Dad?"

"What the hell is going on, Falcon?" Garth demanded in a harsh voice. "What kind of trouble have you gotten yourself into this time?"

"No *trouble,* Dad," Falcon answered in an equally harsh voice. "Mara is a widow and Susannah is sick, it's as simple as that. I'm not asking your approval of my marriage, Dad. I was only offering you the courtesy of telling you about it."

"We want to visit," Candy said.

"No, Mom. That wouldn't be a good idea right now."

"Why the hell not?" Garth said.

"Because I said so!" Falcon retorted, resorting to the words his father had always used to justify every order to his children. "We'll try to be there for the Labor Day picnic." It wasn't much as peace offerings went, but it was all they were going to get. "Goodbye, Mom, Dad."

"Falcon—" Garth roared.

"Falcon—" Candy cried.

Falcon gently hung up the phone. "Well, that's taken care of."

"They didn't sound too happy," Mara ventured.

Falcon tipped Mara's chin up with his forefinger. "It's not their life, it's mine. If I'm happy, it doesn't matter what they think."

"Are you happy?" Mara asked, searching his face for the truth.

His thumb traced her lower lip. It was rosy and plump because she had been chewing on it again. "I'm not sorry I married you, if that's what you're asking."

She lowered her eyes, unable to meet his lambent gaze. But she didn't move away from him. Mara felt rooted to the spot. "You should have told them the truth," she murmured.

"Who knows what the truth is," Falcon said enigmatically.

Mara knew he was going to kiss her. She didn't try to escape the caress. Because she needed it as much as she believed he did. His mouth was gentle on hers, his lips seeking solace, not passion. She kept her mouth pliant under his, giving him the succor, the sustenance he sought.

When the kiss ended, she opened her eyes and was moved by what she saw in his.

He cared for her. He wanted her. And he despaired of having her. It was all there on his face.

Mara wished she could give him ease. But the past intruded and would not be silenced.

It had been easy to blame Falcon for Grant's death, even though she was more at fault than he was. Nevertheless, it was hard to let go of her feelings of rage and hate toward Falcon, however undeserved they were. Grant was still dead, and because of Susannah's illness—which was no one's fault at all—her life had been turned upside down.

There's a great deal of good to be said about Falcon Whitelaw, a voice inside her argued. *He's not a bad man, he just had a little growing up to do. He's wonderful with Susannah. And he makes your blood sizzle. Would it be so awful to give him what he wants from you?*

Falcon saw the conflict raging within her. She hated him. He tempted her.

He was the one who stepped back.

"Good night, Mara," he said.

"Good night, Falcon," she replied.

She didn't want him to go. She wanted him to stay.

Afraid she might do or say something she would regret later, Mara whirled and fled the room.

CHAPTER SIX

"Where have you been?" Mara demanded.

Falcon was astounded to find Mara waiting for him in the kitchen. She had a cup of coffee sitting in front of her. He could tell it was cold, which meant she had been there awhile. He hadn't come home for supper, unable to face the thought of being near her and knowing he couldn't touch. He hadn't been far away, just in the barn, where he had worked soaping saddles that were in better shape than they had ever been, thanks to his restlessness. Was it possible she had been worried about him?

"I was in the barn," he said. "Working on my saddle."

"I thought something had happened to you. It's so late. You're usually in by dark."

"You *were* worried about me," Falcon murmured. "I'm sorry, Mara. I'll let you know where I am next time."

If anyone had told Falcon three months ago that he would have been willing to be accountable to *anyone,* let alone a woman, he would have slapped his knee at the jest and hurt his ribs laughing.

How the mighty had fallen.

Mara rose and crossed to the sink. "Susannah asked about you," she said, as though to deny her own concern.

"Is she all right?" Falcon asked anxiously.

Mara left the cup in the sink and turned to face Falcon. "The doctor thinks she may be in remission."

Falcon stared at her, stunned. Then he whooped and grabbed her around the waist and swung her in a circle. "This is fantastic!"

Mara held on so he wouldn't drop her. "Let me down."

Falcon set her down, but he kept his hands on her waist. He needed to hold on to someone, or he just might float off into space. "I can't believe this is happening. It's too soon. She's only been in therapy ten weeks."

"I know," she said. "It's…a miracle."

Falcon looked at Mara and wondered why she wasn't more excited. "You said *may* be in remission. Is there something you aren't telling me? When will we know for sure?"

"Dr. Sortino wants to do a spinal tap tomorrow. We'll know as soon as he gets the results from the test."

"Susannah hates those back-sticks," Falcon said. His hands tightened at Mara's waist. "They hurt."

"I know," Mara said. "Will you come with us tomorrow?"

It was the first time she had asked him to join her. The first sign at all that she needed him for anything other than his money. "I'll be glad to come with you."

She smiled for the first time since he had come into the house. "I'm glad you'll be there. Susannah has been asking when you're going to come to the hospital with us."

"She has?"

Mara stepped back, and Falcon let his hands drop. "She's very attached to you," she said.

"I'm attached to her, too," Falcon said.

"Well, that's what I waited up to tell you. Good night, Falcon."

"Mara, wait." Falcon didn't want her to leave. He wanted

to hold her. He wanted to sleep with her in his arms. He thought of the ultimatum Zach had wanted him to give her—how many weeks ago had that been?—and knew he still couldn't do it. Not now. Not yet. Maybe if—when—they found out Susannah was in remission he could start making husbandly demands of his wife.

"What is it?" she asked.

"What would you think, if Susannah's feeling well enough, about going to Hawk's Way over Labor Day?"

Mara leaned back against the refrigerator and crossed her arms protectively around her. "Do you really think that's a good idea, for me and Susannah to meet your family?"

"You're my wife," he said. "And Susannah is my daughter."

Not for much longer.

The words hung in the silence between them. If Susannah was truly in remission, it would change everything. Mara wouldn't need him anymore. She would be able to move back to her house in Dallas with its covered porch and its white picket fence.

"I want them to meet you, Mara. Even…even if things don't work out between us. I think you're a very special woman. I've felt that way since the first moment I laid eyes on you."

Mara flushed and shot a quick look at Falcon. "I was a married woman when you first met me," she reminded him.

Falcon's lips flattened, and Mara was sorry she had spoken. She had only meant that he shouldn't have been looking at a married woman that way. She hadn't meant to remind him of the catastrophe that had made her a widow. Falcon turned on his heel, and she knew he would leave the house again if she didn't do something to stop him.

"I've been doing some work in your office," she said as his hand reached the kitchen doorknob.

Falcon turned and glanced at Mara over his shoulder. "What kind of work?"

She gave him a lopsided smile. "Your desk was a little disorganized, and so was your computer filing system."

"You've been working on my computer?" He turned completely around and assumed a pose Mara was coming to recognize as his "I'm King of the Roost and Don't Give Me Any Backtalk" stance, his legs widespread and his hands fisted on his hips.

"I've been organizing," she said.

Falcon raised a skeptical black brow. "Organizing?" Lord help a man when a woman started organizing.

"Come with me, and I'll show you some of what I've done."

Falcon knew an olive branch when he saw one. He willingly reached out to take it. "All right. Lead the way."

Falcon had noticed little improvements around the house since Mara had moved in. Certainly her green thumb was much in evidence. There were potted flowers in the kitchen and trees in planters in the living room.

She had stuck patterned pillows on the leather couch to break up the somber expanse and rearranged nearly every vase into a different arched cubbyhole. The heavy curtains in the living room had been removed so the sunshine filtered in during the day, and gingham curtains had been added for color in the kitchen.

The whole house sparkled with cleanliness. She hadn't been kidding about her ability as a housekeeper.

Which should have made him less nervous about her bookkeeping talents, but somehow didn't.

Mara hadn't completely rearranged his office. He could—and would—have complained if she had. She had been more subtle than that, making small changes, a book moved here, a file moved there. Of course, the spurs and halter he had been repairing had been relegated to a worktable in the pantry off the kitchen.

It wasn't until he sat down next to Mara at the computer that he realized what significant changes she had made in his bookkeeping system. She showed him how she had organized his files so he could see which stud had covered which mare, which cows had been inseminated by which bull. Amounts of grain that had been fed, and increase in weight on the hoof, were also calculated for his beef cattle.

"This is incredible! How did you learn to do this?" he asked.

"I told you I grew up at my mother's knee. I spent a lot of time looking over my father's shoulder, too," she said with a cheeky grin.

"I'm impressed. Why haven't you ever gotten a job doing this for some rancher?"

"I don't have a college degree," she admitted. "I had just finished my first year of school when I found out Susannah was sick."

Falcon was thinking she didn't need a degree to do his bookkeeping. But he could see that if something ever happened to him, she might need an education. "You should go back and finish," he said.

"I can't until I know Susannah is well."

"With any luck, we'll get good news tomorrow. I think you should plan to go back this fall, Mara. I can hire someone to take care of Susannah while you're in class."

"I already owe you too much."

"You don't owe me anything," Falcon said. "I've done what I've done because I wanted to do it. I wish you'd get it out of your head that you have to pay me back."

Falcon didn't breathe, he didn't move. On second thought, there was something she could do for him. She had presented him with the perfect opportunity to ask for what he wanted from her without giving her an ultimatum.

"There is something you can do for me," he said.

"What?" Mara asked.

He hesitated, then took the plunge. "I need a woman, Mara. You're my wife. I want to sleep with you."

She hissed out a breath, but didn't say anything right away.

He reached out and caressed her cheek with the back of his hand. Her eyelids slid closed. Her teeth caught her lower lip and began to worry it.

"I want to give you what you want," she said. "I know I owe you—"

Falcon jerked his hand away, and Mara's eyes flashed open. He rose to his feet and towered over her. The muscles in his jaw worked as he gritted his teeth. "If that's the best you can do, forget it."

She leapt to her feet and grabbed his arm to keep him from leaving. "I'm trying! I have needs, too," she admitted in a choked voice. "But I can't forget who you are. Don't you understand? I loved Grant. And because of you, he's dead."

"Grant was a drunk who killed himself in a car wreck!" Falcon snarled.

All the blood left Mara's face. "Who told you Grant was a drunk?"

Falcon stared at her, not sure what had upset her so much.

"Who told you Grant was an alcoholic?" she insisted.

"An alcoholic? Was he?" Falcon asked, dumbfounded.

Mara covered her mouth with her hand. She hadn't ever said the words aloud. Not to anyone. She had lived with Grant, realized he had a weakness, and tried to pretend it didn't exist.

Falcon grabbed her by the arms. "Are you telling me that you've blamed me for Grant's death all this time when you *knew* he had a drinking problem?"

"He didn't have a problem—"

"Tell me the truth!"

"Yes! Yes, I blame you. He was going to AA meetings. He had quit for almost six months before he ran into you."

"Is that why he lost all those jobs?" Falcon asked. "Was he drinking on the job?"

"I don't know," Mara admitted miserably. "He gave different reasons for why he was let go."

"And you never checked?" Facon demanded.

"I trusted him!" she said fiercely. There were tears in her eyes that betrayed the truth. The first time, or maybe the second, Grant had been able to fool her. But by the sixth or seventh time he was fired, she'd had no illusions left.

"How could you love a man like that?" Falcon asked,

truly puzzled by her devotion to someone who must have caused her untold pain.

She shrugged helplessly. "He was a good father." *When he wasn't drinking.* "And a good husband." *When he wasn't drunk and chasing other women.*

Mara couldn't meet Falcon's intent stare and lie anymore. To him or to herself. It had been easier to blame Falcon than to admit Grant's weakness. Easier to blame Falcon than to admit her own culpability. Because, when all was said and done, she was responsible for Grant's death.

She had known he had a drinking problem. She should have watched him more closely. She should have gone with him.

Mara knew that sort of thinking was irrational. She had read enough since Grant's death, and learned enough in college psychology and sociology classes she had taken, to understand that Grant was responsible for his own behavior. But she couldn't shake her feelings of guilt. She should have been able to save Grant. And she had failed.

"It wasn't your fault," Falcon said in a quiet voice.

Mara's head jerked up, and she sought Falcon's eyes.

"He was an alcoholic. It was his problem. You aren't to blame."

"How did you know…"

"That you blame yourself?"

She nodded.

"Because I couldn't help thinking there was something I could have done to prevent Grant's death. Maybe if I'd noticed how much he was drinking…" Falcon thrust a hand through his hair. "Maybe if I hadn't left that twenty on the table... Maybe if I had stayed with him and made sure he didn't drive home drunk...."

"That's a lot of 'maybe's,'" Mara said.

"Don't I know it!"

"I feel the same way," Mara admitted. "I was his wife. I should have known better.

"After we left you that day, I begged him to call you up and meet somewhere, anywhere besides a bar. He said it was too late for that. He didn't know where to find you to make other arrangements. And he swore he wouldn't be tempted. He swore he wouldn't drink anything stronger than club soda. He had been sober for months before that night, so I believed him. I should have known he wouldn't be able to resist a drink when it was offered to him, especially since he wanted to keep his alcoholism a secret from you. I should have made arrangements to pick him up."

"What about Grant? Doesn't he deserve some of the blame for what happened?" Falcon asked. "Maybe more than *some*," he amended.

Mara thought of all the ugly things she had said to Falcon, all the accusations she had heaped on his shoulders. "I owe you an apology," she said. "Some of the things I said..."

"Apology accepted," Falcon said.

Mara felt awkward. All her animosity toward Falcon had been based on his irresponsible behavior at the bar that had resulted in Grant's death. Bereft of antagonism, she wasn't sure how to interact with him.

"Can we start over from here?" Falcon asked.

"Can you ever forgive me—"

"Can *you* forgive *me?*"

Mara exhaled a ragged sigh. "I'm so sorry, Falcon. For everything I said. I was horrible."

"You were," Falcon agreed.

When her eyes widened in surprise, his lips curled in a roguish grin.

"Sorry," he said. "I couldn't resist."

"Behave yourself," she chided.

They were teasing each other, Mara realized. It was a start. A very good start.

Mara knew there was one way she could show Falcon he was truly forgiven. He had told her what he wanted from her. And if she was going to be honest, she wanted it, too. She reached out, her hand palm up.

"I'm tired," she said. "Let's go to bed."

Falcon arched a brow, but threaded his fingers through hers. "My room?"

She nodded. She didn't want to take a chance on disturbing Susannah. Or on having to explain to Susannah why she was suddenly sleeping with Falcon.

Mara felt unaccountably shy. "This feels strange," she admitted.

"I know what you mean," Falcon said with a rueful twist of his mouth. "I've been wanting to make love to you for weeks. Ever since—"

"Don't remind me," she said, putting a hand to one rosy cheek. "I was an absolute wanton."

"I didn't have any complaints," Falcon said with a grin. When they got to the living room, he tugged on Mara's hand and she followed him around to the couch. He pulled her into his lap and sat there holding her.

She laid her head on his shoulder and let her hand slide around his waist.

"I've been needing this," Falcon said.

"And not the other?" Mara teased.

"Oh, I want that, too. But it can wait."

Mara felt a pleasant sense of expectation. She had been afraid, when she had agreed to give Falcon what he wanted, that he would rush her into bed. She was glad to see he was willing to take his time. She sighed.

"What was that for?" Falcon asked.

"I was just thinking about how badly I've misjudged you."

"So I'm not an irresponsible ne'er-do-well?"

"You did fritter away your fortune," she said.

Falcon stiffened. There was that. He might not have murdered her husband, but he still was not the sort of solid person she might have chosen for a husband. Especially after the bad experience she'd apparently had with Grant. His arms tightened around her. He had done nothing over the past ten weeks to prove he would be a better husband to her than Grant.

Except he had stopped drinking and carousing and spending money like it was water. That had to count for something. He hadn't missed any of those things, either, Falcon realized. Nothing mattered as much to him as Mara. And Susannah. There had to be a way to convince her they belonged together as a family.

"I hadn't planned ever to marry again," Mara admitted.

He didn't want to hear this.

Falcon pressed a kiss to Mara's nape to distract her and felt her shiver. He kissed his way up her throat to her ear and teased the delicate shell with his tongue.

Her hand slid down to the hard bulge in his jeans. She traced the length of him through the denim with her fingertips. He drew in a breath of air and held it.

"Mara," he whispered in her ear.

"Yes, Falcon."

"Sweetheart, let's go to bed."

She didn't answer with words, just rose and headed for his bedroom, leaving him to follow behind her.

Mara knew she was asking for heartache. The more attached she let herself get to Falcon, the harder it was going to be to leave him when Susannah was well. The truth was, she was terrified of getting involved with another man. Falcon hadn't gotten drunk during the past couple of months, but that didn't mean he wouldn't revert to his former behavior sometime in the future. Grant had been sober for months at a time during their eight-year marriage. She didn't yet trust Falcon not to become another Grant.

There was still the awful uncertainty about whether Susannah would survive. And there were no guarantees Falcon wouldn't be claimed by an accident working on the ranch, or driving in his car. How could she dare make any kind of commitment to another human being who might be taken from her?

But, oh, how she was tempted to throw caution to the winds. The more time she spent with Falcon, the more feelings she had for him. He was funny and generous and gave of himself wholeheartedly. He was compassionate and caring. He was a scintillating lover. Such a man would make some woman a very good husband. He just happened to be hers at the moment.

She knew it had been unfair to expect Falcon to remain celibate during their marriage. She owed him tonight, at least. But she wasn't promising more. She couldn't promise more.

Mara stood at the foot of Falcon's bed feeling

awkward, uncertain what to do next. Their previous coupling had been a frenzied thing, more an act of desperation than anything else. She had needed solace and forgetfulness, and Falcon had provided those things in lovemaking that was so passionate it had taken away all thought and left only feeling.

Mara didn't know what to expect now.

Falcon was also aware of how different their joining together was this time. He wanted to show Mara the tenderness he felt, as well as the ardent passion.

"May I undress you?" he asked.

Mara nodded, suddenly shy. Although she didn't know why that should be. He had seen everything before. But she realized, as Falcon slowly undressed her, admiring her with his eyes and his hands and his mouth, that there had been no time before to truly appreciate each other's bodies.

"I want to touch you, too," she told him.

He shook his head. "It would be too distracting. I wouldn't be able to enjoy what I'm doing."

As his mouth closed around a nipple and he suckled, she surrendered to his ministrations. His hands caressed her skin, and the roughness of his callused fingertips raised frissons of sensation wherever they coursed.

Falcon tried to tell Mara with his hands and his mouth how much he adored her, how much she meant to him, how necessary she was to his very life. He wished he was better with words so he could tell her how he felt. Of course the word *love* never entered his head. He couldn't think such thoughts when he knew she hated him. But she had forgiven him. She had no reason to hate him anymore.

Mara was amazed at how her body responded to the

touch of Falcon's hands, the feel of his lips on her skin. She experienced things Grant had never made her feel in eight years of marriage. How was she able to find so much pleasure in the arms of another man?

Mara stiffened imperceptibly, but Falcon was sensitive enough to her response to know something had gone wrong. She was no longer giving herself up to his caresses as she had been a moment before.

"Mara?" he murmured in her ear.

She gripped his waist tightly with both hands and for a moment he wasn't sure whether she was going to pull him close or shove him away. Then her arms slid around him.

"Hold me, Falcon," she said. "Make love to me."

"I will, darling. I am."

Falcon meant what he said. He was making love to Mara. But when he had her under him, and when he had brought her to satisfaction, he did not feel like shouting with joy. He felt like crying instead. Because he knew that what he was feeling for her was all one-sided. He had made love to her. She had submitted to having sex with him.

He tried not to let the despair overwhelm him. There was still time to win her love. There was still time for a happy ending.

He was torn, because as much as he wanted Susannah to be well, he knew her recovery heralded the end of his time with Mara. He would have to find a way, and soon, to convince Mara that she couldn't live without him.

Because he knew now he couldn't live without her.

CHAPTER SEVEN

OVER THE MONTHS he had been forced to stay close to the B-Bar because of his responsibilities toward Mara and Susannah, Falcon had made an astounding discovery.

He liked being a rancher.

His skin had browned in the Texas sunshine, and a fine spray of sun lines edged his blue eyes. His hands had been callused before, but now they were work-hardened. His body had been honed by hard physical labor until he was a creature of muscle and bone and sinew.

He had made hard decisions, and most of them had turned out right. A recent visit to his accountant had confirmed what he already knew. His attention to the details of running the B-Bar was making a difference. Things functioned more smoothly. There was less waste. And the profit margin on the sale of his cattle and horses was higher. To add sugar to the pie, one of the risky investments Aaron had advised him against making had started paying huge dividends.

"If you keep this up, you're going to be rich again," Aaron teased.

Only, it looked like he wasn't going need any of his reacquired wealth to pay medical bills.

Susannah was in remission.

The induction therapy had worked more quickly and efficiently than even Dr. Sortino had hoped. It had only taken ten weeks for Susannah's white blood cells to register normal.

Falcon was amazed at what a difference good health made to Susannah's behavior. She sparkled, she fizzed, she had an absolutely effervescent personality. She was tremendous fun to be with. Falcon teased Susannah that she was so bouncy she was liable to take off someday and go right through the ceiling.

"I don't want to sit still ever again," Susannah said.

"Not even to eat supper?" Falcon had asked.

"Well, maybe for that," she conceded, stuffing a man-sized spoonful of mashed potatoes into her mouth.

When Falcon looked to Mara, to share the humor of the situation, he found her brow furrowed, her eyes dark and despairing. Despite Susannah's good health, Mara didn't appear happy. Falcon dragged her away to the living room after supper to find out what was bothering her. He settled her on the couch and sat down on the coffee table across from her.

"What's wrong?" he asked.

"I want to expect the best, that Susannah is out of deep water," Mara said. "But I can't help dreading the worst, that her good health is a mirage that's going to disappear if I take my eyes off her."

"You have to live for today," Falcon chided.

"I might have expected you to say something like that," Mara snapped.

Falcon flushed. "Once upon a time, I might have deserved that comment," he said. "Not anymore. I'm as anxious as you are to plan for the future." *With you.* "But there's no planning ahead in Susannah's case. She's either going to stay well, or she isn't. There's nothing you, or I, or all the worrying in the world can do to change that."

Mara's eyes were bleak. "You're right," she said. "I know you are. I just can't seem to shake this feeling…"

"Then Susannah and I will just have to do it for you." Falcon set out then and there to put a smile on Mara's face. He enlisted Susannah's aid. "Hey, Susannah," he called to the little girl.

Susannah popped up in the living room like a jack-in-the-box. "What is it, Falcon?"

"I say your mom is more ticklish than you are. What do you think?"

"Ticklish?" Mara said warily. "Who said anything about ticklish?"

Falcon grinned and approached her, hands out-stretched, ready for serious tickling.

Mara jumped up and ran.

Falcon chased her.

When he caught her, he wrestled her to the floor and hog-tied her with his hands, like she was a new-born calf.

Mara was breathless, she was laughing so hard. "Falcon, stop! I just ate supper."

He leered at her like the villain in a melodrama. "She's all yours, Susannah. Have at her."

Susannah tickled her mother in the ribs and under the arms and behind her ears and on the soles of her feet.

Mara laughed so hard she howled. "Oh, stop," she cried through her giggles. "Oh, please, stop."

"What do you think, Susannah?" Falcon said. "Should we let her up?"

"I guess so."

"Of course, this experiment is only half over," Falcon

said, perusing Susannah with a speculative eye. "We haven't seen yet how ticklish *you* are."

Susannah screeched, "Help, Mommy!" but Falcon caught her before she had taken two steps and pulled her into his lap, where he began to tickle her mercilessly.

By that time Mara had recovered slightly, and she rescued her daughter. "I think there's someone here who needs a little of his own medicine," she said to Susannah.

"Yeah!" Susannah said as she launched herself against Falcon's chest.

Her attack knocked Falcon onto his back on the floor, and before he could recover, Mara had joined her daughter tickling his ribs.

Falcon was *very* ticklish.

He howled, he begged, he pleaded. "Please, no more!"

He could easily have escaped their attack at any time. He was bigger and stronger than both of them combined. But Falcon didn't want to escape. He loved being tickled by the two women in his life. He loved seeing their smiling faces and their eyes crinkled with laughter. Their chuckles and giggles and guffaws made him feel warm deep inside.

He let them tickle him until they were exhausted, until they fell onto the Navajo rug on either side of him and sighed with happy fatigue. He smoothed his fingers across the prickly crew cut that was all the hair Susannah had grown back so far. His other hand tangled in Mara's silky black tresses. He pulled them close on either side of him and closed his eyes and wished to be this happy the rest of his life.

But it was only a moment in time and not to be captured or held except in memory.

AFTER THAT NIGHT, however, Mara seemed to let go of some of her fear. She didn't offer a smile often, but Falcon treasured every one. As Susannah regained her strength, she and Mara began riding out to meet him when he was working on the range.

The first time it happened, Falcon reached for his shirt and dragged it on over his sweat-slick body. But Mara seemed to find the dark hair in the center of his bronzed chest, and the droplets of moisture that slid down his breastbone, absolutely mesmerizing. So the next time he just left his shirt off and basked in the pleasure of knowing she found pleasure in looking at him.

Not that either one of them would have acknowledged the sexual tension that sparked between them.

Mara was more determined than ever that she and Susannah were going to return to her house in Dallas. It was safer not to get any more involved with Falcon than she already was. The sooner she escaped his home—and the temptation to succumb to his charm—the better. Now that Susannah was in remission, it was just a matter of marking time, to make sure the cure had taken.

On the other hand, Falcon was encouraged by the fact Mara sought him out when he was working—even though she carted Susannah along as a chaperon whenever she visited him.

Today, Mara had brought along a picnic lunch. They headed for the trees at one of the stock ponds and fought the cattle for enough space to settle down on a blanket and eat.

Falcon knew he would never get a better chance to broach a subject that had been on his mind since his parents had asked when they were going to meet Mara and Susannah. After they had eaten, and while they were lazing around on the blanket in the shade, he casually mentioned his family's annual Labor Day picnic.

"Ever since we've been grown and out on our own, it's been a way for us to get together once a year and exchange news. I've never missed one."

"Can we come, too?" Susannah asked.

Falcon blessed the child for her eagerness. "I'd like it if you did," he said. "I know my mom and dad would like to meet you," he said to Susannah.

"They would?" Susannah said, eyes wide. "Why would they want to meet me?"

"Because you're their first granddaughter." Falcon glanced at Mara from the corner of his eye to see how she was reacting to his discussion with Susannah. Her lips were pursed, and she looked thoughtful.

"Can we go, Mommy?" Susannah asked.

"I don't know, sweetheart," Mara hedged.

"Please," Falcon said.

"Please," Susannah said.

"I suppose we can go—"

"Great!" Falcon said, cutting her off and preventing the qualifications he could see were coming.

"Great!" Susannah echoed, straddling Falcon's belly and jumping up and down.

Falcon rolled her off him so she was caught between him and Mara on the blanket. He had turned on his side, so he could see Mara's worried eyes.

"I'm not really your— And Susannah isn't actually your parents'—"

"Don't sweat it," Falcon said with a grin. "They'll love you. And they'll adore Susannah."

"Falcon, are you sure?"

"Do this one thing for me, please, Mara," he said.

"All right, Falcon," she agreed.

But he could see from the look on her face that she was anticipating disaster. He wasn't so sure she might not be right.

FALCON COULD FEEL his stomach knotting as they turned onto the road that led to Hawk's Way. The house he had grown up in was as impressive as ever, with its two-story antebellum facade, its railed porches and four towering white columns. The drive up to the house was lined with gorgeous magnolias, while the house itself was draped with majestic, moss-laden live oaks. It wasn't until he had returned home after leaving for the first time that he realized the house had been built more in the architectural style of the Deep South than the typical Texas dogtrot home.

"It's beautiful," Mara said. She turned to meet Falcon's gaze and said, "I envy you growing up here."

"It's just a house," Falcon said. But he had a lot of happy memories here.

When they stopped the car in front of the house, they were greeted by an ancient man with long gray braids who was wearing a buckskin vest decorated with feathers and beads. His copper skin was deeply etched with wrinkles.

"Is that a real Indian?" Susannah asked, awed and somewhat intimidated.

"That's Charlie One Horse. He's got a bit of Comanche blood running through his veins. But I promise he's friendly."

Charlie One Horse, the housekeeper who had brought up the Whitelaw kids—Falcon's father and his aunt and uncles—after Falcon's grandfather had died, raised his hand, palm outward, with great solemnity toward Susannah and said, "How."

"Cut it out, Charlie," Falcon said with a grin. "You're scaring my wife and daughter." Falcon was aware of the pride in his voice when he introduced his family to the man who had been like another grandfather to him.

The old man grinned, exposing a missing eyetooth. "Howdy," he said, nodding to Mara. He turned to face Susannah who had retreated behind Falcon. "Sorry if I scared you, Susannah. My name's Charlie. I've got some chocolate chip cookies in the kitchen that I baked myself."

"You can make cookies?" Susannah said with a startled laugh.

"Best damn—" he caught Falcon's warning look and quickly amended "—darn cookies you ever ate. Come on and I'll let you taste one."

Susannah looked up at Falcon for permission and reassurance, which he gave. "I can vouch for Charlie's cooking."

"Only one, Susannah. You don't want to spoil your supper," Mara admonished as Charlie whisked her daughter away.

She turned to Falcon and said, "I didn't think she'd go anywhere with a stranger."

"Charlie doesn't allow strangers in the house. Before he's through she'll be wearing feathers in her hair and war paint on her cheeks.

"Shall we go on inside?" Falcon said. "I'll come back for the luggage later."

To Mara's surprise, there was no greeting party waiting for them in the foyer of the house, nor even in the parlor where Falcon led her.

"This is beautiful," she said as she observed the scarred antiques of pine and oak—all polished to a bright shine—in the parlor. An ancient map was framed over the mantel. "Is this Hawk's Way?"

"Uh-huh." Falcon followed her to the stone fireplace so they could look at the map more closely. "It shows all the various borders of Hawk's Way from the time my ancestors settled here more than a hundred years ago until today."

"It's huge," Mara said.

"It's not as big as it once was," Falcon said. "When my elder brother, Zach, reached his majority, my father carved off a piece of the place and gave it to him for his own. Zach calls his portion Hawk's Pride." Falcon showed the lines that indicated the borders of Zach's ranch. "You can see there's still plenty left for my father."

Mara took several steps away from Falcon. She had been much too aware of the way his shoulder brushed against her back, aware of the feel of his moist breath on her neck, aware of *him*. "Where is everybody?" she asked.

Falcon grinned sheepishly. "We're hours earlier than I told my folks we'd be here. I wanted to avoid exactly the sort of crowd at the door you were expecting."

Mara smiled gratefully. "Thank you."

"Then you don't mind them not being here to greet you?"

"I'd give anything for a shower and a change of clothes before I have to meet anybody," she said earnestly.

"Your wish is my command." Falcon quickly retrieved Mara's suitcase, then returned and led her up

an elegant winding staircase that ended in a hall with
a row of doors on either side. "This is where the family usually stays when they come to visit. This will be
our room."

Mara stopped in her tracks. "Our room? I thought…"
Mara realized she hadn't been thinking at all. She had
slept with Falcon in his room at the ranch, even though
her clothes had remained upstairs in the room next to
Susannah's. Obviously that facade of separation was not
going to be maintained under his parents' roof. "We're
staying in the same room?"

Falcon looked at Mara from beneath hooded eyes.
"I have no intention of telling my parents the true facts
of our marriage. They wouldn't understand. There's a
king-size bed in this room, which is plenty big enough
for both of us to sleep in without running into each
other, if that's what you're worried about."

"Wouldn't it be better just to tell them the truth?"
Mara asked.

"Why? What purpose would it serve? My mother
would be hurt, and my father would be angry and disappointed. I haven't asked much from you, Mara. I'm
asking for this."

For a man who didn't ask much, he had asked quite
a lot lately. Mara had known there were pitfalls to this
trip, she just hadn't known what form they would take.
Now she did. Mara gave a gusty sigh. She supposed she
should have expected something like this.

"All right," she said. "I'll play along with your cha-
rade." Some imp forced her to add, "But I expect you
to stay on your own side of the bed."

Falcon grinned. "You can draw a line down the middle, if it'll make you feel any better. Come on in. This room has an adjoining bathroom, with a great shower."

Mara let him show her around the room, which she learned he had shared with Zach when the two boys were growing up. "His ranch is so close, he doesn't stay here overnight anymore," Falcon explained. "So I inherited the room."

"It's mine now," she said with a teasing smile. "Go away and let me get cleaned up."

"Are you sure you want me to leave?" Falcon asked with a lecherous grin, as he let her push him out the door.

"Absolutely," she said as she shut the door in his face.

Mara turned to peruse the room where Falcon had slept as a boy. The head and footboard of the huge bed were oak. There was an antique wardrobe along one wall and a copper-plated dry sink topped by a patterned pitcher and washbowl on another. An overstuffed corduroy chair with a rawhide footstool at its base was angled in the corner with an old brass standing lamp to provide light to read by. A small, round table held a selection of books secured between two bookends which, she was delighted to discover, were two pairs of pewter-dipped baby shoes. Falcon's and Zach's, perhaps?

The large, sheer-curtained window looked out over the front of the house, toward the long, magnolia-lined drive. There was no lawn to speak of. The prairie had been allowed to run wild.

Like the Three Whitelaw Brats, Mara thought.

It had never crossed her mind to consider how her marriage to Falcon would affect his family. Her mother had died when she was fifteen, and her father had been stomped by a bull he was trying to move from one pasture to another only a year after she married Grant. She had no brothers and sisters, no aunts and uncles.

Falcon, she was discovering, had more family than he could shake a stick at. Mother, father, sister and brother, aunt and uncles. That wasn't all. She had discovered on the drive here that he had numerous cousins who would all be arriving shortly.

Mara took a deep breath and let it out. Could she play the loving wife to Falcon in front of his family? She thought of everything Falcon had done for her and Susannah and knew she could. She need only remind herself of the laughter and joy Falcon had brought to a household that would otherwise have been mired in the somber reality of a life-threatening disease. Oh, yes, she could easily play the loving wife for him.

It occurred to Mara to wonder how much of the adoration in her eyes when she looked at Falcon would be an act.

CHAPTER EIGHT

MARA HAD JUST stepped out of the shower and wrapped a towel around herself when the bathroom door opened without a knock.

"Who—"

"Omigosh! I didn't know anyone was in here!"

Mara stared at the young woman frozen in the bathroom doorway. She had wide-set dark brown eyes that danced with mischief and long black hair tied up in a ponytail with a ruffle of bangs across her forehead. She looked about seventeen. But if what Mara suspected was true, this was Falcon's twice-engaged and never-married twenty-eight-year-old sister.

"I'm Callen, Falcon's sister," the young woman confirmed with a welcoming smile. "You must be Mara."

"I am," Mara said.

Mara didn't know where to go from there. Callen didn't look like she was planning to leave anytime soon, and Mara was too modest to continue drying off in front of her.

Mara realized Callen was giving her a very thorough perusal. "Were you looking for something in particular?" she asked archly.

Callen laughed. "I'm afraid I'm too nosy for my own good," she admitted. "You're not at all what I expected."

"Oh?"

"Falcon's women in the past were…different," she said diplomatically.

Mara knew she should leave it at that. But her curiosity was killing her. "How so?"

"You're very pretty, but Falcon always had an eye for truly beautiful women."

Mara swallowed hard. "I see."

"Obviously Falcon found other things to admire in you besides your looks." Her brown eyes twinkled and she said, "You must have a very fine mind."

Mara saw the teasing smile spread on Callen's face and felt the startled laughter spill from her own throat. It was the first genuine, spontaneous laugh she could remember in months and months. "You *are* incorrigible," she said when she could speak again. "I like you, Callen. Now, what was it that brought you in here?"

"Oh. I was looking for a razor to use on my legs."

"In Falcon's bathroom?"

She shrugged impishly. "He keeps a package of disposable razors in here somewhere."

Mara gestured the other woman into the bathroom. "Be my guest. While you're hunting, I'll just dry off and get dressed."

She closed Callen inside the bathroom and quickly toweled herself off and grabbed clean clothes from the suitcase Falcon had left by the bed. She was wearing no more than a bra and underwear when Callen reappeared.

Callen was holding up a blue plastic razor and had a smug look on her face. "See? What did I tell you?"

"That's great." Mara reached for a turquoise squaw skirt and pulled it on, then added a white peasant blouse and a concha belt. Finally she pulled on stockings and added a pair of short leather Western boots. She shoved her hand through her hair in an effort to shake out some of the wetness.

"Do you need a hair dryer?" Callen said.

"Oh, are you still here?"

Callen sat down on the bed. "I was just wondering."

"What?" Mara said resignedly. Evidently Callen wasn't leaving until she was good and ready.

"What do you see in my brother? I mean, what was it about him that made you decide to marry him?"

His health insurance, Mara thought. There was no way she was going to tell Callen that. "You are nosy, aren't you?" she said instead.

"Uh-huh. You're avoiding the question."

Mara searched quickly for some attributes that would make Falcon seem good husband material. "He's fun to be with. He's good with my daughter. He's patient. He's—"

"Falcon?" Callen interrupted. "Patient?"

Mara nodded. "Infinitely. He's gentle and—"

"Gentle?" Callen interrupted again.

"Gentle," Mara repeated firmly. "And of course," she said with a look of mischief, "he has a *very* fine mind."

Callen laughed.

Mara watched as Callen's glance slid to the bedroom doorway. "Oh, hi, Falcon. How long have you been there?" she asked.

"Long enough," he said with a grin.

Mara turned beet-red. She fluffed her hair over her face and eyes to hide her embarrassment.

"I can see I'm de trop," Callen said as she looked from Falcon to Mara and back again. "See you at supper tonight, Mara." She gave Falcon a sucker punch in the stomach as she scooted past him. "You too, Falcon."

A moment later she was gone.

Falcon closed the door, shutting himself inside with Mara. "Well, well," he said. "I had no idea I was such a good husband."

"I had to tell her something," Mara said as she flung her hair back off her face. Her eyes flashed dangerously. "I thought you wanted us to appear a happily married couple to your family."

"I did. I do," he said soothingly. "It's all right, Mara. You lied in a good cause."

"I wasn't lying," she said quietly.

"What?"

"You heard me," she said, meeting his gaze. "You are gentle and patient and kinder than Susannah and I have any right to expect."

He noticed she didn't repeat her boast about his "fine mind," which he had easily recognized for the euphemism it was. The proof was in the way her breasts stood peaked beneath her blouse, the way her cheeks flushed, the way her eyes observed him, dilated with passion.

He didn't wait for an invitation. He took the several steps that separated them and pulled her onto her feet. He slid one arm around and cupped her buttocks, pulling her tight against him. The other hand he tangled in her wet hair, drawing her close for his kiss.

He was gentle. Achingly gentle, even though what he wanted to do was ravage her mouth. And she responded, reluctantly at first, and then ardently, so he started to lose control. He thrust against her, letting her feel his need. He was having trouble drawing breath, but he didn't want the kiss to end.

There was one sharp knock and the door opened.

"Falcon, I—"

"Dad," Falcon managed to gasp. He kept Mara close, to hide the state of arousal they were both in.

"Doesn't anybody in this house believe in privacy?" Mara muttered with asperity.

Falcon saw the rueful twist of his father's lips. "Sorry for interrupting. Your mother wants to meet Mara. And Susannah is asking where her mother is."

"Is she all right?" Mara asked anxiously, meeting her father-in-law's eyes for the first time.

She would have pulled from Falcon's embrace, but he kept her where she was with the slight pressure of his hand on her spine.

"She's fine," Garth reassured Mara. He focused on Falcon when he said, "We'll be waiting for you downstairs when you're finished with what you're doing."

Falcon flushed. He felt like a teenager caught necking on the front porch. "We'll be down in a minute, Dad."

When his father closed the door, he released Mara. She closed her eyes and groaned. "I have never been so embarrassed in my entire life. What must your father be thinking?"

"Exactly what we want him to think," Falcon said. "That we're a happily married couple."

"When you kissed me, did you know he was coming up here to get us?" Mara asked.

"Would it matter if I did?" Falcon said.

Mara sighed. "No, I suppose not." She had wanted to believe he found her desirable. But after what Callen had told her about his taste in women, she must be a very poor second choice. However, she had known for a long time she couldn't hold a man's attention for long. Hadn't Grant taught her that lesson? They had been married only six months when he started flirting with other women. It had been all of a year before she saw signs that he had taken another woman to bed.

Mara hissed in a breath of air. She hadn't thought for a long time about that night. About the humiliation she had felt when she had confronted Grant, expecting denial and getting none.

"A man needs a woman now and then," Grant had said.

"And what am I?" she had cried, her heart breaking in two.

"You're my wife," he said. "You don't have to worry about me leaving you, sweetheart. But there are itches I have that you can't scratch."

Mara's face had bleached white at the insult. *She wasn't enough woman for the man in her life.*

She had hidden her shame deep. She had been a good wife and mother, and Grant had praised her for those attributes. And he had come to her bed. But that hadn't stopped his trysts with other women. She had known the fault was somehow hers, not his. That if she was just more of a woman, he wouldn't be straying from her side.

Suddenly all those feelings of inadequacy came flooding back. All because her relationship with Falcon was changing.

When she had first married Falcon, she hadn't been worried about the issues that had caused such trouble in her marriage with Grant, because nothing about her marriage to Falcon was real. The normal expectations in such a relationship hadn't existed. Now she feared that history was going to repeat itself. Not that she had seen any signs of Falcon flirting, but if her experience with Grant was any guide, it was bound to happen eventually.

Only, it shouldn't matter to her what Falcon did, because their marriage was only a matter of convenience. Even if her feelings toward him were not as nonexistent as she could wish.

"Mara?"

Falcon had noticed Mara's pale features, the tense set of her shoulders, the way she worried her lower lip with her teeth.

"It's going to be all right. My parents won't eat you," he teased. "I promise they're going to like you."

"Even though I'm not like the women you've brought home before?"

"I've never brought a woman here before," Falcon said.

"Oh. But Callen told me about the kind of women you're usually attracted to," Mara said. "I'm not anything like them."

"Callen's too outspoken for her own good."

"I'm glad she told me. At least now I have no illusions about our relationship."

Falcon's eyes narrowed suspiciously. "What does that mean?"

"It means I know I'm not the kind of woman you would have freely chosen for a wife, and that as soon as it's possible, I'm going to release you from this marriage."

"Aw, hell," Falcon said, tunneling all ten fingers into his hair. "Look, Mara, the kind of woman a man carouses with and the kind of woman he marries are two different animals."

"You don't have to tell me that," Mara said quietly. "Grant explained the situation very thoroughly."

"What do you mean?"

Mara lowered her eyes so Falcon couldn't see what she was feeling. "I mean he explained how I was a good wife and mother, but he needed other women for…for his other needs."

"That bastard."

Falcon crossed to Mara and grabbed her by the shoulders and gave her a little shake. "Look at me," he commanded. When she had lifted her lids to reveal dark, wounded blue eyes he said, "I'm not Grant."

"You could be like him," she whispered. "I've seen you drunk. And that woman who called you—"

"Is that what you've been afraid of? That I'll turn out to be an alcoholic like Grant? Or a womanizer? I'm nothing like Grant! Haven't you learned that by now?"

"You drink—"

"A whiskey now and then," he interrupted. "Alcoholism is a *disease*," he told Mara furiously. "And I don't have it!"

"What about Felicia?"

"What about her?"

"Why would she think she could call and invite you for a weekend on the town if you hadn't encouraged her?"

"Felicia was a flirt of mine," he conceded, "*when I was single*. I haven't even looked cross-eyed at another woman since I married you."

"But you must have needs—I haven't— Grant always said—"

"I'm not Grant!" Falcon interrupted in a voice hoarse with rage. "You're the woman I want in my bed, the *only woman!*"

"But—"

"Don't say any more, Mara," he warned. "I'm leaving. Come down when you're ready. I'd give the whole game away if my parents saw us together right now."

He turned and marched to the door, closing it with a heavy thunk behind him.

Mara was stunned by Falcon's outburst. Did she dare believe him? But what reason would he have to lie? And if he wasn't lying, what was she going to do about it? Did she dare trust him not to hurt her as Grant had? Did she dare let herself begin to love him?

She had to put such thoughts aside, at least for the moment. There was a job to do. She had to go downstairs and play the role of loving and contented wife for Falcon's family.

It was easier than she had expected it to be.

In the first place, Falcon's mother, Candy, was a dear. Mara could see how the Three Whitelaw Brats had gotten so spoiled. Candy was an indulgent and adoring mother, and she had her husband twisted around her little finger. Mara was amused at the solicitous treatment the tall, rugged cowboy gave his wife.

She had trouble keeping all Falcon's relatives straight. Honey and Jesse Whitelaw were there with Honey's two older boys from a previous marriage, Jack and Jonathan, and their daughter, Tess. Falcon's Aunt Tate was there with her husband, Adam Philips, and their two grown daughters, Victoria and Elizabeth. His uncle Faron Whitelaw and his uncle's wife, Belinda, had come with their two adopted teenage sons, Rock and Drew. It was a boisterous, motley and exceedingly noisy crowd.

Mara's main concern was that Susannah not get tired out. She watched her daughter carefully, but Susannah basked in all the attention she got from her cousins-by-marriage. Toward the end of the evening, after a supper that culminated in a food fight in the kitchen while the dishes were being washed, Mara separated her daughter from Rock and Drew and started upstairs with her.

"Come back when you've gotten her settled," Falcon's mother said. "We'll be gathered in the parlor in front of the fire."

Mara couldn't find a polite way to refuse. "All right."

Susannah was so keyed up, Mara wasn't sure she would ever get her settled. Her daughter's hazel eyes were feverishly bright and her cheeks were flushed. Mara pressed her hand against Susannah's forehead, fearing the worst.

Susannah shoved it away. "I'm fine, Mommy. Don't worry about me."

Mara forced herself to smile. "That's what mothers do best," she quipped.

Susannah bounced onto the bed and shoved her feet under the covers. "I can't wait until tomorrow," she said. "Drew said he'll take me riding. They have lots of ponies here! Can you believe it?"

"Now, Susannah, I don't know—"

"Please, Mommy. You have to let me go! Everyone's going!"

"I haven't been invited."

"It's just for kids. No grown-ups allowed."

At that moment Falcon stuck his head in the door. Susannah's room was across the hall from theirs, and would eventually be occupied by several other children. "Everything all right in here?"

"Falcon, tell Mommy it's all right for me to go riding tomorrow."

Falcon turned to Mara and solemnly repeated, "It's all right for me to go riding tomorrow."

"Not *you!*" Susannah said with a laugh. *"Me!"*

"Wasn't that what I said?" Falcon asked.

Susannah snorted in disgust. "Mommmmy! I want to go!"

"It really will be safe," Falcon reassured Mara. "The older boys and girls will take care of the younger ones."

Mara didn't have the heart to refuse Susannah. She pursed her lips ruefully. She had no business judging Candy's indulgent behavior toward her children. Look how lenient she was with her daughter!

"All right," Mara conceded. "You can go."

"Yippeee!"

"If you get a good night's sleep," Mara qualified.

Susannah pulled the covers up under her arms. "Turn out the light, Mommy, quick. I'm ready to go to sleep now."

Mara kissed her daughter on the forehead, using the opportunity to reassure herself that Susannah didn't have a fever. To her surprise, Susannah felt a little warm. "Susannah, are you feeling all right?" Mara asked.

"I'm fine, Mommy. Really, truly I am!"

Falcon crossed past Mara and pressed his own kiss to Susannah's brow. "Good night, pumpkin," he said as he turned out the lamp beside the bed.

He had left the door open, and he and Mara headed for the stream of light from the hallway. He closed the door behind them.

"I hope the other kids don't wake her up when they come to bed," Mara said. "She needs her rest."

"I'm sure they'll be quiet," Falcon said.

"As a herd of buffalo," Mara said with a sideways glance at Falcon.

He grinned. "You're probably right, but the only other choice was to put Mara in with us. I thought she would have more fun with the other kids."

And they would have the privacy that a newly wedded couple should want. He didn't mention that to Mara. She had already coped with enough friendly badgering from his family this evening to know he was right.

"How are you holding up?" he asked her as they headed back down the stairs. "My family can be a little overwhelming."

Mara shot him an arch look. "A *little* overwhelming?"

He grinned. "All right. They're a riot looking for a place to happen." He put a hand on the back of her neck and kneaded muscles that were tight with strain.

Mara groaned. "Lord, that feels so good!"

"Want to come back upstairs with me now? I give a killer back rub." And he was dying to give her one.

Mara hesitated, then shook her head. "I promised your mother I'd come back downstairs."

Falcon turned her to face him. He settled both hands on her shoulders and began to massage the tenseness he found there. He had the satisfaction of hearing Mara moan and watched as her eyes drifted closed in pleasure. "She'll understand if we both disappear," he murmured in her ear.

Excitement shivered down Mara's spine at Falcon's invitation. She was tempted! So tempted. She opened her eyes and saw him looking down at her, his eyes hooded, his nostrils flared. She knew what they would end up doing if she followed him up the stairs. In his parents' house. With his whole family waiting for them in the parlor.

"I don't want everyone leering at me tomorrow morning."

"They wouldn't dare—" Falcon grimaced. They

would. He and Mara would be teased mercilessly. "You're right," he said, starting her back down the stairs. "Let's go join the multitudes."

Falcon seated Mara on the floor in front of the fire and settled himself behind her. His arms slid around her hips, and he pulled her close. They had arrived just in time to hear Candy finishing the story of how she and Garth had met and fallen in love, complete with fairy-tale ending.

"That's the most outrageous pack of bullsh—"

"Zach!" Candy admonished. "Keep your cynicism to yourself."

"I want to hear the story of how Falcon and Mara met," Callen said.

Mara stiffened. She hadn't expected this. She shot a frightened look over her shoulder at Falcon, who shook his head once, very slightly, to let her know there was no escape. To her relief, he was the one who undertook the task.

"It's really very simple," he said. "I was walking down the street in Dallas when I spied this absolutely stunning woman on the corner."

"You're kidding, right?" Callen challenged.

Falcon shook his head. "That's exactly the way it happened. Only, the next thing I saw was her daughter, and then a man joined her," he recalled.

A hush had fallen on the crowd.

"Who was the man?" Callen asked.

"He was an old friend of mine, a football teammate from Tech," Falcon said. "He was Mara's husband, Grant Ainsworth."

"I remember him," Garth said. "I met him in the locker room after one of your games."

What happened to him?

The silence was pregnant. Falcon said very matter-of-factly, "Grant was killed in a car accident. It was a year later before I saw Mara again, but I knew I couldn't let her walk out of my life again. I asked her to marry me, and she said yes."

"How romantic," Candy said with a sigh. "True love conquers all."

Falcon realized Mara was squeezing his hand so tightly her fingernails were cutting into his skin. He made himself smile at her. "I've been doubly blessed," he continued. "I got a daughter in the bargain."

"And a pretty little minx she is," Charlie One Horse contributed.

"Falcon told us Susannah has been sick," Candy said to Mara. "But she seems so well now."

"She has—had—leukemia. It's in remission."

"Thank God for that," Candy said.

The discussion shifted to Callen, and the fact that for the first time in years she didn't have a man at her side.

"And thank God for that!" Mara heard Garth mutter.

Mara watched Candy put her fingers over his mouth to shut him up and hiss, "Garth! Be good."

The evening wound to a pleasant close, as couples settled back together to watch the fire burn and to drink a glass of whiskey or brandy or some sweet liqueur. No wine drinkers here, Mara thought with an inner smile. But then, this was the frontier, where things were harder, the elements harsher and life was lived to the fullest.

She caught herself yawning and looked quickly to see if anyone had noticed. To her chagrin, Falcon's father was staring right at her.

"Time for bed," he announced.

She started to say, "I'm not tired" and realized she was. Falcon had to haul her to her feet. Her knees felt like jelly.

"Come on, sleepyhead," he said. "We've got a big day tomorrow."

"We do?" Mara said. This day had seemed quite big enough.

"Picnic. Football. Frisbee. Croquet. We've got games to play."

Mara snickered softly. "That we have, Mr. Whitelaw. Games no one else even knows about."

Falcon swatted her on the fanny. "Save the cynicism," he said. "I get enough of that when Zach's around."

Mara undressed in the bathroom and put on a thick terry-cloth robe before she ventured into the bedroom. To her relief, Falcon was already under the covers. To her chagrin, his bronzed shoulders were bare.

She narrowed her eyes suspiciously. "Are you wearing anything under those sheets?" she asked.

"Pajama bottoms," he said.

"Oh. Well. That's okay."

"I'll be glad to take them off," he volunteered.

"Thanks, but no thanks." Mara turned off the light before dropping her robe beside the bed and slipping under the covers. She was aware that she wasn't alone in the king-size bed. It seemed to have shrunk. She could hear Falcon breathing, even believed she could feel the heat of his body.

"Good night, Mara."

"Good night, Falcon."

Mara stared at the ceiling, not the least bit tired.

Ten minutes later she said, "Falcon? Are you awake?"

"I am now."

"I like your family."

"They like you, too."

Mara shivered. But she wasn't the least bit cold. "Falcon?" she whispered.

"Why are you whispering?" he whispered back.

"I don't know," Mara whispered. "I don't want to wake anyone."

"I'm the only one in here," Falcon said, "and I'm already awake. Is there something you wanted to say to me, Mara?"

Mara heard the irritation in his voice and wondered what had caused it. "I guess not."

Falcon flipped the light on. He sat up and the sheet dropped to his hips. Mara's eyes shot to the expanse of bare flesh he revealed.

"What is it?" he demanded. "I'm awake, and you have my full attention."

"I was just wondering if you'd still be willing to give me that back rub."

"Why didn't you just say so? I'd be glad to." Falcon scooted over and ordered, "Turn over onto your stomach."

Mara did as she was told. Falcon quickly straddled her at the waist and his hands came down firm and sure across her shoulders and began to massage the sore muscles there.

"How's that?" he asked.

"Mmmm," she murmured.

"How about getting this nightgown out of the way?" He pulled the thin straps of her silk gown off her shoulders and shoved the garment down below her waist, freeing her arms. "There," he said with satisfaction.

Mara had a sudden realization of what she had done. What she didn't understand was why she had done it. She knew where this encounter was heading, and she had to make up her mind quickly whether she was going to let Falcon make love to her.

There was no doubt he was ready and willing.

His hands caressed as well as massaged, and as her languor increased she knew her resistance was decreasing.

"Falcon?"

"Yes, love?"

Mara shivered again as he murmured the endearment against her ear.

"Would you like a massage when you're finished doing me?"

Falcon chuckled. "I would love one," he said. "Just as soon as I finish doing you."

She gasped as he slid his hands beneath her and cupped her breasts, teasing the nipples into tight buds with his fingers. "Falcon?" she whispered.

"Why are you whispering again?" he whispered.

"Because I haven't got the breath to talk," she admitted.

For a long time, neither of them said anything. They spoke with their hands, with their mouths and with their eyes.

When Mara drifted to sleep, she was snuggled tightly in Falcon's embrace. She refused to question the right or wrong of what she had done. For now, he was her husband, and he wanted her. And she loved being with him. Maybe she had heard one too many fairy tales this evening.

Tomorrow was soon enough to let reality creep back in.

CHAPTER NINE

A SINGLE RIDER galloped hell-bent-for-leather toward the Whitelaw mansion. He leapt from his horse before it had even stopped on its haunches and raced toward the crowd gathered under the live oaks in back of the house.

"Falcon!" Drew called. "Falcon!"

"I'm here, Drew," Falcon said, racing toward the teenager. "What's wrong?"

Mara was sitting at a picnic table with several of the other wives. When she heard Drew's cry she jumped up and ran toward him. "What's wrong?" she repeated only a moment after Falcon.

"It's Susannah," Drew said, his eyes huge and worried. "She's hurt. She fell off her horse."

"Oh, no!" Mara cried. "How bad is it?"

Falcon clutched Mara hard around the shoulders to keep her from seizing Drew's shirt and shaking him. "How is she?" he asked Drew.

"I couldn't tell," Drew confessed. "I left her with the others and rode back to get help. She seemed fine when we started out. We asked her if she could lope, and she said yes."

"She's a good rider," Falcon confirmed.

"But she fell off!" Drew said. "We weren't even going very fast."

"I'm sure you weren't," Falcon consoled the inconsolable boy. Falcon gave Mara a push toward his mother's already-outstretched arms and said, "Keep her here."

"I want to go with you!" Mara said fiercely.

"Wait here," Falcon replied, his voice like granite. "I'll bring her back to you. Call the family doctor and make sure he's here when I get back," Falcon told his father.

Garth nodded.

Mara let Candy lead her into the house. To her relief, Falcon's mother didn't ply her with platitudes like, "I'm sure she'll be all right." They sat together in silence in the kitchen, each with a cup of hot coffee in front of her that neither touched.

It seemed ages before Falcon returned. He had Susannah in his arms.

"She wasn't hurt by the fall," he said quickly, before Mara had a chance to be frightened by her daughter's ashen complexion. "At least, not more than a few scratches."

"Then what's wrong with her?" Mara demanded.

Falcon's blue eyes were bleak as a winter day. "She has a fever. And her lymph nodes are swollen."

Mara felt a chill slide down her arms. "No. No!"

"I think she must have fainted. That's why she fell from her horse."

"This can't be happening," Mara pleaded. "Please, God, nooooo!" she wailed.

"What is it?" Candy asked her son.

Falcon's lips were pressed flat to keep them from trembling. He wasn't sure he could speak past the constriction in his throat. "I think the leukemia is back."

Falcon could say one thing for his family, they rallied around in times of trouble. Zach flew the three of them back to Dallas in his private jet, while Callen promised to drive their car home for them. Garth phoned Children's Hospital to tell them to expect Susannah. Candy volunteered to pack their clothes and send them along with Callen.

The rest of Falcon's cousins and aunt and uncles promised to pray.

Falcon only managed to keep Zach from staying with them at the hospital by turning on his brother like a rabid dog. He bared his teeth ferociously. "Leave us be. We can handle this better alone."

What he really meant was *I don't want you to see me fall to pieces.* He felt like he was already in pieces. Mara wasn't in much better shape. He wanted to be alone with her somewhere in a dark place and put his arms around her and lay his head on her shoulder and comfort her and be comforted.

Zach settled a succoring hand on Falcon's shoulder, which was tensed hard as stone. "You don't have to go through this alone."

"Don't stay," Falcon said starkly. His eyes glittered with unshed tears. His throat had a huge lump in it. If his brother was there, if he had someone to lean on, he might break down completely. If he was alone with Mara, he would have to be strong for her. He would be able to stay in control.

Zach tightened his grip momentarily, then let go. "Call us," he said. "We want to know how Susannah is doing."

Falcon nodded. He couldn't manage any more speech.

Zach swept Mara up in a tight embrace, as though to

lend her strength, then let her go. "She'll be all right," he whispered in her ear.

Mara whimpered, the sound of a suffering animal. "Thank you, Zach," she grated out. "I needed to hear that."

Even if she knew it wasn't necessarily true.

When they were alone together, neither Mara nor Falcon seemed to be able to reach out to the other. They sat down in chairs next to each other in the hospital waiting room, but they didn't touch.

At long last, Falcon broke the silence. "Even if it is the leukemia back again, that doesn't mean she won't eventually get well," he said, as though to convince himself.

"But she'll have to start all over with those awful treatments," Mara said in a low voice. "She'll be sick again. And lose the hair she was so pleased to be growing back."

Mara reached out a hand, and Falcon grasped it. They clung to each other in a way people do when they know there is strength and fortitude to be found in the other grasp. Mara raised her eyes and met Falcon's steady gaze. It gave her courage to face whatever was to come.

He isn't like Grant. He's nothing at all like Grant.

The revelation came to Mara in those few seconds like a star bursting and shedding great light. Grant had never been there for her when she needed him. He had never offered her strength. He had never been a rock to which she could cling in times of trouble.

Falcon hadn't reached for a bottle in times of trouble, nor sought out another woman. He had reached for her. He had come to her.

That wasn't the end of her epiphany.

Why, I love him, she marveled. Mara stared at Falcon as though seeing him for the first time. How had he come to mean so much to her? When had she started caring more for his pain than for her own? When had she started wanting him to love her back?

Her thoughts were cut off by the arrival of Dr. Sortino. Mara knew before he said a word that the prognosis was not good. She rose to her feet, still gripping Falcon's hand, and waited to hear what the doctor had to say.

"The leukemia is back."

Four words. Four frightening words.

Mara bit her lip to keep from crying. She pressed her face to Falcon's chest as though to escape what was happening.

There was no escape.

"We've got her stabilized," Dr. Sortino said. "We'll start the therapy again within the next few days. Don't despair," he said. "Children often have a relapse and then recover completely."

Mara lifted her head and stared at him with liquid eyes. "But some don't," she challenged.

"Some don't," he conceded reluctantly. "We'll have to wait and see."

"Can we see her?" Falcon asked.

"You can look in on her. She's sleeping now. The nurse will show you to her room."

He left then, without saying more. But Mara had heard quite enough.

"Hold me," she said to Falcon. "Hold me."

Falcon needed to feel the warmth of Mara in his arms. Because he was cold. So cold.

"She'll be all right," he told Mara. "She has to be."

But when they saw Susannah lying in the hospital bed, her face almost as white as the sheets, neither could manage an optimistic word. They grasped hands and held on.

"Your pony is waiting for you to get well," Falcon whispered to the sleeping girl. "And your mommy needs some more tickling," he said. "And I need you home to bounce around the house," he said in a choked voice.

He turned to Mara, and this time she took him in her arms and comforted him. His powerful body shook with silent sobs that were all the more intense because he fought them, even as they escaped.

Mara reached out a hand and touched her daughter's cheek. "Good night, Susannah," she whispered. Then, to Falcon, "Let's go home."

There was no question of staying in separate bedrooms. Falcon never let go of Mara's hand. He led her to his room and silently undressed her then undressed himself. He laid her on the bed and joined her there, twining their bodies together.

"I need you," he said.

Mara knew what he was asking. She gave herself to him, gave him the comfort and reassurance and love he needed, and took it in return. It was a gentle joining of two bruised souls who sought solace in each other's bodies.

Mara's heart swelled with love, and she gave Falcon a part of herself that she had kept hidden somewhere deep inside for long years—ever since Grant had told her she was not enough woman for him. For Falcon she could be more, was more, because he sought more from her.

Falcon lay beside Mara and realized that he felt far more than physical satisfaction. There had been a difference in their lovemaking this time, subtle but detectable.

Mara had held nothing back. She had been lightning and fire in his arms, and he had found himself burning in her embrace. He knew now that what he felt for her was more than lust, or mere affection, or even admiration. He loved her, body and heart and soul.

He wanted to say the words. He needed to say them.

I love you, Mara. I want to spend my life loving you. I want you to have my children. Susannah needs brothers and sisters to play with. I'll make you both happy. I promise it.

But he didn't say any of those things.

She was already asleep.

DURING SUSANNAH'S SECOND bout of induction therapy, any discussion of Falcon's and Mara's life together, their future, was held in abeyance. It was as though Susannah was the glue that held them together. Neither was willing to contemplate what form their relationship would take if something should happen and she should disappear from their lives. It might be too painful to remain together as a couple, because each would see in the other's anguished eyes a constant reminder of what they had lost.

In spite of that, their love grew. It happened in small ways, over many days.

They shared duties taking care of Susannah, relieving each other when one had reached the end of his patience with the sick child's petulant whining on the one hand, or was unable to endure another moment of the little girl's tremendous persistence in the face of her debilitating illness on the other.

They spent their nights together making love. Neither spoke the words each privately thought. They told each other of their love in the only way they were allowed. Because there was no question of committing themselves to each other until—unless—Susannah recovered.

Mara made a point of getting up each morning with the sunrise, as Falcon did, and making him breakfast.

"I can do this myself," he said. "I know you're tired."

She traced the shadows under his eyes with a gentle hand. "And you're not?"

"Some sex goddess keeps me up half the night with her demands on my body," he teased.

"Remind the sex goddess you have to work in the morning, and I'm sure she'll leave you alone," Mara replied pertly.

Falcon pulled her into his arms and showered her face with kisses. "I'd rather miss the sleep," he said, snuggling his face against her hair.

Mara felt loved and cherished and appreciated.

"Get going, you've got work to do," she said as she shoved him out the kitchen door.

Sometimes, late at night, after he had made sweet love to Mara and she had fallen asleep, Falcon returned to his office. He wanted Mara to know she would be getting a husband who was financially responsible if she agreed to extend their marriage beyond its current artificial structure. He was planning for the future, something that hadn't interested or concerned him before Mara came into his life.

One night Mara awoke and found herself alone. She sought Falcon out and found him in his office.

"What are you doing here in the middle of the night?" she chided. "You need your sleep."

He was sitting in the swivel chair in front of his desk,

and he circled it to face her. Because it had become second nature to find comfort in his arms, she settled herself in his lap and twined her fingers in his hair, pulling his face down to hers for a tender kiss.

"Now," she murmured against lips that were warm and wet against her own, "tell me what's going on. Are we in financial trouble? Do I need to go back to work as a short-order cook?"

"No," he said, perhaps too emphatically. "The whole reason I'm spending time at this desk is to secure our future together in a way that will leave you free to be home with Susannah." *And any other children we have.*

Falcon hesitated, aware he had crossed an invisible line. When Mara gave him no encouragement, he backed up again, into neutral ground. "I'm just making sure the ranch is run well and reinvesting what money I have in less risky ventures."

"You're a man who needs risk in his life," Mara said in a quiet voice.

"Not this kind," Falcon objected.

"Then let me see if I can provide another kind," Mara said, as she bit the lobe of his ear. Her hand slid across his naked chest and down toward the pajama bottoms he wore in case he had to check on Susannah during the night. He was already hard by the time her hand got to him.

"Mara," he warned. "It's nearly dawn. I have to get dressed and go to work in an hour."

"We've got a whole hour? That should be enough time for what I have in mind."

A moment later she was on her back on the floor of his office, and he was inside her. Their loving was stormy and tempestuous, full of risk, and she climaxed twice before he was finished and lowered himself, chest heaving, to the carpet beside her.

Falcon groaned. "I'm sorry, Mara. I didn't mean to be so rough."

She took one look at the love bite she had left on his shoulder and laughed. "I'm sorry, Falcon. I didn't mean to be so rough, either."

ONCE, DURING THOSE weeks and months while their lives were on hold, Mara took herself back to the house she had bought because of its location on a quiet, tree-lined street where children played. She was amazed to see it was just an ordinary house. There was nothing particularly special about it. Yet, keeping this home was one of the reasons she had been willing to marry Falcon Whitelaw.

She let herself in and wandered through the house. It felt empty, despite the furnished rooms. She wondered what it was that had made this place seem so much a necessary part of her life. And realized it wasn't the house, but what it had represented. Permanence. A place of belonging where memories could be made.

This house wasn't a home. A home was where people lived and loved. Home was where Falcon and Susannah were. Home was the B-Bar Ranch.

Mara threw herself on the bed in her room and wept. For all the might-have-beens with Grant. What would their life have been like if only…? There, in the house where she had sought the happiness she had been denied in her marriage with Grant, she let go of the past. Her first love was dead and buried. He no longer had the power to hurt her.

The only question now was whether she had the

courage to put aside her past fears and reach out and grasp what she wanted. It meant taking risks. She might be hurt again. She might not live happily ever after. It all came down to a matter of trust.

Did she trust Falcon Whitelaw—who less than a year past had been an irresponsible, carousing, ne'er-do-well—to offer her a future filled with happiness? Or would a lifetime with him be filled with trials and tribulation? Had he merely been on his best behavior for the months they had spent together? Would he revert to form once Susannah was well?

Mara sat herself down on the edge of the bed and dropped her head into her hand. There were no guarantees. She was going to have to take a chance. She was going to have to make up her mind one way or the other. Because she knew that the moment Susannah was out of danger—and she *would* be someday soon—Falcon was going to starting asking questions and demanding answers about their relationship.

And she would have to answer yes or no.

CHAPTER TEN

"HI, MOM. I'M AT the hospital."

"Falcon? What is it? Is it bad news?"

"She's in remission."

"That's wonderful, Falcon!" his mother said. "Oh, I'm so glad for all of you!"

"Tell Dad for me, and Zach and Callen." Falcon didn't think he could handle talking to all of them. He was having trouble keeping his voice steady as it was.

"How's Mara?" Candy asked.

"She's fine."

"When will we see you again?" Candy asked.

"I don't know, Mom. Everything is pretty hectic right now. I'll call you again when things are more settled. Okay? I've got to go now."

"Goodbye, Falcon. Take care of yourself. Give our love to Mara and Susannah."

When things are more settled. Falcon wasn't sure how soon that would be. Certainly not until he had an answer from Mara about whether or not she was willing to end their sham marriage and start a real one. Although, since the day of Susannah's relapse, there had been nothing halfway about Falcon's commitment to his wife. Mara had given him hope that she felt the same way he did, but until the words were spoken, nothing was *settled*.

It had taken the full amount of time—Christmas

had come and gone—for the induction therapy to work a second time. Even Susannah welcomed the "backstick" that had resulted in the news that she was in remission again.

"We're going to take things a little slower this time," Mara gently admonished her daughter as they rode home from the hospital. "No more bouncing off the walls."

Falcon winked at the little girl. "You'll have to settle for bouncing on the beds," he teased.

Mara shot Falcon a warning look. She had almost lost Susannah the last time. She wasn't taking any chances with her daughter's health now that she had been given a second lease on life.

Falcon had different ideas about what was appropriate behavior for Susannah's present state of health, and during the next few weeks, the two adults were constantly at loggerheads over what Susannah could and could not do.

"You can't keep Susannah wrapped up in cotton batting," Falcon argued.

"I can, and I will!" Mara retorted.

"She's a little girl. She needs to run and play."

"What if she gets sick again?" Mara said, her heart in throat.

Falcon pulled her into his arms and rocked her back and forth. "We'll make sure she rests, but she has to be allowed to live as normal a life as she can, Mara."

Mara knew Falcon was right. She was being overprotective. "But I'm so scared," she admitted in a small voice.

"I'm here," he said. "I'll watch over you both," he promised.

It was as close to a declaration of love as he had ever

come. He wanted to go further. He wanted to say the rest. But Mara stopped him.

"I know you'll take care of us," she said. "But I wonder sometimes if it's fair of me to ask it of you. This isn't what you bargained for when you married me," she reminded him.

"But I—"

Again, she cut him off. "I don't want to think about the future. I want to do what you advised me once before. I want to enjoy today for what it brings and forget about tomorrow. Maybe when I know Susannah is going to get well, I'll think differently. But now…now life is too uncertain."

When she said things like that, how could he talk to her about their future together? But neither could he let what she had said pass without challenging it.

"Do you really mean to put your life on hold for however long it takes Susannah to get well? She won't be truly in the clear unless she stays in remission beyond the five-year mark. *Five years,* Mara. That's a long time."

"I know," she conceded. "When you put it that way, I know I'm being ridiculous. But I need a little time to start believing there will be a future for us—for me and Susannah."

He was achingly aware he was not included in her picture of the future.

"A year," she said. "If Susannah stays in remission a year, I'll let myself hope again. But it's too dangerous to believe in the future before then. You do understand, don't you, Falcon?"

He did. All too well. Mara wasn't going to make promises to him or to herself that she wasn't sure she would be able to keep. He wanted to say they could have a life together even if the worst happened, and Susannah died. But he discovered he couldn't voice even the possibility that the world might lose a free spirit like Susannah. She had become as dear to him as though she were his own flesh and blood.

To anyone watching from the outside, they appeared a perfectly normal, happy family over the months of winter that led into spring. In fact, Susannah quickly got well enough to misbehave. That created a whole new set of problems for Mara and Falcon. They were no longer merely caretakers for a youthful invalid, they were parents trying to raise a responsible, honest and self-sufficient child.

Falcon found himself sympathizing with what his own parents must have gone through with him and his siblings. Susannah had gotten used to being waited on and catered to during her illness. The first time Falcon insisted she pick up her damp towel and put it back on the bathroom rack, she responded as the spoiled child she had become.

"You do it," she said.

Falcon wasn't sure what to do next, but he wasn't about to let an eight-year-old order him around. "Pick it up, Susannah. Otherwise, you can go to your room and spend the rest of the morning thinking about ways you can help do your share in this family."

"You're not my father," Susannah shouted back. "You can't tell me what to do!"

Falcon stood stunned, appalled at the child's apparent dismissal of the role he had played in her life over the past nine months. Surely no real father could have been more kind or considerate, more loving or caring during her illness. But children, he was learning, can have short, selfish memories.

"Susannah Ainsworth! You apologize to Falcon this instant!"

Mara had overheard the entire conversation and was appalled at her daughter's devilish behavior. "You will pick up that towel and hang it back on the rack. Then you can go to your room and stay there the rest of the morning!"

"I'm sorry, Falcon," Susannah said in a petulant voice. Then she turned to her mother. "If I've picked up the towel," Susannah reasoned as she sullenly hung the damp towel on the rack, "why do I still have to go to my room?"

"Because you were rude and disobedient," Mara said.

"Why do I have to do what Falcon says?" Susannah complained. "He's not my real father."

Mara looked quickly at Falcon's face, which had hardened like stone, then back to her daughter. She was the one who had forced Falcon to remain on the fringes of her and Susannah's life. She was the one who wanted everything on hold until she was good and ready to move forward. She had created this situation, and the time had come for her to resolve it.

"Falcon *is* your father in every way that matters," Mara said. "He has the right to tell you what to do. And you have the duty to obey him and to treat him with respect."

Susannah turned wide, hazel eyes on Falcon. "Are you really going to be my real father?" she asked, her tone more curious now than belligerent. "Forever and ever?"

Falcon shot one desperate look at Mara, wanting to be able to say yes, and knowing that he hadn't the right.

Mara knew she had to make a decision. "Yes, he is," she answered for Falcon. It was easy, she realized, so easy to say yes to a lifetime with Falcon.

Their glances caught and clung for a moment. Mara almost gasped at the powerful emotions she saw in Falcon's eyes. She knew then she had done the right thing. She was committed to this man. For better or worse. For richer—and he was beginning to spend money like Croesus again—or poorer. In sickness—and there might be more of it for Susannah—and in health. It only remained for the words to be spoken between them.

Only, now that she had taken a step off the edge of a treacherous cliff, Mara was terrified that Falcon wouldn't be there to catch her.

"All right, you can be my father," Susannah said in the way children have of accepting momentous occasions with aplomb. "I'm sorry, Falcon," she said, this time with more contrition in her voice. She crossed to him and put her arms around his waist and said, "Actually, I'm glad you're going to be my father for real and always. I guess I sorta like you a lot." Then she looked up at him with an innocent, angelic face and said, "Do I still have to go to my room?"

Falcon swept the little girl into his arms and gave her a tremendous hug. "God, I love you, Susannah. I'm so glad you're my daughter for real and always." Then he set her on her feet and said, "And yes, you still have to go to your room."

Susannah grimaced. "All right, but if I stay in my room this morning, can we go riding this afternoon?"

Falcon shook his head at her persistence. He sent a questioning look to Mara as if to say, "All right?" When she nodded, he said to Susannah, "Sure. You use the morning to think, and we'll go riding this afternoon."

"Yippee!" Susannah said as she hopped, skipped and bounced away.

In an exaggerated motion, Falcon wiped his brow with his sleeve. "I have great respect for my parents when I see what they coped with from the other side of the fence."

"It isn't easy knowing the right thing to do or say," Mara conceded.

"Did you mean it, Mara? That I'll be Susannah's father for now and forever?"

Mara flushed. "Yes," she said in a whisper. "If you want to be."

"If I want to be? How can you even ask? I *love* Susannah." It would only take another breath to say *And I love you.*

Mara never gave him the chance. "I've got a lot to do this morning if I want to be free to ride with you and Susannah this afternoon," she said.

She backed up a few steps, then turned and almost ran for his office. She was like a skittish filly that had walked up to his hand to take the sugar he held out to her, but at the last moment had taken fright and run. Like the filly, he knew she would be back. Because once a creature had developed a taste for sugar, it was an irresistible lure.

It wouldn't be a bad thing to wait a little while and give his jumbled feelings time to sort themselves out. And give Mara time to realize that he would be there, waiting with his hand outstretched, whenever she was ready to move forward in their relationship.

At least the suspended animation in which they had lived for the past nine months was coming to an end. But Falcon wasn't taking anything for granted. He wanted the words spoken. He wanted things decided once and for all. And if he moved slowly and carefully enough, there was just the chance she would come to him today.

Just before lunchtime, Susannah came running into the kitchen. "Can we go riding now?" she asked. "Patches needs some exercise."

"What do you say, Mara?" Falcon asked. "Shall we go riding now, or after lunch?"

Mara finished wrapping the last of the sandwiches she had been preparing. "I've put together a picnic to take to the stock pond," Mara said. "But mind you, no racing!"

Falcon and Susannah raced the last few hundred yards to the stock pond, with Mara flying close behind.

"Whew! I have to admit that was exhilarating," Mara said with a laugh as she slid off her horse.

"I'm hungry," Susannah said. "Can we eat lunch now?"

"Sure. Untie the blanket from behind your saddle and I'll get the food." Mara began untying the saddle-bags on her horse.

Falcon quickly relieved her. "I'll do this. You can help Susannah spread out the blanket."

All of them ate like they were never going to see food again. Replete, they settled back lazily on the blanket and watched the shapes on the ground made by the broken shadows of the leaves.

In a very short while, Mara and Falcon were treated to the sight of Susannah sound asleep on the blanket between them.

"She seems to tire so easily," Mara said as she chewed worriedly on her lower lip.

"Most kids her age take a nap, don't they? Or would if their parents could get them to slow down long enough. She's fine, Mara. Try not to worry so much."

"I do try!" Mara said. She rose from the blanket and walked a few steps away, where they wouldn't disturb Susannah's slumber.

When Falcon came up behind her and circled her waist, she leaned her head back against his shoulder. This felt good. This felt right. She wanted to stay married to Falcon. She wanted them to be husband and wife. But was that fair to him? What if she had trapped him by the things she had said this morning. What if he didn't want to stay with her and Susannah after all? She had to know the truth.

"I took advantage of the situation this morning," she said. "If you want out of this marriage, all you have to do is say so."

"Oh?"

Mara couldn't tell from that one quiet word whether Falcon was relieved or infuriated by what she said. But his hands had tightened uncomfortably around her.

"I can't breathe," she protested.

His hold loosened, but he didn't let her go. Neither did he speak. Maybe he did want out.

She continued, "When Susannah asked if you were going to be her father forever and ever, I said you would. But we've never talked about forever, Falcon. I made the choice for you. I know that's unfair, and if you want to be free of us, of both of us—"

He whirled her around and clutched her tightly at the waist. "Look at me, Mara."

But she couldn't. She was afraid.

He caught her chin between his fingers and forced it upward. He tightened his grasp and demanded, "Look at me."

He waited until she looked up at him before speaking again. His eyes were narrowed, his gaze fierce. A muscle worked in his jaw. This was not a weak man. This was not a man who would let her fall from a cliff. He would be there to catch her.

"I want to be Susannah's father," he said in a harsh, grating voice. "Very much."

"That means you'll also be stuck with me," Mara said with a breezy laugh that somehow got caught in her throat.

Falcon let go of Mara's chin and caught her by the shoulders. "I love you, Mara. I want you to be my wife, forever and ever."

Mara's heart soared when she heard Falcon's declaration of love. But she had to make sure he knew what he was getting into. "Are you *sure?*"

There was a silence that sent Mara's heart to her throat.

Falcon was shaken by Mara's third attempt to set him free. Didn't she hear what he was saying? Didn't she realize how much he loved her? There was only one thing that could possibly change his mind about staying married to her, and that was if she didn't want him. He needed to know that Mara loved him. He needed to hear the words. But he didn't dare ask her outright. What if she said no?

For the first and most important time in his life, Falcon found himself at a loss for words with a woman. "Mara, do you— Is there a chance that— Is it possible—"

"What are you trying to say, Falcon?"

From the blanket behind them a little voice piped up, "Falcon wants to know if you love him, Mommy."

"What?"

Both adults shot startled looks at the little girl, who was lying on her stomach with her head perched on her hands and her legs waving in the air.

"I thought you were asleep," Mara said.

"Well, I'm not," Susannah replied. "Do you love him, Mommy?" she demanded.

Mara flushed, and Falcon feared the worst. He tried to get the words past a constricted throat, tried to offer her the divorce she so obviously wanted. Fortunately he was too distressed to speak.

Because the next words out of Mara's mouth were, "Yes, Susannah, I love him very much."

Mara and Falcon exchanged glances that shouted hosanna and hallelujah, before Falcon pulled Mara into his arms for a possessive kiss. A moment later, Susannah was tugging on his shirt, demanding to be included in the family embrace.

"Love me too, Daddy," she said. "Me, too."

"You too, Susannah," Falcon assured the little girl. "I'll love you and your mommy both, forever and ever."

Falcon met Mara's eyes and they spoke without words. They might not have forever with Susannah. There were no guarantees of long life and happiness. But whatever time they had together, they silently vowed to live to the fullest.

"Let's go home," Falcon said. "I want to make love to my wife," he whispered in her ear.

"Yes," Mara replied in a soft voice. "Let's take our daughter and go home."

* * * * *